Grey Matters

WALKING GREY: Book 1

by
Rachel DeFriez

Two Cents Publishing

First Two Cents Publishing edition May 2013

This book is a work of fiction. Names, characters, places, and incidents either are products of the author's imagination or are used fictitiously. Any resemblance to actual events or locales or persons, living or dead, is entirely coincidental.

ISBN-13 978-0-9893459-0-3
ISBN-10 0989345904

For Natalie, Janie, Elizabeth, Connor

Prologue

The Zombie Apocalypse.

We've played the video games, seen the movies—the blood, the gore, the disgusting creatures ripping people open with claws and teeth, pulling out guts like link sausage, shoveling fistfuls of organs into their putrid mouths. We've cheered or cringed when the hero went after them with a pair of hedge clippers, and a purple-grey, bloody-mouthed head rolled across the floor. The really terrifying zombies, the fast ones, the ones that chase you down, tackle you, start tearing off chunks of flesh while you scream, they made us shiver. And the predators, the ones whose only brain function is tenacious, vicious, savage stalking, they haunted our dreams. I read the books, had the nightmares: the rabid ghouls gashing my flesh as I clawed at the ground, desperately crawling away, only to come nose to toe with the rest of the pack, blood dripping off their chins, and guts smeared on their torn pant legs. I woke up sweating, gasping, wondering if they were out there.

But that doesn't even compare to the real horror. The real horror, the soul-wrenching terror, is when you wake up one morning and the bloodshot eyes, the sick purple-grey skin, the ghastly cravings for human flesh…they're yours. No, you're not having a nightmare. You *are* the nightmare: the monster, the enemy—and the target.

Chapter 1

They bash our heads and chain us up because we're different. Well, maybe knowing we would happily throw on a bib, rip out their guts, and devour them like hotdogs on a stick, without the stick—or the bib for that matter—probably has something to do with it. Maybe I don't blame them. No one really wants to hang out with a girl whose idea of a Slurpee is grey matter and blood splashed in the snow, hold the straw.

I used to be like them—not the same, not by a long shot. I was different the way everyone wants to be different— like everyone else, but bigger, brighter, and better. Little kids used to stop me in the mall and ask for my autograph. They thought I was Taylor Swift until I got the Z-Virus.

All I have to do is crawl out of the dark, through the trap door under the third pew from the front on the left, and I can remember what I was. I do that sometimes on clear nights, when the moon breaks through the jagged panes of broken stained glass, frightening the bare walls.

When I drag my suitcase up, the moonlight highlights its frays and dents. It's pretty much trashed: only one of the zippers works, and the handle is half broken. It's more grey than black now and wobbles on one wheel. But inside, I still have my tiara. Yeah, there are at least fifty jokes about that waiting to make someone's milk shoot out their nose. But there's also a letterman jacket in there. I lettered in track my sophomore year: ran the women's 400m and the 4x4 relay. That's one thing that hasn't changed: I was a beast back then, and I still am. I may not look like Taylor anymore, but I am swift.

On the team, I could compete with most of the boys. My boyfriend Bridger was never freaked out that I could outrun him in Capture the Flag. But he was an amazing golfer and I suck at golf, so it evened out.

It never seemed to bug Bridger that I was smarter than he was too. 3.98 GPA, none of those lame standard classes—all AP—except for the couple of electives I took so Bridger and I could have a class together. He wasn't much for studying. Sometimes I wrote English papers for him. It wasn't all that hard. He only needed a "C" to stay on the golf team.

I run my fingers along the jagged white edges of our picture from the Track Awards Banquet. The night I ran, I stuffed it in my jacket pocket—for company, I guess. It's pretty wrinkled and Bridger's foot is torn off in the corner, but I can still see how cute he is. He brought me lavender roses to match my dress. He looks so hot in black. We made an awesome couple. Sometimes it seems so odd that we ever broke up. It was Julie that told me he cheated on me over the summer while I was gone to Dallas. Like I could just let that go.

One of the guys on the boy's track team, Chase somebody-or-other, was nice enough to step in and take me when he heard I wasn't going with Bridger anymore. Chase was fun and all, but we all knew he was gay, so it wasn't like anything was going to happen between us. It just wasn't the same without Bridger.

Sometimes, here alone in my hole, I wonder if the cheating really mattered that much. Sometimes I wonder if it's possible to actually die from loneliness.

I smell like I'm dying, like old French cheese but ten times worse. You get used to it. The old church is perfect camouflage. The leaky basement floods the whole building with a lovely mildew, rotting wood scent. You'd actually have to have Z-Virus caliber senses to sniff me out over the smell.

My muscles are anything but dying, which comes in handy sometimes when I'm really hungry, or really angry—or really scared. My after-school Karate classes come in handy too. My mom wanted to put me in ballet. (Sometimes, Mother *doesn't* know best.) I did both.

I pull my white puppy out of the suitcase. Bridger gave it to me before prom. I can cuddle up to the fur, close my eyes, and pretend I'm still at home, lying on my taffy striped comforter, falling asleep to the green glow of the plastic stars pasted to my ceiling. But then my finger sticks in the little rip of his tail and I remember the soldiers. That first night, the night I lost everything and everyone, loops over and over in my head like a scene from a horror movie.

The soldier, who isn't much older than I am, rifles through my suitcase while the old square-faced officer watches.

The oldest of my younger brothers wanders in, looking horrified that my parents are sending me away with soldiers. "Go upstairs, Cory," my dad barks. Apparently, this wasn't a family decision. My dad twists him by the shoulders and pushes him up the first stair. His foot climbs, but his eyes are on me. I nod, breaking out my best "I got this" smile.

Soldier boy pulls out Puppy Pudd and tosses him onto the marble tiles in the entry. Breaking away from my mom, I dive to scoop him up. I'm not going to let them take anything else away from me. The soldier catches the stub tail as I yank the dog away. My heart rips with the seam. "NO!" I scream, falling to my knees. My mom shoves herself between the soldier and me. Cory swears and starts back down the stairs, running smack into the flat of my dad's palm.

"Evelyn is taking the puppy!" My mom looks hard at the old guy. The graying pallor of my skin, the purple tint growing under my eyes and along my lips, the red spider veins creeping through them, making the green of my irises pop—it all scares the crap out of her—but she's still my mother.

The air is tense until the old guy nods and soldier boy tosses me Pudd.

They escort me out to a Z-V Institute van while my mother cries into my father's shoulder on the front porch. The streetlights snap on. My dad's frown is barely visible in the yellow light. I can hardly blame my parents. I have three little brothers and a baby sister who sneaks into bed with me. They can't risk waking up one morning to find their daughter has become the big bad wolf and made a midnight snack of her little sister.

I climb up into the van. At the sight of all the equipment, I suddenly feel hunted. This is supposed to be the humane thing—take me to an institute where doctors are hard at work studying the infected, trying to find a cure to contain the virus. But I can tell, from what I see hanging above the seats and folded up in the corners, that I'm not human anymore, not to them: hooks and chains—those aren't humane.

Fear is my friend. It kicks in hard, something even more than adrenaline. Before soldier boy has time to click the lock into place, I kick the door back in his face—basic Karate move. The metal plate flies off its hinges and knocks him flat. I have my suitcase in my hand when I jump, but I let go, so it clatters to the ground and lies forgotten in the street.

Landing clear of the orphaned door, I sprint towards the empty lot that leads into the trees along the golf course. The quiet suburban evening explodes in a volley of cracks. It's the first time I've ever been shot at.

My mother's screaming fades in my ears as I race over curbs, into the dirt and weeds, towards the ravine behind the bluff. The gunshots stop abruptly. Glancing back towards the yellow beam of the streetlight, I catch a silhouette view of Cory wrestling the shooter and my dad wrestling Cory. The old sergeant screams at his soldier while the figure of my mom, shadowed in the bright light of the open front door, sinks to her knees on the porch. That image burns itself into my brain and I know I can never go back. It's too dangerous for all of them.

I guess I really am turning into some kind of animal. My survival instincts take over. I head for underground, amazed at how quickly I've left them all behind, and how I feel more like I've taken an afternoon stroll than sprinted a 5K. Three feet into the park drainage pipe, my feet stop short at the sound of rattling. My heart juggles a beat. Anything that makes odd noises in dark places freaks me out—mice, cockroaches, crickets, beetles, snakes—especially snakes.

I shouldn't be able to see the rattler. I've been inside this pipe before, with Bridger in the afternoon, looking for the thrill of something dangerous. Even at midday, the pipe is pitch black after the first couple of feet. I guess I can now confirm that ZVs have night vision. The viper is coiled up, his beady eyes fixed on my knees. Something snaps inside of me. I grab at him as he lunges for me, his mouth open. My fingers clamp around his neck; his jaws swing around to bite my fist. Ripping through the flesh with my teeth, I bite his head off and spit it out. It hits the metal pipe with a happy little clang. This insane urge to take a bite out of the wriggling body dangling from my fingers seizes me. Hurling the fleshy thing after the head, I flee down the metal tube, disgusted by myself.

The pipe ends at a reservoir field where the kids play soccer. Probably seems bizarre, but I don't want to be too far away. I want my suitcase.

Creeping through unfenced backyards, I make my way home from the other side of the street. They couldn't have expected this much trouble. I was a voluntary committal. I watch, crouching in the neighbor's bushes, as they yell into a phone before packing up and heading towards the golf course. My suitcase is still in the street. As I pass, I scoop it up.

The street lamp bathes our house in shadows and shallow yellow. In the side yard, the glow of my nightlight funnels through my window. It is definitely not unlocked; I've always been too afraid of the dark to leave it open. (Yeah, I'm afraid of the dark. Hilarious.) The window is full length, long enough for any stranger off the street to walk through. We don't live in the scary part of town, but my mom is always suspicious of the constant parade of construction workers in our subdivision.

A glimpse from the edge of the window frame shows my mom sitting hunched over in the chair she used to rock her babies in. It's in my room because she's too sentimental to give it to a thrift store even though we don't need it anymore, and because it matches the Maplewood furniture I inherited from her grandmother. My room is more of a mausoleum than a bedroom. I guess that's appropriate now.

There's already been plenty of noise in the neighborhood. Not wanting to add to the drama or draw a crowd with the sound of shattering glass, I tap my fingers lightly on the windowpane, and then a little more insistently. Finally, my mother wipes her eyes and looks around the room. I tap again and touch my nose to the glass.

My mother jumps out of her chair, one hand on her mouth and the other on her heart. A few seconds too late, I realize that a face like mine in the window, on any night but Halloween, is a heart attack in a bottle. I step into full view before she can faint. The moment of recognition melts the tension on her face. Rushing to the window, she slides it open and fidgets with the screen, muttering, "Baby, oh baby, my baby, Evelyn!"

"You okay, Doris?" my dad yells from the family room.

"A spider. A big one. I'll get it." She practically drags me through the gap.

"They were shooting at you!" she whispers, grabbing me close to her. "Shooting at my little girl. I was so afraid. I thought you…" She bursts into tears. I hold onto her for a while, knowing it's probably the last time I'll be able to get this close to another human, another human who is actually pulling me close and not pushing me away. When I feel like I might cry, I pull back.

"I need to get some things, mom…before they come back."

"We'll hide you, honey. I won't let them take you. I didn't know they'd bring soldiers. I thought they were doctors, that they'd help you." Tears fill up her red eyes again.

"You can't hide me, mom. They know now. They'll come and get me, just like they came to get Bridger."

"I wish you'd never met that boy." She's so miserable, I almost want to tell her Bridger and I never had sex, that the virus isn't transmitted that way. But I don't.

"Well, I did meet him. And I'm infected. I'm a ZV, mom."

"You're not anything like them, sweetie." She puts her hand on my cheek and bites her lip. "You'd never hurt us."

The snake in the pipe and the wicked burst of adrenaline flash through my mind. "I might." My mom's face crumbles into disappointment like I just told her I was planning to have sex on prom night or something (which I wasn't). "We're lucky this has been slow. It could get worse." I disappear into my closet and grab my letterman jacket. I'm going to need warmer clothes if I'm going to be out all night…every night.

There isn't much in my suitcase so I grab a book from the top shelf, in case I have some time on my hands. A couple of photos and the dried flowers of my corsage tumble down with my tiara. I just stare at the crown for about thirty seconds—as long as it takes for my whole life to flicker through the facets of the fake crystals. I stuff it and the pictures in the pocket of my jacket before my mom can see that I care about the life that died when I got the virus. She can't do anything about it, and she'll want to.

"Can I get you something to eat? Some food to take with you?"

"I'm not hungry." It's a lie. I'm not hungry for what she has in the kitchen. We both know it. Awkward silence, pierced by the sudden outbreak of an argument between my twin brothers Josh and Jeremy.

"I got it first. You have the broken one."

They have two of everything. "The broken one is yours. It's blue. Mine's green."

Then the duet: "Mom!"

My mom ignores them; she looks hurt again. "I thought it was hard feeding you when you became a vegetarian." She tries to lift the weight of a one-ton-brick-of-a-shitty night with a feather. I try to help by cracking a half-smile. She looks confused and then covers the awkwardness. "Where will you go? Can't you tell me? How will I get things to you?"

She still doesn't get it. She still thinks I'm her baby, that she can take care of me. "I don't know where I'll go, mom!" I turn on her. She looks a little scared, so I grit my teeth and breathe deeply. "You can't try to find me." She starts to object and reaches for me. I back away, trying to keep a grip. "You don't know what you'll find if you do."

With both hands flattened together, she covers her nose and mouth like she's offering some kind of desperate prayer. Her eyes mist up. It looks like she's trying to keep her whole body from collapsing in on itself. I guess I'm still a little human, still alive, because I feel like I'm dying. "I'll try to get you a message or something, so you don't worry," I say.

She reaches for me, but Amber's voice travels through the hallway. She's the fifth child and twelve years younger than I am. By the time my mom had Amber, the rest of us had already worn her out. Amber's *my* baby.

"Mo-o-o-m. Mommy. When is Evelyn coming back? I can't go to bed until she reads me a story."

"I have to go," I whisper, breaking away from my mom and heading towards the window. Amber's little body appears in the room as the remnants of my former life disappear into the scuffed-up suitcase. Behind me, the headlights of the Z-V Institute van flash through the grey dimness of the front yard.

Chapter 2

I'm one of the few kids in Eli that knows about the hide in the old church. Ironically enough, it was Bridger that showed it to me. It was just before we broke up, that weekend his brother Preston came home from basic training. Bridger was always jealous of him. He was taller, faster, on all the teams, brilliant…and really good-looking, in a scruffy kind of way.

The night of Bridger's Homecoming pool party, when I was playing volleyball, Preston joined my team. We both raced into the trees and bushes after a wild volley and when we came out, I was holding the ball and Preston was holding me. Bridger went through the roof. I didn't blame him; Preston's dreamy. It probably didn't help that he used to tell Bridger that I was too good for him, and that, if I were older, he'd date me. What really got to Bridger was that we could both tell Preston meant it. But he went off to college and joined the National Guard and I haven't seen him since. It wasn't real, just an "older guy" crush.

Bridger made a point of telling me he took me to the polygamist hide because Preston told him he couldn't. It's an old Mormon church that the Methodists bought before they built their new building over on 2nd Street. The FOR SALE sign has been out front since before I went to high school. Eli's barely a two-church town. There's just not enough difference of opinion here to make a third.

Bridger's grandpa was the last Minister. He showed him the trap door under the third pew on the left before they moved to their new building. The underground room was obviously left over from polygamy days when the old geezers were hiding out. Bridger's grandpa thought someone ought to know about it, in case some little kid ever went missing and they needed to check it. But they never told anyone about it either, because they didn't want any kids hiding in there and getting hurt. Bridger's family and I might be the only people in Eli that still know about it.

Sometimes, when I'm sitting here in the dark, alone—night after night, week after week—I think about the other freaks that hid here before me. Seriously, what kind of virus was snacking on *their* brains? Personally, the idea of polygamy is as awkward to me as salivating when I get a whiff of that heavenly medium-rare-steak-at-a-summer-BBQ scent the uninfected have; but then, I haven't ever actually tried to eat anyone. Now that I'm a ZV, though, I guess I really shouldn't judge. Freak by choice or freak by nature. Either way, I'm glad the hideout is here.

I'm not sure why Bridger didn't use this place. He ran before I did; his symptoms showed up a lot faster than mine. I think Preston gave him a heads-up when the National Guard helped clean up the outbreak in Provo and the rumors about the Institute started up.

A half a dozen of the infected couples came from a high school down there. I guess they tracked it back to some archeological dig in Egypt sponsored by the university. But there were a handful of cases at a high school in Salt Lake. The high schools seem to be ideal breeding grounds for the virus. They have pretty tight medical screenings at all of them now.

The Z-V Commission commandeered every K-9 patrol they could get their hands on. Dogs can sniff out a ZV before he even knows he's infected. The National Guard stepped in to help with screenings so all the parents wouldn't freak. Students can't get into a building without getting sniffed by a dog or having one of those thermometer thingies jammed in their ear. The first noticeable symptom is a drastically dropping body temperature.

The ZV Comm started a bunch of ad campaigns trying to convince people that the risk of contagion was really low, that the media coverage was just a bunch of hype. Channel 2 News started doing human-interest stories on "Living with the Z-Virus." The virus spread so sparsely because it needed a teenage couple, and only a very small group seemed at risk. After the swine flu frenzy fizzled out, people thought this was more of the same—a nightmarish disease that other people get—and went off and got their flu shots. They stopped taking much notice of the occasional infection in the small towns that sprawl along the mountains for miles. By the time Bridger and I got infected, there hadn't been a reported case for months.

Of course, by then, the few that managed to get themselves infected were running away before their parents could book them a stay at the Institute. That's when the gangs started popping up.

One church-Nazi dad got the idea he could "heal" his infected daughter with faith, prayer, and righteous living. Seemed to be going well, until the virus hijacked her brain. She woke up one night, made a sushi snack of her little brother, and went AWOL. It was one of the few cases, since the original outbreak of the virus, of a ZV actually eating someone. After that, the father decided the only way to "heal" a ZV was with a bat. He put together a search party and watched them beat the crud out of his daughter when they found her.

It's hard to judge them; she still had pieces of her brother in her hair.

That's when the Z-V Commission authorized the Z-V Institute to apprehend and institutionalize all reported cases of infection. And that's also when it became every fanatic's holy calling to seek out the cursed and send them to Hell or the Institute. I decided I couldn't risk staying home anymore, even if my symptoms were slow in showing. I told my parents to call the Z-V Institute.

The moonlight catches on the crystals in my tiara and sprinkles candy light on the concrete walls around me. The old church is one of the first places they searched when kids started running. A gang broke in here one night a few weeks after I ran. I nearly peed my pants, but they headed straight for the basement and didn't bother with the main chapel. They probably think we can't go in churches or something. I wouldn't put it past them since they're convinced that infection is the "wages of sin." At least their delusions are working *for* me for once.

I've got pretty much everything I need here—everything but food. I'm starting to feel the hunger again. It's not like before, eating three times a day—twice on a diet. The hunger drives me to distraction every few days, but I only have to eat once. It's pretty quiet outside, one of the benefits of a small town—not much traffic after ten p.m. Now that it's nearly winter, with warmer clothes, some mittens to cover my hands, and a scarf wrapped around my neck up to my nose, I can walk around at night without causing a frenzy. My hair isn't falling out, thank God, since it was always my best feature anyway. The first thing in my suitcase was a brush.

Sliding away the last board in the floor, I listen for a few minutes before I crawl out. Crickets, drops of rain crashing into the overgrown flowerbeds, the rustle of a breeze in the quaking aspens, the creak of the walls—my hearing is as sharp as my night vision. Whatever else the virus is doing, it's turning me into a night predator. No sign of people. My feet clear the opening. The board falls snugly back in place.

There's a little basement door in the back of the building. The cement stairwell leading down to it is overgrown with trees and bushes and makes a great covert exit. The night has a crisp, nippy look to it. Shifts in temperature don't really faze me; the virus has mostly affected my skin. It's like my skin is getting just enough blood to survive, but not enough to heal. It looks ghostly pale, with a tinge of grey from the dirty purple blood running inside me. I have to be really careful not to damage it.

One of the city trails leads to the old millpond and avoids the streets lit by lampposts. It's the first place a gang of ZV bashers or Institute Snatchers would look for a stray one of us, and the last place any of us would hide. We have Gavin S. Tanner to thank for that.

Gavin is the son of John K. Tanner, one of Salt Lake's wealthiest businessmen and son of former US Congressman

Scott C. Tanner. He lives in a big mansion in Federal Heights. His aunt is a reporter for Channel 2 News. Gavin's girlfriend got sniffed out in class one afternoon about the same time Bridger started showing symptoms, during the second wave of the virus. The Snatchers—it's written in bright gold letters on their uniform: SNCHR, Security and Non-Cooperative Host Retrieval—came calling at the mansion that evening. Gavin's left arm got broken in the scuffle. Of course, that's not going to heal, and his dad was pissed.

John K. Tanner has an army of lawyers, bank loads of money, security cameras, bodyguards; you name it. End of story—the courts ruled they couldn't arrest someone or commit them just for being sick with an STD. The virus isn't contagious enough to be deemed a public threat. ZVs have to actually be proven, in court, to be a nuisance or engaging in criminal activity before they can be picked up and locked away. The Commission pulled back and now Snatchers can only grab ZVs off the street as runaways or vagrants until the Appeals Court can overturn the ruling.

So now dumpster diving is a crime. But a girl has to eat.

I can't believe my luck. There's some homeless guy rummaging through the big dumpster. That's a little odd for Eli because most of the homeless hang out in Salt Lake at Pioneer Park near the shelters. But an early case of ZV hunted a few homeless in the park and now some of the transients have moved out to the suburbs. No one actually uses this mill anymore, but the town broke down and put the dumpster there because everyone was dumping stuff on the lot anyway.

I crouch behind a clump of weed-infested boulders and watch the guy in his dingy red jacket and moth-eaten beanie sift through the dumpster's *plat du jour*. Oh yeah, I had French—four years, Advanced Placement, top 1% of my class. Lot of good it will do me now.

The guy seems kind of finicky. He picks stuff up, sniffs it, tosses it aside; doesn't seem to find anything worth taking. I'm waiting, watching like a cat. If I had a tail, it would probably be waving behind me. Not all ZVs can do this, by the way. Once the virus really takes over, there's no hunting and stalking, just blind, shuffling, tenacious descent upon anything that smells uninfected. I'm not anywhere near that. If anything, I've become a hunting machine.

After a few minutes of motionless patience, I see what I've been waiting for. A stray dog wanders up to see if the guy will share. The eyes of my prey flash golden in the moonlight. I feel the adrenaline rush and saliva oozes around my tongue.

As I spring out from the boulders, my nose catches a whiff of dead skin on the breeze, and my eyes snap towards movement in the brush around the mill. I'm not the only ZV here. It's going to be a race between the two of us, but I'll win. I can tell by the shambling behind me that the other ZV is further gone than I am, but not enough that he can't run.

I'm diving for the mutt when the bum realizes I'm there and lets out an ear-piercing scream. The stray dog bolts and my hands come up empty. I'm so mad when I stand up that I growl at the homeless guy, who's much younger and cleaner than I thought he would be. He cowers as I swing my fist just in time to punch the other ZV who has finally caught up. The zombie stumbles backward.

"Get the hell out of here," I yell at the bum in the red jacket. I may look like a ZV, but I don't eat like one—not yet. The bum stumbles away, tripping over his own feet. The other ZV is up and after him, but I throttle him with my arm. I don't want to hurt him, but I don't want him hurting anyone else either.

"Eat...gotta eat...smell the meat. Starve!" he gasps, struggling against the chokehold.

I recognize the voice.

"Bridger?" He's still struggling. "Bridger. Look at me!" I grab his cheeks and yank his face around to look at mine. He's had a rough go of it. There's a big gash on his chin. It looks fresh and old at the same time. "It's me. Evelyn." I look hard at him, holding his head tight. He stares back at me like Amber when she's trying to remember her address but the numbers and letters are all a jumble. His eyes refocus with recognition. Bridger is still in there.

I can't help myself. I throw my arms around him and hug him like I used to when he'd take me to scary movies. Right about now, I don't really care about who cheated on whom. Bridger makes me feel warm for the first time in a long time, the way he always did, even though I know I'm cold.

"Ev'lyn. I thought…I thought…I thought…" Apparently thinking is easier than speaking. "Ev'lyn…Institute." He's really struggling. I'm a little terrified by how far gone he is.

"I ran, Bridger. I wasn't smart like you were. I actually got in the van first. They had chains and metal hooks…and other stuff that made me sick to look at it."

Bridger stares at my face and my mouth like I'm speaking half one language and half another. I wonder if not all the synapses are firing in the right order. He nods, though, like he gets the gist. This is the first time I've ever been up close and personal with another ZV. It makes me want to cry—that face I stared at in Health, the lips I kissed under the glowing, green plastic stars of my bedroom ceiling, they're sagging, washed out, dying.

"Hungry, Ev'lyn." His face darkens and he scowls.

I pet his hair back. Just touching another kid like that, like when we used to on the couch watching DVDs, slows my breathing and I feel…I feel…I just feel.

The break-up wasn't pretty, but I was totally smitten with Bridger once. It's been months since I've touched anyone, months since my mother hugged me and I slipped out the window, out of humanity, and into the solitary confinement of my cache under the third pew. I don't think I've spoken out loud either, except to Puppy Pudd. I read to him now, instead of Amber.

I shake my head while I look in my ex's face. Even ghoulishly pale, with a festering gash on his cheek, purplish circles drawn around his eyes, and bluish lips, he's still damn hot. Maybe my standards have slipped. With my face this close to his, I can smell the reek of the open sore and feel the clammy hollowness of his skin. My insides seize up and my eyes sting with the rush of touch from another person. My arms melt from a grasp to an embrace.

A deep breath shuts off the path between my brain and the collapsing going on in my chest. Lacing my fingers in his, I start off towards the thicket around the pond where I know the strays hang out. Bridger trails behind like a little kid. I feel more like his babysitter than his ex.

"Let's get you something to eat. You're all skin and bones." My mother used to say that to me. I shake off that image.

Some of the cats and dogs are starting to recognize our putrid scent as a predator. It'll be tougher to catch something without a human decoy. But I'm no amateur, and if I play it right, we might catch a newbie when it sneaks in to investigate the odd smell.

"Man gone," Bridger grunts.

"Is that what you were after?" I get irritated. No big surprise. I was always yelling at him about something. That's one of the reasons we broke up in the end. "You can't go around eating people. The gangs will hunt you down. If they don't whack your head off with a baseball bat, they'll drop you off at the Institute and chain you up like a rabid dog."

"Dog." I'm not sure if he's making a dinner selection or just repeating what I say. The conversation is such a novelty that I go with the menu choice option.

"Yeah, I'll share a stray with you." I feel almost like a teenager again. I was always the responsible one who did the homework. I found us the job at the frozen yogurt place. "You have to be careful," I go on explaining, "that you don't get someone's pet. They'll come after you for that too. I mean, with the strays, we're helping everyone out. The Humane Society doesn't have as much work, right?" That's not really true. It's perfectly legal to buy and eat a slaughtered cow or chicken from the grocery store, but it's a crime to slaughter a stray yourself and eat it.

I look back and Bridger nods. I think he's smiling. "Dog," he says, but his face cramps up.

"I know. It's like eating macaroni and cheese when you can smell filet mignon on the grill. But you can live on it. I'll show you which pieces to eat. I don't think you're in any shape to help with the hunt though. You might have to wait for me. Or maybe we can use you to get them running in my direction."

I'm so caught up in the forgotten novelty of a conversation with another person that I don't even notice when the Z-V Institute van rolls up in the dark behind us.

Chapter 3

We try to run, but the Z-V Snatchers are all over Bridger, hauling him into their death mobile. I twist around and go after the one that grabbed me. My legs are super strong. I knew what I was doing when every other girl in my second-grade class was hip-hopping, and I was kicking butt with the boys in Karate. Bones crack when the Snatcher finally hits the ground. I think I broke his leg. All the hunting and fighting have worked up the virus in me. I have this insanely powerful urge to kneel down and rip a bite right out of his belly, right through the protective suit, right in the spot where my mom used to blow raspberries on my tummy when I was little…right in the spot where I used to tickle Amber.

"Don't eat me!" he groans.

Fighting against the viral instincts inside me, I look around for Bridger. He's nowhere in sight. They're so stupid with their prejudices. They sent one Snatcher after the girl and the other two after the boy. Idiots. Bridger is down to about the mentality of a toddler. A well-armed grandma could have handled him. I abandon the guy with the broken leg and sprint through the weeds to the van. As I race past the driver's window, he shoves his door open and yells to his buddies. In the back of the van, the others are tying up the closest thing I have to a friend. I snarl and they turn.

"Don't shoot her, Joey!" the taller guy yells to the driver in camouflage. Without taking my eyes off them, I back away towards the trees that surround the mill yard. "If she took Williams out," he yells, "she must be fresh. The doc's gonna want her alive. Get Williams in the van!" Joey runs for the injured Snatcher.

The two Snatchers that captured Bridger are wearing heavy black suits and the gloves Animal Control wears to protect themselves from bites. The smaller guy's suit isn't done up all the way. I catch a little snip of a dingy red jacket hanging out. His eyes meet mine. Something told me the homeless guy foraging was too convenient—they're setting traps for us now.

I should just run. There's no way they can catch me and my hideout is pretty secure. But I can't walk away from Bridger, not like this.

"Ev'lyn...dog..." I hear muffled moaning from the bed of the van. The door is still gaping wide open, waiting for them to toss me in. The Snatchers climb out, brandishing poles and bags, never breaking eye contact with me.

"Bridger, come on. You gotta get out of there!" I yell. He's struggling in one of the bags.

Williams cries in pain as Joey drags him. I have to go through these other two losers to get Bridger, but I'm not sure I can take on two at once. I'm no Lara Croft.

"I'll work around behind while you distract her." The big guy has the bag in his hand, the kind they use to throw over a wild animal's head to catch it. He blurts out his plan like I'm some dumb beast that doesn't know what he's saying.

I play along, pivoting slightly, watching the Snatcher by the van, but never losing sight of the guy with the bag while he tries to get behind me. When the two are far enough apart from each other, I spin around and spring on the Snatcher with the bag. He doesn't know what hit him. I toss him into a patch of knee-deep dry weeds. I don't want to hurt anyone. I just need to get him away from the van long enough to fish Bridger out of it.

Of course, the other Snatcher is functioning on the conviction that my driving goal in life is to sink my teeth into his liver and enjoy a little moonlight dinner out. He launches himself into the back of the van, yelling, "Go. Go!" I think he's warning them away from me. Why can't he catch a clue, see that I just want Bridger, and toss him to me?

Then the movement from the shadows in the trees catches my eye. The Snatcher who played decoy is not abandoning his buddy with the bag; he's caught sight of a whole gang—at least half a dozen ZVs—closing in on the guy. I'm totally stunned. I had no idea there were that many ZVs roaming around Eli. Now I've got more than Bridger to save. I race for the Institute man I just tossed into the weeds. He's got a nasty gash on his head like he slammed right into a rock. Unfortunately, he's not dazed enough to let me hoist him up without a fight.

The van starts backing out towards me. The back doors are still open, waving back and forth as the driver stops, shifts into drive, and turns sharply towards the street. The field around the old mill is a maze of abandoned farm equipment, boulders, trees, and now zombies. The driver has to stop every few yards and maneuver around the obstacles. If I'm fast, I might get to the van and maybe toss the Snatcher in before the mob of ZVs turns him into meatloaf. If I'm lucky, I can manage to pull Bridger out too.

The plan is all good, except for the ZV leading the rabid mob; he seems to be pretty fresh. He runs like I do, and he's not carrying a dazed, unwilling Snatcher on his back. My hand reaches for the back door that's still flopping open as the driver accelerates through the brush. The van crashes to a halt when it slams into some debris.

The leader of the ZV gang tears the door off, dives in, grabs the Snatcher's foot, and pulls him out screaming. He tears a chunk out of his neck with his teeth; blood flies from the ripped vein. He tosses the gushing man to the other zombies who swarm to the scent of fresh blood. Revulsion and hunger clash in my guts and shiver up my spine as the van shifts into reverse. I heave the reviving Snatcher on my back into the van and backpedal out of the way.

"Give me the zombie!" I yell. The Snatcher stares back at me like I'm speaking Russian. I tear the other door off myself. The wheels throw up dirt as they fight for traction in the mud. I dive for Bridger's foot, hoping to pull him out.

At the same time, the other ZV, apparently not satisfied with his Happy Meal, wants a double stack. Growling and snarling like an animal, he launches himself into the van again and grabs the Snatcher I've just busted my back to save.

The van lurches forward, the rush of the screaming Snatcher's body sliding towards his death sweeps me out in its wake. I lose my grip on Bridger's ankle. The van shoots away, over the curb and into the street, as the ZV alpha, the Snatcher and I tumble into a seething mass of feeding ZVs. The Snatcher hollers bloody murder as the zombies break away from the wasted carcass of the decoy in the red jacket and tear with claws and teeth into fresh meat.

It's a frenzied free-for-all. The man is a bloody, limp mess in seconds. The ZVs slash and snarl at each other. I stumble away since I know that when ZVs get injured, they don't heal. I don't want any part of this, even though I'm famished. I guess that means I'm still mostly human.

I can't look at the Snatcher's eyes. A minute ago, I would have gladly busted him up to get Bridger back, but now, all I can think of is how I can't save him. I turn away, humiliated, lost, revolted.

What's really gnawing at my gut is that this time it's not just the stuffed puppy the boy gave me that the Institute has torn and ripped from my hands, it's the boy himself. The tears feel like they're gushing up from my chest. I thought that the need for human touch was gone, but no, it was just seething in the dark corners of my heart. Meeting Bridger cracked the dam, and now it's gushing out.

The ZV leader grabs my arm. His fingers smear my sleeve with blood.

"Not hungry, baby?" he teases.

"As a matter of fact, I'm starving. I'm just not a monster."

He surveys the raging horde and shrugs. "They're not monsters. They're just animals. They don't think anymore. They feed the need."

My mouth hangs open for about a second because I have no words to respond to that kind of callousness. Shaking my head, I let it go in favor of anger because my eyes are still following the fading red taillights of the van. "That was my friend Bridger in the back of that van. They're going to take him to the Institute. Do you have any idea what they do there?"

"Sort of, but, calm yourself. The kid was so far gone, there's not much more they can do to him that the virus hasn't already done."

Outrage forces me to finally look the alpha in the face. I jerk my arm away when I see who's holding it. Greyson Childs.

Greyson Childs is the biggest tool on the planet. The virus always infects a couple. That's why they think it's an STD. Of all the jerks in the world, the guy holding my arm truly deserved to catch a sexually transmitted disease. His virus partner used to run track with me. By the time her symptoms were showing, Greyson had moved on to someone else.

"Where's Julie?" I demand, reminding him I was not on his side of the break-up.

At least he hasn't forgotten her name. He squints a little to recognize me in the darkness, then smiles, "Evelyn. Evelyn Cross?" I guess girls lost their heads over the thick blond hair, the full lips, and the square jaw, before they were set in pasty grey. He's not my type, most zombies aren't, but I can see why so many of my classmates got taken in—his amber eyes, even bloodshot and purple-tinted around the edges, are sexy. He knows I don't like him. It wasn't a secret.

"Evelyn Cross. I'll be damned." He smirks and shrugs, folding his arms across his chest. "Julie went fast. They've probably got her chained up in a padded cell, doing experiments on her brain." He looks me up and down and I'm pretty sure the scowl I feel inside shows up on the outside. "But, you're lookin' damn hot for a ZV." He nods appreciatively. "You and me, baby. We are the future." He reaches out to touch me again and I shove him away.

"If there's only you and me, there is no future."

That's when the gang of ZV bashers shows up. I smell them over the carnage: the sweet, spicy smell of untainted meat. Both our heads jerk around at the same

23

time. Whatever's going on with me, that makes me the way I am, is going on with Greyson too. He was one of the first infected. His brain should be toast by now. He should be wandering aimlessly in search of meat. Instead, he's leading a bunch of full-fledged ZVs around like a mom on a field trip.

"C'mon. Get out of here. It's a gang!" I grab one of the girls feeding; she hisses, claws at me, and jerks away. Talk about conflicted. These ZVs are disgusting—they just ate two guys alive; they're covered in blood. But they're also sick and they're sitting ducks—okay, vicious, carnivorous ducks. But they need help, and not Z-V Institute help—someone-who-cares help.

The gangs aren't here to help. They're here to live out their Call of Duty, zombie-killing fantasies. "We have to get them out of here," I hiss at Greyson. The gang sees us and starts running. There are about twice as many of them as there are of us. I look at Greyson, expecting him to signal some kind of retreat to get his tribe out of here.

He doesn't even give his friends a second look. He clamps his fingers around my arm and starts hauling me away. I pull up, yanking my arm back. If he's not going to save them, I'll have to.

The gang starts whooping and catcalling. They've got baseball bats, shovels, and axes. One of the ZVs that I reach for bats me away; he's too engrossed in devouring a chunk of liver. I try again because I think I recognize him—it's Chase, the kid that took me to prom. He was a cross-country beast and pretty bright guy. He looks like he might be fresh. "Chase. It's me. Evelyn Cross. We have to go now. C'mon. There's a gang!" He looks up from the piece of guts he's tearing at, as if he recognizes me, but then the girl next to him tries to grab the meat out of his hand and they go at it with teeth and nails.

"Believe me, Chase can take care of himself," Greyson yells over the snarling, and tugs at my sleeve.

Another ZV stands up and runs, growling at the vigilante gang. They stop and converge when he reaches them. The poor sick slob has no idea what he's in for. He's just following blindly the viral urge that drives him. A bat slams him in the stomach and doubles him over. They all laugh as the guy with the shovel swats his butt and knocks him face forward. A big, burly kid with an axe hacks off his leg below the knee. The ZV grunts and growls with each attack, but just keeps trying to grab himself some fresh meat.

"*It's just a flesh wound.*" I recognize the attacker's voice over the bad British accent; I also recognize his shape. It's Gordon Roberts. He's on the football team, not because he's an athlete, but because he's mean. General laughter rocks the gang.

My guts are churning. I wish I could throw up. Being human isn't all it's cracked up to be.

"How can they do that, when there's not even a virus controlling their brains?" The other ZVs don't notice the groans of one of their own. "You're going to leave your friends to that?" I cry as Greyson drags me away.

"You don't get it, do you?" He pulls me along, ignoring the carnage going on behind us. "They're not my friends. They're dead. I just let them hang around and feed until they're too far gone to escape. That way, I don't get killed or hacked up like that." He points a thumb over his shoulder. "They're decoys."

Sucking in a breath, I run, but I'm not running *with* him. I'm running *from* him.

Chapter 4

Greyson's no slacker, but I really am fast. He loses me at the Calder's field. Outside the church, I hide in the ragged bushes for a while, just to be sure. Call it instinct, but I don't want him to know where I'm hiding. I would, however, like to know where *he's* camping out with his friends…no, his "decoys." Those poor ZVs he's herding are no better off than frogs hanging out with the biology teacher.

The moon is gone and the street has been empty for a while. Wind rattles the dead leaves, bugs click and twitter in the still of the night. It's really late, but I can still see the nightlight in Madi Calder's window.

I used to babysit her. She loved me and I'm pretty sure I was the only girl in the neighborhood willing to babysit at the funeral home. The only way I could talk her into going to bed was to tell her I knew the secret of keeping the dead people downstairs in their coffins. She was sure the corpses got up and walked around as soon as the lights went out. I used to do this special spell, sitting with my legs crossed and my palms pressed together in front of her bed until she fell asleep. I never did tell her parents my secret.

When I think I've lost Greyson for sure, I slip down the stairwell. The basement door closes quietly behind me. When I moved in, one of the first things I did was oil the hinges.

In the cubby, all my clothes are strewn on the floor and I start sorting through them. What's the best outfit for breaking a friend out of an asylum? No way I'm going to sit here safe in my little hideout while the Institute "doctors" torture

Bridger. He's still human—disgusting eating habits, maybe—but human.

My pale skin has an eerie glow in the dark. I stare at my hands and think of holding Bridger's. He was like a little kid, losing his speech, grasping at thoughts, limping. I try to hold it together, but a little tear slides down my cheek, my chest feels too small for the fat pain inside. That boy and I weren't just a couple; we were friends. I swipe at the drop on my face. The virus is eating Bridger alive and we caught it together. I should be as far gone as he is. I wonder what freak of nature is making me stronger instead of devouring me from the inside out.

I try to figure out why the virus god "smiled" on me, and I can't come up with an answer that makes sense. If I were home, my mom would tell me that bad things happen to you so that you can feel sorry for other people when bad things happen to them; and good things happen to you so that you can help people that bad things have happened too. I guess both apply to me. *Dans le royaume des aveugles, le borgne est roi. In the kingdom of the blind, the one-eyed man is king.* Maybe I'm like this so I can save Bridger.

My mom's not here, but I straighten up my pile of clothes before I leave because I know she'd be mortified if she came in and found it a mess. I'm amazed at how many books I have—not just that I have them, but that I've actually read them. It seems that time to kill and reading go together. Yeah, I caught the double meaning there. That's not what I meant.

The books arrived special delivery via Cory. That probably wasn't a family decision. There's a big, old maple tree on the very edge of the Calder's field, right where the fence meets the canal. It got hit by lightning a few years back and now the center has a bunch of hollow dead spots. Cory and I used to hide fruit snacks and juice boxes in there so we could stay out and play longer.

On my birthday a couple weeks ago, I found Baby Oscar in the tree with a big bow around his neck. Bridger gave the doll to Amber. I'm not sure which one of us got more presents from him. Sometimes, I was a little jealous. Anyway, she named her baby doll Oscar after the little kid that the demon kidnapped in *Ghostbusters*. Amber loves Baby Oscar and here he is with me. I can't think about that.

I figure the all-black ensemble I'm wearing is best, and I want to cover every inch of skin that I possibly can. Good thing winter arrived early. The cold doesn't really register for me, but it means I can cover up like this without making anyone suspicious. The daylight is rough. My eyes and skin can't take the ultra-violet.

After sticking a pair of sunglasses in my hair, I settle in to wait until just before dusk tomorrow. With some spare change, I'll catch the Trax up to the university where the Institute is. The trains don't run this late, and I can't go in broad daylight.

To pass the time, I rearrange my library. Books help, but I'm dying for a real person to talk to. No one has really bothered to set up a support group for lonely ZVs. The refreshment table could get complicated.

I guess my dad warmed up to the idea of the underground post because he sent me Kafka. I'm not sure what made him think I should read *The Metamorphosis*; maybe he thought reading about some guy that turns into a giant cockroach and gets rejected by his whole family would make me feel better. Maybe it did. At least, someone else out there knows how this feels. And maybe feeling bad for someone else for a change *does* help. A few pages in, I fall asleep.

Gnawing, cramping hunger wakes me up the next day. I read some more, trying to ignore the groaning in my guts, and the monster growling in my brain.

By the time the day is spent enough to leave, the hunger has turned to pain. I'm still annoyed that dinner got away from me the night before. I'm going to have to forage. Good thing I'm wearing black; foraging is never a little white sundress affair.

Eli was mostly farmland about twenty years ago, but when the city overflowed, farmers sold off their fields to build mansions. Later, they started building on the side of the mountain. A few of the old-time Eli families held out, or maybe they didn't have cropland to sell. In between the subdivisions are these huge lots with creaky old houses surrounded by overgrown shrubs, hiding from the world and the invasion of the city folks. One of those houses sits smack in the middle of my back-road route to the Trax station. The backyard looks like a farm tool cemetery. Stray dogs and cats love the place.

Only trouble is, Gordon Roberts lives here. He's a big-time gang member. The year I lettered, Gordon showed up at track meets to do the shot putt. Almost everyone noticed the bruises, but no one said anything. We all knew his dad got drunk and laid into him. I guess being a bully is contagious, or genetic. In junior high, he had a crush on me, but I wonder what he'd do now if he saw me. Don't really want to find out.

A stray dog is sniffing around the Roberts's back porch. Not much of their garbage makes it into the city bin. With plenty of cover and no one around, that dog is as good as dinner. The problem with dog is, what the bug inside of me really wants is people—I crave them like I used to crave chocolate during my period. Since people don't eat dog, dog doesn't taste anything like people, doesn't taste like chicken either—more like cardboard. Beef, or pork, or even chicken—those I can get by on because people *are* what they eat; and people eat beef, pork, and chicken.

I'm close enough to grab the dog when some heavenly scent comes wafting out of the broken screen on the kitchen window. No, it's not apple pie, but it might as well be. In my infected mind, the dog disappears from the scenery. I'm willing to risk a brutal beating and permanent maiming to get what's on the kitchen counter. What I'm doing, where I'm going, who I am; it's all gone. The only thing that exists is that smell and me getting it.

Sliding between the bushes, I make my way up onto the porch. The dark screen door is too opaque to see through. The coast is clear; I sense it. No one will see me go in. I wince as the screen door screeches. It might as well be an alarm that screams: *One of those deadly ZVs is breaking into the house! One of those deadly ZVs is breaking into the house!* As if the door isn't enough of an announcement, the saggy floorboards groan beneath me.

"Gordon?" a whiny voice calls from the back of the house. The air dies in my lungs. "Daddy told you to get out and mow them weeds. They better not be there when he gets home."

The kitchen is tiny. Dirty dishes, rags, clothes, ripped-open envelopes, old fruit, and trash clutter the counters. I can't see what's drawing me. ZV vision isn't x-ray. Whatever it is, there's a huge knife sitting next to the plastic it's wrapped in. The blade flashes in the light of the setting sun coming through the sink window.

My fingers stretch for the counter while my eyes keep a close watch on the hall door. The floorboards in the dimness beyond moan rhythmically—someone heavy is lumbering towards the kitchen. I lunge for the knife as the bulk of the intruder fills the tiny doorframe. His mouth opens to scream but nothing comes out. It's Gordon's little brother Marlow Junior. Little is a relative term. Too big to fit through the opening straight on, he's a walking all-you-can-eat zombie buffet—deep-fried and slathered in margarine spread.

One stab, a slice, a grab, and it's done—not the kid, the plastic bag—although it's like the knife has a mind of its own and really wants to slash that tender, juicy belly. I force the blade through the bag, grab the spoils on the counter, and I'm out the door, fleeing the screams of bloody murder.

Warm, sticky fluid seeps down my arm from the gooey delight in my hand. The scent is more than I can take. The second I hit the cover of trees and brush by the creek, I'm on my knees shoving the meat into my mouth. I can feel it smeared across my cheek and dribbling onto my chin. It's like the satisfying sensation of stepping into a hot bath on a freezing cold morning the day after I've run the 400. I lie flat on my back in the grass and soak it up.

Chapter 5

The Trax runs directly north and south through the city. Eli lies about twenty blocks south of the end of the line, so I have to walk to catch it, keeping to the trees and the little back roads. You never know when an idiot with a bat will be randomly roaming the streets. Even though it's almost impossible to tell I'm a ZV when I'm all decked out in my cool weather gear, if one of them gets close enough to catch a whiff of me, the game is up. Gobs of perfume help, but my nose is super sensitive so I'm paranoid that other people can smell me too.

I washed the leftover slime off my fingers in the creek before I headed for the train. The bag on the counter was full of some kind of cow organs: liver, kidney, who knows what else. I figure that's why they tasted so heavenly. The virus craves whatever comes from eating organs.

My whole body just wants to shut down and digest, so walking is a challenge, but sitting still would be a huge mistake. Whatever else he did, I'm sure Marlow Jr. waddled off to alert his brother to the invasion of the evil zombie girl.

It's an odd hour for going into the city; most people are coming home. Only a kid and some older lady in a scarf are heading for the station when I get there. A couple of teenagers ride up on bikes about the time I'm stepping onto the platform. The train pulls in, the doors open, and people spill out. Looking over the railing to the parking lot, I see a K-9 ZV dog trot out of a car and head towards the stairs I just came up. It's the cutest black lab and his ears twitch as he sniffs at the air. His partner leans down and pats him. "What you got, boy?"

He whines, tugging his leash forward into the knotted crowd walking towards me. I'm not about to wait and pet the doggy, but I can't risk him getting on this train either. The platform has two entrances: one at the front of the cars, and the one I'm exiting at the back.

I'm a quick thinker. That's how I ace pop quizzes that I didn't even study for. It's no big deal to carve a little cut into the flesh of my palm with my thumbnail—or should I say claw. I seriously need a manicure. I just haven't seen them flashing the "zombie special" at the salon recently.

By the time I pass the two kids toting their bikes, there's a nice little pool of purple blood trailing down my thumb. I casually walk past the tangle of people and brush the blood onto one of the biker's jeans as he fights his way up the steps. Circling back, I'm halfway up on the other end of the platform before I hear the barking frenzy and the crowd screaming. As I slip into one of the front cars and the train pulls away, I catch a glimpse of the mayhem. No worries. They'll stick a thermometer in the kid's ear. He'll be fine—I hope.

I'm the only one in my car for a while as the train heads back to the city. Once we get downtown, I'll have to jump onto the other line that runs east to the mountain and the university. The ride lasts a good thirty minutes. I find parts of an old newspaper and settle in to read in a corner seat near the doors.

The Z-Virus stories don't even make the headlines anymore. The "Z" really stands for Zoser. It was the media that started calling it the Zombie Virus.

ZOMBIE VIRUS MAY NOT BE SEXUALLY TRANSMITTED

While the virus requires a couple to incubate, new research suggests that sexual contact does not lead to infection.

I could have told them that.

In the face of new evidence to the contrary, local church leaders reaffirm the position that infection is God's punishment.

I can't help but roll my eyes. The couple thing has worked out well for them. They've been trying to outlaw teen dating for years now. Another article, in much smaller type, catches my eye:

NEW ZOMBIE VIRUS IMMUNITY GENE
Dr. Vern Christensen, MD, Head of the Z-V Institute, confirmed the recent discovery of Z-Virus carriers who appear to be immune to the terminal effects of the virus. "Normally, the Z-Virus hijacks the brain and consumes the organs in the host, resulting in death. But we can now confirm that a few rare ZVs resist these late-stage, terminal developments indefinitely." Dr. Christensen warned that these immune specimens pose a much more serious public threat, withstanding the more debilitating effects of the virus, and also demonstrating heightened physical abilities. According to Sudhir Nicolas Vadlamani, MD, PhD, Senior Official of the CDC and Head of Research: "In a select few hosts, the virus shuts off some systems, but enhances others allowing the host to become a more effective predator."

My whole body shivers as the train pulls into a station. That's me. I'm becoming a predator.

Even though my skin is dying, my nails are sprouting out of control; they're thick and long, and not in a pretty way. I'd kill for a mani/pedi right about now. Well, not really kill; it's just a figure of speech. I don't hunt people.

A few pages in, another headline catches my eye: **Court of Appeals Upholds Ruling on ZV Rights.** Seems the Z-V Commission isn't too happy about that. The case is on its way to the State Supreme Court—a lot of good that does me now.

At the next stop, a mom with a perky brown ponytail hauls a baby stroller and a three-year-old onto the train. She looks my way and then opts to sit at the other end of the car. The electric train hums away while she arranges the kids around her.

"Is daddy gonna be at the zoo, too?"

"Yep, it's a special night so daddies can come," she answers, tucking blankets around the baby. "Remember the fireworks?"

The little boy nods. He has a big plastic tiger in his fist. He waves it in front of his sister's nose. "Grrrrr. The tigers will eat you for dinner, Mimie!" His sister wiggles and giggles at the excitement in her brother's eyes.

The mom leans over and wrinkles her nose at Mimie. "The tigers are in cages, baby, and they've already had their dinner." She pulls the boy onto her lap, nuzzles his nose. "Maybe they should put YOU in a cage, wild boy."

I can smell them all the way at the other end of the car. Thanks to the snack I devoured before I got on, I don't feel like running off the train to get away from the impulse to feed. What actually does make me feel like running off the train is that the boy is just a little younger than Amber, and when I was little, my mom used to chase Cory and me around, threatening to make witch stew out of us in the bathtub. My eyes sting and I shield them from the light with the paper.

I hate to think about what it means that the guy who was going through the trash, who seemed awfully picky for a dumpster diver, was actually one of the Institute Snatchers. Do they know about me? This article makes it seem like they know there are some of us who don't progress and actually go into some kind of hyper mode. Maybe they know about Greyson. If he's out there with his gang, hunting people, they've got to be gunning for him. Maybe I stumbled into the trap. And what the heck did the guy mean, "She's fresh. The doc's going to want her alive"? It makes my skin crawl just thinking about it—even though my skin doesn't really crawl anymore. I flip back to the article because it gives me the creeps:

Dr. Vadlamani is confident that if they can gather some of these semi-immune specimens for study, "the chances of isolating those genes and synthesizing an antibody or inoculation increase dramatically."

With my eyes closed and my face behind my hand, I try to swallow the word "specimen." They're looking for "specimens" like me. I glance out the windows as the train pulls into the stop in Green City.

Green City is anything but: there's not a tree in the place, nothing but concrete, weeds, rocks, and potholes. It's a town where you don't get off the train unless you have to because you live there. In the bright lights of the station, the city in the background fades to a black void. Somewhere out there is the empty lot where a father watched a gang beat his daughter to a pulp. Anyone with Z-Virus knows to avoid this place like the plague. Churches here encourage gangs to wipe evildoers off the face of the planet. If I lived here, I'd probably be locked up in the Institute right now.

When the virus first broke out, they hauled the first few "lucky" couples into quarantine right away. The Z-V Commission set up a facility in the old burn unit near the university hospital. They slapped on the name Z-V Institute and transferred all of the patients out of the regular hospital.

When the rumors about "experimental testing" started leaking out, the occasional victim went missing instead of checking in. Parents were afraid their own kid would show up in the night and eat them. That's when the gangs formed to scour Green City clean.

My parents and I, law-abiding citizens that we are, called the Institute.

The doors slide open and two Neanderthal guys hop into my train car. My body flips into survival mode. They're wearing letterman jackets and carrying baseball bats. There's dried purple blood splattered on the white leather sleeves. Technically, legally, they can't hunt us down, but no one seems to care much when a ZV turns up smashed to pieces. They just put it down to the natural progression of the virus. The gang members can't really brag about their feats of carnage, so they wear bloodstains like medals of valor.

I slide down in my seat, slip my glasses up on my head, and turn my face out the window, pretending to sleep. A thick sheet of hair falls over my profile. If they only see my hair, there's no way they'll peg me for a ZV. I can barely see them from the corner of my eye. Every now and again, I take a peek. They clomp their way to the other end of the car and find a seat. It creaks under their weight.

"Smells like shit in here—and perfume." The burly blond guy grumbles. I hold my breath, hoping that if I can't smell me, he can't.

"Hey, it's not me, dude."

"Did I say it was you?"

The brunette with a hooknose makes some woeful pretense of whispering confidentially, but I can hear him clearly on the opposite end of the car: "Probably that kid's got a load of shit in his pants." He raises his voice, obviously talking to me. "Hot date tonight, baby?" He cracks up.

I don't respond. My hands are shaking. Their bats tap out of time on the floor as the train pulls away. I wonder if there are still stray ZVs to be hunted in Pioneer Park. My heart stampedes; my body gets drunk on the adrenaline the blood is serving up. The transfer station up to the university is two stops away.

The little boy gets up and starts walking back towards me. He's hopping his tiger over the seats. "I'm going to the zoo," he announces when he's about a seat away from me.

I don't move. I can feel everyone's eyes on me. My head pounds like it's going to explode. I can smell the little boy. I wonder if children are tenderer than grown-ups and then cringe at the thought. My mother read me too many child-eating witch stories when I was a kid.

"I'm going to the zoo!" the boy yells at me, much louder this time. I don't know whether to say something so he'll go away, or just play dead.

His mom's voice reaches across the car and leashes him in. "Zachary, come back here. That girl is trying to sleep."

I breathe deeply like she's right. If only they knew just how *not* asleep I am. Zachary runs back to his mom, and the beat of the bats tapping against the floor mixes with the shuffle of his tennis shoes.

The blond guy nudges his buddy and says, "You know Nicky?"

"Nicky Coles. That kid that hunts with us from over in Eli?"

The train rattles through an intersection. "Yeah, that's the one. His brother Joey is in the Guard. He was driving the zombie mobile last night," blond thug says.

"Yeah, what's up with that? Since when does the Guard hunt zombies?"

"Since they found a new breed that's faster and stronger like a super killer. But get this: the disease doesn't eat them up slowly. They don't go brain dead. They talk, they think, like you and me. You can't tell anyone. The military's not officially involved. But think about it. If they could put that virus in a soldier?"

The bat stops tapping while they both stretch their pea-sized brains to imagine. "Joey told Nicky he thinks they want that Doc Christensen who's heading up the zombie research to find what makes these new freaks immune so they can bottle it and feed it to soldiers."

"Damn super army," hooknose drools.

"Joey said they almost caught one last night. They went after it out in Eli..." My ears perk up and my stomach drops. Blond guy just keeps going, "...some guy that's been leading a group of them around eating up all the homeless bums. They spotted him in Pioneer Park a couple weeks ago."

"If you ask me," hooknose interjects, "them ZVs are doin' the city a favor. Keep all that worthless trash off the streets."

"Yeah, whatever. They sent a guy into the dumpsters to try and draw out the pack leader. The gang showed up, all right, but there was some girl, too. They didn't know about her."

I shrink in my seat. If they look at me, they'll see me shaking. I'm breathing so hard that I feel like the air is roaring out of my nose. Suddenly, I feel fifty feet tall and twenty feet wide. I shove my face farther into the corner of the train.

"You mean she was one of them ones they're looking for?" hooknose asks. He's not too bright.

"Talking and everything. Joey got a good look at her. Watched her pick a guy up by the pants and toss him about twenty feet; broke his leg." *I'm pretty sure twenty feet is an exaggeration.* "Said she was talking like you and me: tall, really sexy like an Amazon. He thought she was just a regular babe, at first, until she tried to suck the guy's brains out through his ear."

"Amazon, huh?" They sit quietly for a minute while my brain tries to figure out if I can get out of the car before they make me out for who…what I am. "You think those zombie chicks can still do it?" hooknose asks, scratching the side of his lip with his thumbnail. He's obviously the less evolved of the two creatures.

"Do what?"

"You know—do *it*?" he hisses and then glances my direction. A cold rush washes through me. "I mean if they're, like, superhuman now…"

"Are you a total dipstick? That's how you get the virus, idiot."

"Oh, yeah."

The bat stops tapping again. Lights flash through the car. We're coming up on a station. My speed is my asset. I'm calculating a run for it.

"So, what happened? Did they get her?"

Blond guy stands up. I hold my breath. "No. The zombie gang showed up with the one they were looking for. By then, the ninja zombie chick had ripped the guts out of one of the Snatchers and fed him to the zombie mob."

This is such a load of crap. If they ever catch me, they'll tear me apart and I don't even eat people. The thought of it makes me want to puke. I can't help it if the way people smell makes me drool.

The train slows into the station.

"Joey thinks she and the male zombie are together—like a couple." The other one nods like he knows exactly what his goonmate is thinking. "When he showed up, he pulled the other Snatcher right out of the truck and fed him to his gang."

"Filthy SOB!"

"They got the other ZV that was hunting with the girl though. It was still talking. The doc was pretty happy about that. Came and congratulated Joey himself. Guess they don't get many fresh ones."

"Gotta kill those ones. There's no bringin' them in," hooknose agrees.

They chuckle. "Yeah, Doc wanted to know all about the girl, wanted to know if Joey thought they could find her again."

"Not a bad night," hooknose steps off the train.

"Wish we had that kind of action around here. Been a long time since we brought in a live one. All we ever get are the old, stale ones. It's about as fun as taking down Betty White." Blond guy takes a swing at the light post as he walks by. The clang ripples through the station and into the car as the door closes. I shiver in the vibration.

Chapter 6

The bushes around the Institute prickle so I'm glad I wore long sleeves. Up to now, I've done a pretty good job of protecting my skin.

The faded marks from the letters for the burn center underneath the Zoser Virus Institute letters are still vaguely visible. The building is pretty old, brick with a windowed emergency staircase at the end.

No one is coming in or out, and there are only a few cars in the lots—mostly black Institute vans and SUVs. I guess they decided they needed something a little sportier when they started having to chase us down. The army Humvee out front worries me. An old army base sits across the street from the university; they use it for the ROTC guys now.

What surprises me is how unprotected the Institute looks. They're clearly not expecting me. Then again, they probably don't have to work too hard to keep people out. I'm sure they're much more concerned about keeping the inmates in than keeping the public out. If I have my way tonight, that's going to change.

I'm crouched in the greenery for about an hour before it starts to look like the night shift might be coming on. I figure sneaking in with the rush is my best option. My scarf is wrapped so high up my face, it looks like I'm either a mummy or allergic to the cold.

When I slip inside the building, I realize that getting back out is going to be the real challenge here. The place has boxes scattered everywhere like they're still moving in. People in scrubs are wandering around looking confused. There are a couple soldiers, but they don't look like they're expecting any kind of action.

Not too far behind the receptionist, who is chatting up a guy in camouflage with a big, fat handgun stuck to his side, are some over-sized metal doors. Even though they have warnings—QUARANTINE AREA – ANTI-VIRAL EQUIPMENT REQUIRED – AUTHORIZED PERSONNEL ONLY—some guy all dressed up with a mask and a jumpsuit walks right by. The guard and the receptionist don't even glance at him. But the exit, that's a different story. There's a line of the day shift waiting for the security to work them over like Arabs at an airport. I'll need a separate exit strategy.

Keeping a few steps behind, I follow a girl about my size into what looks like a locker room, where there's a whole shelf of jumpsuits and masks. My accidental escort grabs a set and steps into a changing room. This looks promising, so I follow and suit up. My reflection explains why the soldier didn't bother to check the guy going in. First of all, why would anyone voluntarily walk into the zombie ward? Second, even if he did want to check me out, I'd have to shed all this gear that I just put on for him to see anything. I'm pretty sure the smell can't get through the suit, either. I'm golden.

My new friend heads for the door and I follow. She doesn't go through. She's staring at my hair. "I'm sorry, I don't think I know you," she says, holding the door but standing right in front of it.

Okay, maybe not so golden now.

"What's your name?"

Think fast. (That's what Honors students do.) "Ev...uh Evelyn. I'm new."

"They didn't tell me we were getting anyone new." It's difficult to tell through the goggles and mask, but she sounds mad. "How am I supposed to make a decent schedule if they don't even tell me who's working? Did they send you over to personnel in the hospital to fill out the paperwork and do the screenings?"

"Uh... Well, I'm not really working...I'm doing an internship. Psychology. I'm mostly just observing."

"Yeah, but you're going to have to sign the forms. I swear the zoo runs better than this place. Wait here and I'll find out what I'm supposed to do with you." She leaves me standing in the doorway and stomps across the hall to some offices past the reception desk.

Like I'm really going to wait.

I follow the next guy that opens the big metal doors. He nods and smiles like he knows me. It's my hair. My mom calls it the Rapunzel effect. (Actually, she called it the Farrah Fawcett effect, but we didn't know who that was—my mom graduated in the 80's—so she changed the name.) When the guy turns down a corridor, I cut the other direction and duck into an open doorway that leads to a room that looks empty: OBSERVATION ROOM 3.

The dark room is not empty, though I wish it were. I don't need a camera, because what I'm seeing will be forever imprinted on my nightmares. Even though I'm wearing my mask, the stench slams into my nose, and my hand flies up to cover my mouth. There's a ZV in here. A projector flashing one picture after another catches my eye, but I don't look at the screen right away. What I do notice is a boy strapped into a metal chair, connected to electrodes by a metal cap that spurts and fizzles in the dim light. At least I think it's a boy. I'm only judging by the length of the hair, or what's left of it.

Not even his parents would be able to recognize him. One side of his face has been smashed, probably with a baseball bat. His jaw hangs loose around the wire in his mouth. With the flash of a new slide, the chair whizzes, the body and muscles jolt and convulse, and the teeth knock and rattle against each other. But that's not the worst. I expected the lips, skin, and eyes to be all the wrong colors. What I didn't expect was for the lower parts of the arms and legs to be shooting out at odd angles from the straps holding him down. Purple-black ZV blood splotches his limbs. One of his legs is half gone and fractured bones slice through the dead skin.

I want to throw up, but I'm wearing the suit and the mask. I rip at it to get it away and luckily my hands are too clumsy. I turn away and swallow the acid, try to collect myself, and force my emergency cool to kick in. Three deep breaths and I think I can face him again. I'm wrong. I turn away, close my eyes, and count to ten. When I turn back, I avoid his face and focus on the locks on the metal wrist restraints. The least I can do is get the poor guy out. He's obviously dead—really dead.

"Oh, that was fast." A nasal male voice from the door freezes me. I thank my lucky stars I couldn't get my mask off. I get ready to slam the owner with a good kick to the head and wish I had checked the room for the fire evacuation chart and the emergency exit. Chances are they didn't really put that much effort into assuring the safety of the occupants here, but it seems like there'd have to be something for the staff. "I only called a few minutes ago for cleanup. The key to those cuffs is over there on the wall. You can just take the body down to the lab. Dr. Christensen will want the parts—" he chuckles, "—what's left of them."

He thinks I'm the cleanup crew. My hand reaches for the key, realizing gratefully that I must look like every other grunt in the place, and there's no way he'll pick up my stink over his patient's.

"Man, I thought he reeked before we started the therapy." I'm a little confused because the man speaking to me is not decked out in antivirus gear, just scrubs, and he's totally unfazed by the horror sprawled out in the chair. We might as well be looking at a monkey in the zoo. He's disconnecting the headgear where bits of skin have fused to the metal.

"Therapy?" I can't stop myself from asking.

"Yeah, they brought this specimen in last night with the talker. He was nearly done for, so Vern sent him over to us to test out the therapy."

"Is that what the projector and the electrodes are for?"

"Oh, yeah, I better shut that down. Don't want to waste the power, least not until we get that military funding. Are you new?" I nod my head and relax a little. It's my hair. It distracts boys, no matter how old. It's probably all he can see of me.

"Psych intern," I explain.

It disturbs me that this guy can be around the carnage without even flinching. *How much of this does a human being have to see to get this calloused?* "This should be interesting for you, then." He points up at the pictures flashing on the screen. For the first time, they draw my attention. Food: pictures of steak, potatoes, salad, chicken, pie, cakes, a little girl licking an ice cream cone. The chair rattles and the wrist I've just freed flies on its own. I gasp and jump back. "Sorry about that," the guy chuckles. "The machine's up a little high. This one was already so far gone, Vern— Dr. Christensen—told me to go ahead and test the limits."

Behind my mask, my mouth is hanging open. "You…You…You hook them up and show them pictures of real food. And then…what? When the pictures of people come up…?"

"As soon as the sensors pick up any undesirable reaction—hunger responses, salivating—to an inappropriate stimulus, the machine delivers an electrical current to the subject." He nods and shuts down the projector and the chair from a control panel. "Basic Behavioral Modification Electric Shock Therapy. But this specimen was so far advanced that we just set the machine to fire whenever the wrong picture came up. We didn't think his neural responses were still sufficiently sensitive to react properly." I notice a pad of paper and pencil on the desk next to the chair. Someone must observe the whole torture process.

"What went wrong?" I ask, afraid to know.

The guy frowns a bit, clearly mystified. "Nothing." He shakes his head and picks up the pad of paper, surveys the markings. "Looks like the viral-infected brain is less tolerant to the charge than we projected. But the reaction to the inappropriate stimuli was decreasing measurably. So, it looks successful."

The door swings wide and a gurney powered by a couple of large anti-viral suits rolls into the room. The cleanup crew tosses what's left of the boy onto the sheet.

"That's going down to the lab, not the incinerator. We still need some stats off of it," the doctor reminds them. He turns to me, "Well…uh. What was your name?"

44

I use the cleaning supplies from the cart in the corner and wipe down the area while I debate whether or not to lie. "Evelyn," I respond. I figure if I tell the truth, I'm less likely to slip up.

He reaches out a gloved hand. "Dr. Hickman, Brent." I shake his hand. "I'm Dr. Christensen's assistant and Head of Behavioral Reconditioning. Well, Evelyn. It's your lucky night. I'm going to get you in on something big. Did you hear about the talker they brought in?"

"Yeah," I stumble, "I think they were talking about him in the dressing room."

"Would you like to get in on that surgical investigation?"

"Most definitely," I respond, half astonished at my good luck and half scared witless for Bridger.

Chapter 7

The corridors reek of antiseptic with just a hint of ZV that seems to hang in the fumes. I'm pretty sure the staff here is used to the smell by now and won't even register my personal *eau de zombie*. Dr. Hickman chats with me non-stop all the way to the elevator at the end of the hall. He's an information junkie, the kind of guy you can't ever trust with a secret because the potential ego boost of divulging it is too sexy to resist. I'm just what he needs to follow him around all day—a student minion to gaze in awe at the peacock spread of his superior knowledge.

"This surgery was scheduled for tomorrow morning, but Dr. Christensen wants to get inside the specimen's head and organs before deprivation from other sources of nourishment forces the virus to accelerate its consumption of the host organs." The way he talks about Bridger like he's not the boy I went to junior prom with, like he doesn't have a mom, like he's not alive or human, I'm seriously tempted to rip this doctor's stomach out and eat it in front of him.

"Don't you have to talk to him first?"

The guy looks at me like I'm a half-wit. "Why?"

"I don't know. Find out his history? Who he is? I mean…he can talk. Couldn't he tell you something about how he got the virus? I don't know…I'm not really a doctor…but it seems to me you could probably get some pretty valuable information from him."

Dr. Hickman laughs. "All that convoluted research on the origins of the disease. Yeah, we already wasted a whole day on that. Dr. Christensen's research assistant, that Indian kid,

Vladami, Vilamani...don't know why they can't have normal names. If they're going to live in America, they ought to have names Americans can pronounce."

"Nicolas Vadlamani. I read about him in the newspaper."

"Yeah, well he does all that dry, interviewing, observation shit. Dr. Christensen and I handle the juicy stuff. We like to get to the meat of it." He laughs at his own gross wit. The muscles tense in my jaw. I'm trying desperately to swallow the urge to bite his head off—the literal way. We've reached the elevator and he pushes the up button.

I play into his game, keep up the charade. "Thanks so much for getting me in. You don't know what this means to me."

He nods condescendingly, but I can tell by the way he straightens his shoulders he's really pleased that I'm such a suck-up. "It means your Psych professor is going to be taking lessons from *you*. Hook your bike to my bumper, Evelyn. You'll graduate a high-value commodity." The door pings and opens.

"Thanks!" I'm worried that the irony in my voice might be too obvious, but I keep going: "Dr. Hickman, I know I'm just a student, so I don't know all the process yet, but don't we stand a better chance of curing the virus if we find out where it came from? How it's transmitted?" We step into the elevator. I'm a little worried about him catching a whiff of me in an enclosed space. We both spot the drops of fairly fresh, purple-black blood on the floor. He rolls his eyes disgusted and I thank the zombie gods for the cover. The blood stinks more than the cleaning products.

"A cure. Is that what they're telling you? You think those army stiffs are hanging about out there and the pentagon is sniffing around with a pen in its hand because we're looking for a cure?" He snorts. The door closes. We're alone in the elevator. "Let me tell you something, little girl. There's a new breed, a strain that enhances the host, makes it a better predator, but doesn't destroy it. That's what we're after. They saw one last night when they picked up this talker. We think they may be a virus pair, but the male manifests a significantly higher rate of deterioration than the female. That's why we

47

want a good look at the virus inside this kid. We get that strain, and the military will be camped outside our door with money in their hands."

I close my eyes and concentrate on breathing so I won't explode. It's my fault they're going to cut up Bridger. If they'd never seen me, they might be more interested in helping him fight off the virus or finding a cure.

Who am I kidding? These wackos would dissect their own mother for fun.

The virus capitalizes on my rage; my hunter instincts seethe and rattle the chains in my head. Sweat breaks out on my brow underneath the goggles. "Don't you need the boy's parents to sign something? Authorize the surgery? Seems like someone ought to be worried about him."

Hickman sneers down at me. I can see he's rethinking the grand and glorious privilege he's bestowing. I backpedal. "I guess they're not really human anymore."

"You haven't been in here long enough, yet. You still think of them as people. They're mindless, vicious filth."

"But he's just a boy—a boy who's sick. He needs help."

"Tell that to the two Snatchers that got slaughtered last night trying to bring him in." The elevator door opens. We take a right and head down a long hallway. I take note of the emergency stairway at the far end of the hall before we turn down a small corridor and walk through a set of metal double doors marked SURGICAL CENTER.

Three or four tagged nurses and a couple of anonymous, fully suited nondescripts like me nod respectfully as Dr. Hickman passes. I follow him into a locker room like the one I changed in downstairs where he suits up. His suit is monogrammed.

Operating Room 1. The door swings wide and from behind Dr. Hickman's bulk, I get my first glimpse of Dr. Death. Dr. Vern Christensen is tall and thin. Not the kind of thin that comes from a healthy workout and a good diet, the kind of puckered thin that comes from not liking anything. He has that nasty receding chin and a hooknose that makes him look like a bird—a bird of prey. He's about to dig his metal claws into Bridger with the help of some loud-mouthed, bossy nurse that keeps barking at the poor intern in the room.

Dr. Christensen looks up. "Dr. Hickman. Glad you could make it."

"Wouldn't miss this, Vern. Just finished up over in rehab."

"How did that go?"

"Not well for the zombie." They both laugh. Hickman explains his night's torture session to Christensen while I distract myself from my homicidal thoughts by surveying the room. One small window with bars, a counter, a sink, and a closet...

The nurse takes over arranging a table of nasty looking sharp tools and dismisses the medical intern—and then I see Bridger. He's lying on a surgical cot close to the wall, strapped in with restraints across his forehead, waist, wrists, and legs. He's hooked up to an IV.

I'm afraid they hear me gasp. They've shaved Bridger's head and drawn lines and incision marks on his skull and abdomen. I can hear water dripping somewhere. My arms cross mechanically over my stomach and my legs feel like they want to buckle. And then the door opens behind us and we all shuffle to the side. I use the distraction to turn away from my friend on the chopping board, brace myself against the counter, and breathe deeply, focusing on what has to be done, not on what's going on.

"We still need a few fluid samples," the newcomer announces. He has a faint Indian accent, the emphasis slightly on the wrong syllable.

When I turn back to look at him, I can't help but wonder what the heck a guy like him is doing in this Nazi experiment hole. He doesn't have the face for it. On Christensen and Hickman, I can see the lines, and the set of the eyes, that speak hypocrite plastered over villain. But this other man can't be more than a few years older than I am, maybe the same age as Preston, Bridger's big brother. And there's warmth in his face—it's molded the lines, just like meanness has molded Dr. Hickman's. I know the newcomer is important because his name is scrawled across his coat: Dr. Nicolas Vadlamani.

He pulls some vials from his pocket and wraps a plastic band around Bridger's restrained arm. "Okay, pal," he says, looking in his face. "You're going to feel a prick here 'cause you haven't been sedated. It shouldn't be too bad, though. Your skin has lost most of its sensation." He draws a few vials of blood while the "doctors" joke about the electric shock therapy. I focus on the restraints and how they're latched and unlatched so I don't have to hear what they're saying, but it's too awful to ignore.

"By the time we're finished with this one, it won't be good for much more than your therapy trial," Dr. Christensen quips.

I squeeze my eyes shut and grit my teeth. They're planning to murder him slowly, piece by piece. And no one cares—no one but me. My eyes lock on the vial slowly filling with fluid from Bridger's veins. The blood is darker and more purple than it should be. That's part of the reason we smell bad. Bridger growls and thrashes in his restraints. He's probably starving. The assistant notices his pain.

"Thanks," he puts his hand on Bridger's head, pets his scalp where his hair should have been. "You're helping us more than you can comprehend."

I want to cry. I want Dr. Vadlamani to put his hand on my head too, look me in the eye and see me—me, Evelyn—the way he sees Bridger.

"The anesthesiologist hasn't hooked him up yet?" Nicolas asks. He's holding the IV tube at the head of the bed. He looks concerned. "I think he's already gone home for the night."

"We're going to postpone that until after some of the initial brain probes," Dr. Christensen announces. "We want to gauge some of his cerebral responses. We'll be doing non-sedated vivisection in this evening's phase of the surgical investigation."

"But what about the pain?" I blurt out, even though I know if I have anything to do with it, Bridger will be long gone before they get anywhere near him with one of those scalpels.

They all turn and stare at me perplexed. When the answer doesn't seem to be obvious or relevant to them, Nicolas speaks up. "You're not seriously going to cut into him without anesthesia? He's still almost totally functional. He's going to feel everything at some level!"

"That is the point," Dr. Christensen snaps and turns away derisively. "And who is our guest?" he asks Dr. Hickman, nodding in my direction.

Igor looks a little disturbed that I've embarrassed him in front of Dr. Death. "New Psych intern. Helped with the cleanup after the electro-therapy. Evelyn, this is Dr. Christensen, Head of the Z-V Institute." By his tone, he's trying to impress on me the importance of shutting up and sucking up to the good fortune of being here.

I nod respectfully. "Thanks for letting me be here." At the sound of my voice, Bridger starts fidgeting in his restraints. "I had no idea we'd get to see some of the surgery up close. I've heard so much about your work. It's fascinating." I choke the words out convincingly, but I really feel like I'd be doing a favor to the entire ZV community, not to mention the world in general, by breaking my diet and making a Scooby-snack of these two slime buckets.

Dr. Christensen nods like I might have won him over. I can tell his ego would deluge a football field if it were popped. Dr. Hickman nods; his eyes crinkle up like he's grinning under his surgical mask. Nicolas looks like he smells old cheese. He's about to protest when Bridger moans, "Ev'lyn?"

They all look at him. Nicolas looks at the doctors and explains, "That's the name of his virus mate."

"Ev'lyn...help."

It's about a two-second delay before they all look at me. The most logical move at this point is a round kick. *See mom. Karate is much more practical than ballet.* I take out Dr. Christensen first. He slams into the tray of surgical supplies that fly like shrapnel through the room. Everyone ducks and covers. Christensen is out cold and bleeding from a cut on his head. He won't be doing any experimental surgery tonight. Hickman gets stabbed in the hand. I can only hope it's the one he does surgery with. He looks like he's going to come after me, so I haul him up and toss him at the sink. His head slams into it and he falls in a heap to the floor.

The nurse cowers in a corner at the head of the bed, and, of course, Nicolas, who got knocked over when the tray crashed into the bed, is shielding her with his body. He's reaching for some kind of blade that clattered to the floor by him. I run around the bed, and stomp my hand on his wrist before he can grab it. The nurse screams, so my time is up. My ears pick up the cluttered rustle of running in the hallway. With my foot firmly on Mr. Stunning's arm, I release the latches on Bridger and haul him up out of the bed.

"Ev'lyn, help. Ev'lyn…bad…doctor…bad."

"I know, Bridger. We gotta get out of here!" I grab his arm and pull towards the exit, but he resists, tugging me back towards the nurse on the floor.

"Hungry…Ev'lyn…hungry."

Using both arms, I rip him away from the cowering humans and shove him to the door. "Go. We don't have time for that. Go!" He stumbles towards the knob. I'm following, but I can't help myself. I turn back around and drop to my knees in front of the face of kindness.

I pull my mask off and Nicolas gasps. My heart sinks. He's never going to look at me the way he looked at Bridger because I'm not restrained. I thought he was different, but he's not. I'm a vicious animal to him and I'll never be anything else, but I desperately want to be.

"I'm not going to kill anyone. Not ever. I'm here for my friend. That's it." I turn away and head towards Bridger, who can't quite figure out the complicated workings of a door handle. Then, I don't know why, I turn to Nicolas once more. "Help us." And then Bridger and I are out the door.

It's like trying to run a fire drill with my little sister in the middle of a toy store. Bridger wants to grab and eat every panicked piece of personnel we run into. Alarms scream as I drag him towards the stairs. At the opposite end of the building, the elevator dings and a couple of camouflaged soldiers dive into the corridor. I'm pretty sure we're gonna be dead because they have these ginormous guns. I make a desperate dash for the emergency exit anyway. Being shot has to be better than being chopped up like a worm in Biology 101.

Dr. Death stumbles out of the surgical room, holding his head, and growls, "Don't shoot them. Don't shoot. Talkers. I need them alive. Catch the damn things!"

Yeah. He wants us alive so he can kill us slowly and painfully. Once we're inside the stairwell without distractions, Bridger keeps up. The door behind us crashes open. I fly over the last steps to the landing with my friend trailing behind. The door below us squeals and footsteps flood the stairwell. Trapped. The stairwell is lined with a huge column of windows. Apparently, I'm going to have to risk some skin damage…or worse…if we're going to get out of this dungeon.

For a brief second, the thought crosses my mind that I could turn Bridger loose on them and make a run for it. That's the virus talking—violence works it up. The bio-suit will protect me. I crash my elbow into the window, ducking as the glass flies. A muffled gunshot rips the air above us. Bridger jerks, moans, and stumbles.

"Shit!" Wrapping my arm around his waist, I propel the two of us out the broken window. *How high up can we be?*

We fall, fall, fall. We roll. Nothing snaps. I scramble for Bridger. I can hear them at the window. "Are you hurt, Bridger. Can you run?" He rolls over like a sack of potatoes. The dart protrudes from the side of his neck. It's going to be harder to get away with him on my back. My arms encircle his chest; he's about six inches off the ground when I hear the crack of the gun from the jagged window above.

The dart penetrates my suit, right along my spine. Another crack from the window; another jolt—in my neck. I stumble. Another crack; a crimp in my thigh. As the parking lot lights fade into darkness, Bridger weighs my arms down, and only one thought floats about in the fluid void. *Those are going to leave marks.*

Chapter 8

Tugging on my wrist. "Greyson. Don't touch me!" Squirm…can't move. Scream…no sound. Eyes flutter against the light. Where am I. Thirsty. Nausea. So tired. Nothing.

* * *

My eyes flutter. Too bright. Drool on my cheek. Arm stuck. Can't wipe it. Where am I? Nausea. White light. Antiseptic. Kaleidoscope focuses to white tile. Who's touching me?

"Evelyn?" Female voice. Don't know whose it is. Head stuck. Blurry face in front of my eyes. Surgical mask. Face disappears. "Dr. Vadlamani. I think she's finally coming around."

New face. Familiar ripples of attraction. Drool still on my cheek. Confusion. Embarrassment. "I can't wipe my face," I mumble.

"Let me help you." Face disappears. Hand with tissue arrives, brushes cheek.

Dry heave. "I think I'm going to be sick."

"Gloria, get this head restraint off. What were they thinking? You don't head restrain someone after heavy sedation. She's going to choke on her own vomit."

Hands by my head. The jingle of latches. "They were afraid she'd bite." Gloria is nervous. I can smell her. But the thought of eating brings the bile to my throat.

My head is free. I lean up and retch. A kidney shaped-plastic bowl appears in front of my mouth. A hand supports my neck and lifts me forward towards the bowl. More wiping. I lean back, exhausted. The doctor hands the bowl to the nurse, who takes it, making obvious efforts not to come anywhere near my mouth's striking range like I'm some kind of poisonous snake. The bowl gives her the perfect opportunity to make a strategic exit.

The Institute. Didn't escape. Drugged. Bridger. It all floods back.

"What happened to Bridger?" I cough out.

"The young man, your friend, he's your virus partner, yes?"

"It's not sexually transmitted. I'm proof." I'm not sure why I thought that was the most important thing to tell him right now when my vocal cords are crusty as fried chicken. "He's my friend. We broke up before the symptoms started to appear."

"You never engaged in sexual intercourse?"

I don't want to talk to him about this. "Where is he? He got hit by one of those darts."

"The soldiers were a bit zealous in their efforts to apprehend you. I'm afraid you were hit by three of them. You've been out for a few days."

He's avoiding my question. My stomach starts churning again. "Where's Bridger?" His lips go thin and his brow creases. He doesn't want to tell me. "What did they do to him?" My hands shake in their restraints.

"I couldn't stop them," he apologizes.

I turn away and the tears start flowing. I can't wipe them.

"I had to pull some strings in Atlanta at the Center for Disease Control just to keep Dr. Christensen away from *you*." He reaches over and wipes the tears from my cheek. I jerk my head away. "Don't worry, Evelyn, you have two sets of guards outside, checking each other. Agent Mitchell is from the CDC in Atlanta. He won't let anyone in here without clearance from me."

"Don't worry?" I snort bitterly. "Are you blind. You do realize I have the Z-Virus and I'm strapped to an operating table?" I have every reason to be a bitch here, but I shouldn't be. At least, I'm not "it" to him. Hearing my name on his lips thaws a few of the places that have grown cold in the last few months.

He puts his hand on my forehead and strokes back my hair. I feel it again, the melting inside that I felt when I saw him pet Bridger like he was a little boy, the way I pet Amber. "I'm not letting anyone near you," he promises.

I'm doing my best to stay in control of the viral impulses, but those words trigger all the bitterness of months alone in a hole under an abandoned church. They well up and choke me. "It's not real!" I spit at him, turning my head to accuse him of everything that's happened to me. "You're only nice because I'm chained up." I squint ruefully at the stunned look on his face. Did he think I couldn't see? Couldn't feel? Wouldn't know? "I saw the way you looked at me when I broke Bridger out. You're afraid of me, just like them. I'm just a vicious animal on the loose. You want to tap on the glass, but you don't want me out, roaming free, prowling." I jerk my head away, out from under the pressure of his touch, the only thing I can do.

His hand hangs in the air and then falls to his side. He doesn't try to force it back on me. I'm not sure if I wish he would, or if I'm glad he doesn't. "You think I *want* you chained up?" he replies, his mouth hanging open and his brow crinkling for a second before he adds, "You think the look on *my* face when I saw *your* face was *fear*?"

I snort and shake my head. I can't believe he's still keeping up this act of being my friend...and yet, somewhere deep in a place of my heart that I haven't felt for months, I kind of hope it's not a charade.

"I wasn't afraid, Evelyn." He crouches a bit closer to my level on the bed, almost whispering. "I was stunned, stunned at my good fortune." He glances at the door. The nurse still hasn't come back. He leans farther over the bed, so he's looking right into my eyes. "I need your help."

My eyes narrow as I take a deep breath, trying to slam the window on that little corner of my heart that was starting to sniff at the fresh air. He said something just like this to Bridger, right before he extracted a couple of syringes full of blood from his restrained arm. "I know," I respond, shifting my eyeballs to keep his from gazing into my soul. "You want to cut me up so you can help them create some super soldier." Anger is easier to deal with than whatever chemical cocktail he's trying to stir up in my veins. I rattle my arms and legs in their restraints, meet his eyes again with the stone behind mine, challenging him. "That's why I'm all chained up like this."

He stands up and leans over me, refusing to back down. He's totally serious. "You're all chained up because I knew when you woke up, you wouldn't know where you were, you'd be scared, and you'd run. I didn't want you to run until I had the chance to talk to you. I didn't want you to run and give them another excuse to shoot at you…or worse." His voice resonates with reliability like books slammed on the library desk. "I need your help, Evelyn. I saw how you were with Bridger." The mention of my ex's name brings tears to my eyes again. "You're kind; you're brave; you're loyal." He hesitates and his eyes dart to the door. He almost whispers, and I can hear the tragedy in his voice. "I need your help to save my little brother."

Wait. What? I didn't see that coming. "What does your brother have to do with anything?"

"He's infected. He's not much older than you. Our parents…" he turns his head away as his voice cracks, "…are dead. I'm all he has," he whispers, his shoulders drooping.

Suddenly everything changes. Everything changes because my mother still loves me. Now I know why this guy talked to Bridger like he was a small boy, someone's son; why he talks to me like I'm a person, not a monster.

"We all need your help." He straightens up and looks down at his feet as if he's not sure he wants to tell me more. "ZVs have become a serious threat. The situation has escalated. There was a killing spree last night in Eli."

A rush of adrenaline sets my heart pounding. I bite my lip, not sure I want him to tell me more.

"A dozen or more are dead." He reaches down; a latch snaps and my left arm is free. I'm too worried to do more than use my freedom to cover my mouth. Up until now, there have only been random incidents of ZV homicides. The infected have mostly been the victims, not the attackers. Moving around the table, Dr. Vadlamani unsnaps the last of my restraints.

"We think it's the other immune boy, the one like you. He's highly functioning, rational, calculating. He's organized a group of them."

"Greyson?"

"Is that his name? He has them pack hunting. When they attacked, the adults died; the children died or he kidnapped them. We don't know why."

Suddenly the idea of Amber at the mercy of Greyson brings the nausea back. I lurch up, my hand over my mouth. The doctor grabs the bowl again, but nothing comes out. I haven't eaten for a while. When I've got control of my gag reflex again, I stutter, "Amber? My family—my little brothers…my parents, are they…are they okay?" The whole reason I left, cut my human ties, lived in a hole for months, was to protect them.

He shakes his head. "I really don't know. I wish I could say they were fine. But the reports are confused and unreliable. This is the worst thing that could have happened. Everyone is panicked. We're running out of time for research and finding a cure." I can see he's desperate. "Please help me, Evelyn," he begs. "You're my brother's last chance. It's going to get ugly."

The words aren't processing because the scene in the movie has altered too quickly for me to catch up. I'm staring at the faucet, watching the water drip out, seeing Amber's face in every little drop before it disappears inevitably into the sink, crashing against the metal.

The warm touch of Dr. Vadlamani's hand in mine brings me back to the white tile of the hospital room. "The military wants to cut you up and see what makes you tick. But I need your help more, and I think I can help you in the process. We can help each other if you don't run from me."

Most of what he's saying is spiraling in a cloud in my brain. The main pieces getting through are images of my town being terrorized, dozens of dead, and my family in the middle of it. Greyson and his group of rampaging ZVs can destroy forever any chance the rest of us have of getting better, or even of just not getting our heads bashed in. I've seen enough of the video games and movies to know what happens once people get scared. I have to keep a grip on the emotions stirring up my animal survival instincts and do whatever I can to stop the insanity from spinning out of control.

I concentrate on the white sheet under my legs and grip the sides of the bed. "I won't run."

He nods. "I knew you wouldn't, once you knew."

Our eyes meet. We both want to say something, but neither of us knows what it is.

"Are you hungry?" he finally asks.

Embarrassment. "I'm still a little nauseous."

"That's the tranquilizers. Let me get you some fluids. It's important to stay hydrated."

Three strides and his hand is on the doorknob.

"Dr. Vadlamani?" I whisper.

He turns back with a smile that would melt an iceberg. "Call me Nicolas...or Sudhir. My family calls me Sudhir, but most Americans prefer Nicolas."

My eyes drop, and I feel a confusing flutter inside. My fingers reach up and sweep the long bangs out of my face and then trail down a thick, tangled strand. I don't really know how to say this, so I just grasp at the most obvious way. "Nicolas, don't let them shave my hair." His eyebrows go up. It sounds vain, I know, especially right now. But, I can't stop seeing Bridger lying on that table, lines drawn over his bald scalp. They want to dissect me; they want to see what kind of worms are floating in *my* brain. "It's all I have left," I explain, swallowing hard.

His jaw tightens and he nods. "Believe me. As long as I have anything to say about it, they won't touch a hair on your head." Oddly enough, I do believe him.

Chapter 9

Puffy white clouds float across the sparkle blue canvas of my windowpane. Marshmallow animals and toys frolic across the afternoon sky, then dissolve before my eyes. My cheeks are damp; Bridger's gone, probably smoke drifting out the Institute chimney. My family might be dead—or worse, infected.

My IV tube dangles aimlessly from a sack of fluids. The corner behind the door feels safer than the bed. Alone in my hospital cage, I am a wild cat cowering away from the glass that separates me from my new zookeepers. At least I have my clothes back. The hospital gown gave me the creeps. In my tank top and jeans, I feel more like a person. My sweatshirt, gloves, and glasses are folded neatly on the top shelf of my closet.

When I bury my head in my knees, I see Amber stretching out her little arms for me to pick her up, my mom and dad laughing at dinner, my brothers playing swords. I can't picture them gone. I thought I was alone before, a solitary little rowboat on a huge blank sea, tossing and rolling. But knowing my family was out there kept me from sinking. Holding my breath, I grasp at the floating possibility that my family got out. They need to know that I'm not like the others. I want them to know that I haven't turned yet. My mind catches hold of the image and it buoys me up. The need to rescue my little sister, make sure she's okay, brings me to my feet. I pace the room.

When sounds of padded shuffling in the hallway drift through the door, I peek out the window. On one side a uniformed guard stands armed. On the other, a guy in a suit sits tapping at the screen of an iPhone. The handgun strapped to his side peeks out from the gap in his suit coat. I'm still not convinced they're here to keep Dr. Death out. It looks a lot like they're here to keep me in.

A man in scrubs and a mask is headed up the hallway towards my door with a tray. My eyes dart around the room seeking a weapon. My claws and teeth are lethal, but lethal isn't what I'm going for. A wooden plunger in the bathroom suits my purpose. I grab it and duck back into the corner behind the door.

I haven't seen Dr. Vadlamani—Nicolas—since he hooked me up to the IV this morning and I fell asleep. I have two bandages on the insides of my elbows that weren't there before he put me out. I'm such a dweeb. I'm furious with myself for actually letting him talk me into trusting him. He probably didn't want to have to fight me to draw the blood samples. He's just so hot and it's been like forever since anyone was nice to me, I totally bought it. I need to grow up and realize that nobody helps anyone unless there's something in it for them. It's dog eat dog, or…no, that's really too gross to say. But I can't run because I told him I'd stay, and some part of me wants to believe that he really wants me to help him save his brother.

The guy coming down the corridor stops in front of the guards. I grip the handle of the plunger, my palms going sweaty, this sinister instinct to pounce invading my veins. If the guy in the corridor is hostile, I can take him out with my "weapon" before he realizes I'm not strapped to the bed. I will *not* eat him.

The door opens and a bootie-covered foot slides into the room, past the slab of metal that separates us. I stay crouched, but brandish the plunger like a bat, holding my breath. A tray appears. My muscles tense to spring. My mind runs through plan A: through the window, around the parking lot, and down to the Trax. Plan B?

"Evelyn?" My shoulders drop, and the breath rushes out my nose as the face appears around the door. The eyes belong to Nicolas. My head thumps back against the wall and my eyes close as I breathe in again.

Nicolas scans the room, looking first over towards me in the corner with my deadly weapon, and then towards the bed and the sink. "Oh. I'm so sorry," he apologizes. "I'm sorry; I didn't mean to frighten you."

He apologizes for scaring *me.* That's new.

"I just wasn't thinking. I get caught up in my work sometimes and I forget." I have no idea what he's talking about. He sets the tray on the bed and hustles out of the room. The door swings shut behind him.

I can smell what's on the tray. It's not human, but it's tasty—like warm toast and butter when you're starving. It's organ meat, something like the package I grabbed off the Roberts's kitchen counter. I have this urgent need to run over and shove it all in my mouth before he gets back, but something tells me that wouldn't be ladylike. More than I want to gorge myself, I don't want to add to the endearing "Bride of Frankenstein" impression I've already made.

The door swings open again, and Nicolas rolls a couple of chairs into the room. His mask dangles around his neck. "I forgot these rooms are so barbaric." He scoots a chair up to each side of the bed, still made up tight enough to please my mother, the bed-Nazi. "Most of the patients don't seem to mind." He stumbles on the sentence. "I mean, they're all mostly brain dead. The virus is the only thing keeping them alive." Instead of tossing the guts to me like roadkill in a jail cell, he motions me to the chair like it's prom night and we're dining at Fleming's Steak House.

I don't dare look at him but take a seat. "What is it?" I ask, latching my hands together so they don't reach out and grab. There are knives and forks. The knife is sharp. On his side of the tray, it looks like he's got some sushi or something.

"Well, I'm not sure you're aware because you were unconscious, but this weekend was Thanksgiving. I managed to commandeer some of the 'delicacies' from the kitchen."

"Turkey guts?"

"I know it's not exactly where your tastes run…"

"I don't eat people." I reach for the knife. I notice him watching me. I stop and meet his eyes. "I don't." He drops his gaze.

I cut off a dainty little piece of gizzard, or liver, or whatever it is like I'm some princess. He uses his fingers and dips something that looks like a California Roll into sauce and pops it in his mouth. He watches me cut and eat, an ogre at a tea party. "How do you do it?" he asks.

"What?" I set down my knife and fork. Here it comes. I can't stop it. "I just have to accept the fact that I'm a monster now; that stupid jocks don't want to get into my pants, that they want to beat me to a pulp with bats; that doctors want to cut me up like a rat, that my parents are afraid of me..." I look towards the window. The clouds are gone—nothing but blue skies. "...that I'm afraid of myself."

Nice. I just vomited the pent-up emotion of what it's like to be me all over his nice sterile scrubs. *That was pretty. Now maybe psycho chick can go back in her hole and let normal girl do the talking.*

I turn back and concentrate on the freak feast in front of me. "You get used to living alone. You figure it out. It's easy." I saw off a large chunk of innards and shove it in my mouth. When I look up with my mouth full, I'm expecting a condescending nod, a bit of a frown, something like the face my dad made when I was six, and he told me to "suck it up" after a horse we stopped to feed bit my fingers and I had to ride my bike all the way home before I got any sympathy or First Aid.

Instead, Nicolas looks like he's about to cry. I look away again. "I really just wanted to know how you control the urges of the virus so well. But since you brought it up, you should know, Evelyn, you're still beautiful."

Even with my cheeks stuffed with turkey guts, my hair tangled and matted from lying strapped to a bed, and no make-up, I really want that to be true. That's the delicate, broken part of me that I wrapped up right after I got sick. I wrapped it in the soft tissues of my heart and hid it deep, deep in a box, in the black corners of my mind. I can't look at it or I'll fall apart. And now he's unwrapped it and it's there in his eyes, the sunlight from the blue skies shining off of it. I cover my eyes with my hand. Somehow, I'm not hungry anymore. How does he always do this to me?

I pull myself together. "Yeah, I was thinking of entering the Miss Corn Cobb pageant this year." The bitterness inside makes me want to jar him, make him take back all the nice boy crap he's feeding me so I can despise him for trying to make me believe he cares about me. "For the talent competition, I thought I'd rustle myself up some tough cowboy and devour him on stage. What do you think? Too showy?"

Instead of fading, the look in his eyes sinks deeper. He can see right into me. I look back down at my plate, clenching my fingers together, jamming the tip of my tongue into my teeth because my eyes feel tight and heavy like a storm cloud ready to burst on the mountain that dares force it up. The blue skies in the window laugh at me when I look away from Nicolas.

He leans across the table, drops his hand onto mine, shelters it. "Not everyone is blinded by the virus. Some of us can still see the person behind the symptoms."

I pull my hand away. "I'm just a disease. That's all. It's nice of you to try and pretend, really it is, but why don't we all just do a quick reality check, note the ghostly pale skin, the purple tint to my eyelids and lips, not to mention the claws for fingernails, and accept that I am a freak? The only reason you're not screaming and calling for security to blow my brains out is that you need my disease to help your little brother."

He doesn't flinch. "The reason I'm not screaming and calling for security is that you promised you'd stay and help, and I believe you. Because you're a decent human being who cares about the people you love."

I stare at him, waiting to see the flash of deceit cross his face. Just for a second. No one can hide the fear, not all the time—not even my mother. My leg starts tapping maniacally. It does that when my history teacher is droning on and on and the bell's about to ring. "Is that why you took my blood without my permission?" I hold out my arms, calling as witnesses the two tape and gauze bandages that adorn the insides of my elbows. "I thought you had to have permission to take someone's blood. Or do *human beings* no longer have control of their own bodies?"

Finally, he looks mortified. My lips crack into a smile, but I don't feel it. I'm not sure I wanted to win this argument. "The one arm is from the IV," he explains, coughing a bit. "With the extra tranquilizers we needed to monitor you carefully; and you needed the fluids." He bows his head and runs his fingers through his thick black hair that curls up on the ends and falls back, not far from where it started. "I did take a couple vials of blood." His face pleads with mine. "I had to. It was the only way I could keep Dr. Christensen and his gang of butchers away from you. I needed the blood to get the CDC down here with some extra security. There's a chance your blood has some natural immunities in it that we could work with." He drops his eyes and shakes his head. "It couldn't wait until you woke up. After last night, it may be the only thing keeping you off the surgical table."

I've seen the look plastered to his face before. Amber looked like that when I caught her painting herself with my 75-dollar-a-bottle foundation. Of course, I had to forgive *her*. But, Nicolas is a grownup; he doesn't get off that easily. I rip the bandages off. Angry, red dots stare back at him. "They're going to leave marks," I say. "I guess you'll be trying to tell me they're beauty marks?"

"I'm really sorry. I couldn't see any other way." He shakes his head miserably. "Dr. Christensen was hell-bent on cutting you open after you knocked him flat on his butt. He's not accustomed to being put in his place, especially not by women."

"Why am I not shocked?" Nicolas has this annoying way of reminding me that I owe to his unreasonable generosity and goodwill the fact that I'm sitting in this chair and eating off the bed instead of lying strapped to it with my head shaved. I have to swallow hard, and I can't look him in the face, but I manage to choke out, "Thank you." Glancing up, I watch him sink into the back of his rolling chair. The torture is over. "Thank you for keeping them off of me. And thank you for Bridger. You treated him like a person, not a science rat. That's why I promised to stay. That, and my family."

"Man," he sighs in relief, "you had me going. I was beginning to think there was no way I could cure the disease that's stuck in your head and telling you no one can see you anymore."

"Most people can't." I grin reluctantly. He's doing it again. The guy missed his calling; he should have been an actor. I shrug and can't stop myself from asking, "You're really not grossed out when you look at me?" I watch him carefully for the twitch, the crack in his poker face that tells me he's lying. It never comes.

"Why would I be? You remind me of my little brother. He's been sick for a while now. He's like you in that the disease doesn't progress, only he's not stronger; he's weaker. I need to find out why. I need to compare the two strains."

He is really good. "You can have all the stinky blood you like out of my veins, but let's try to limit the puncture wounds to less conspicuous spots."

His lips curl into a small smile. "I appreciate your generosity. It's not that simple, though."

"Complications?"

"Two actually."

"I'm all ears." I lean back in my chair. "I'm willing to do whatever it takes to help you find a cure for your little brother…" I sit back up again and lean as far over the table as I can so he knows I'm serious, "…but then, I want you to do whatever you can to help me find my family."

He folds his hands together on the bed and his jaw clenches up while his eyebrows furrow down. He can't look at me. My knee starts bouncing again. Around me, the room shrinks. Where I am, why I'm here, who he is, all of it vanishes, sucked away in the silence. "Where's my family, Nicolas?" I ask, tensing my arms against the bed so I won't shake.

He can't look me in the eye while he tells me. "Your house was one of the first ones hit. It was all over the news."

Long pause. I start sandbagging around the edges of my heart and my brain. I can feel the flood coming. "Your parents are dead and…" the sound of his voice fades in my ears as the blood rushes up to my head, some kind of cushion against the blow of what I'm hearing. "…your twin brothers were found with them."

My gaze can't meet his either. I'm staring at the wispy clouds on the blue canvas. They stretch for the other side of the window but fade before they reach it. My eyes swell up like dried sponges doused in a wave of the incoming tide. Squeeze them and the saltwater rushes out in torrents. The lids can't stay open any longer; it stings. I blink, turning back to Nicolas. A blob of water tumbles down my cheek. My hands grip the sides of my chair and I speak slowly, trying to control the quiver in my voice. "Amber? My little sister?"

"Missing, along with the oldest of your three brothers," he whispers. He pulls a newspaper from the big pocket of his coat and lays it on the bed between us. Photos of my parents are there with the twins, Jeremy and Josh. Further down the page, I see Amber's first-grade picture smiling back at me along with Cory's picture. "They think they were taken. Because of her age, your sister was most likely kidnapped by the gang."

I gulp, conjuring up a picture of my dad, repeating over and over, *Don't dwell on what's happened, just about what you can do about it. Don't try to kill the snake while the victim dies from the bite.* My dad never let us wallow. I take a deep breath, hold it, and clench my jaw.

Nicolas stands up, reaches across the bed, and puts a hand on my head. I shove it away before it can release the tide welling up inside me. "I'll leave you alone for a few minutes. Can I get you anything?"

"No. Don't go. Just tell me how I can find them. Help me!" My eyes follow him as he walks around the bed. He reaches for me, but I shove my rolling chair back and stand, bringing myself almost to his height.

"You need some time to mourn. You've just lost your parents and your brothers."

"I don't have time to mourn. I still have a little sister and brother out there. I've been on my own for months now. I'm used to it. Cory's a big boy. But Amber's little. She needs me. She's always needed me."

"Look, I'm not lying when I tell you that I know how it feels. My parents died in an accident. I wasn't at home when the police found me and told me. My first instinct was to get home to my brother. It falls on you, the need to protect what's smaller than you. But you need to say good-bye to your parents before you can trust yourself to take their place."

He's doing it again. He finds my weak spots and pokes at them with his warm, pointed words. I can feel the melting: drips, and then trickles, and finally the flood, and I'm leaning on his chest, and that horrible sound of my whole body ripping apart is coming from my mouth in sobs, and his arms are trying to hold me together.

Chapter 10

Sleep. It's what I do when the world is teetering—lie still and let the planet turn until I'm back in the center again and the sickening spin slows down. It's what I do when the nightmares I dream up are less painful than the ones I'm living. I slept through two whole days when the track coach cut me from the 9th grade District finals because I ditched practice to see a concert with Bridger. The band was lame and Bridger got busted for smoking a clove cigarette.

"Evelyn?" A warm hand covers mine. The fingers slide underneath my palm. My eyelids flutter and squint. The room is bright. The hand belongs to Nicolas.

I struggle up to my elbows. "Where's Amber?" I ask rubbing my eyes. "How long did I sleep?" It's dusky dark out my window.

"Most of the day. Don't worry about it. You needed it."

"Don't worry about it? Don't worry about it!" Throwing my feet over the side of the bed I land a little tipsy on the floor and steady myself with a hand on the bed. "Tell me, Nicolas. Just exactly where is this infected brother of yours that you seem so anxious to take care of? Because my sister has been out there with a bunch of zombies for over a day now!"

"Okay, that's not what I meant. And just so you know, my little brother Smaran is here."

Suddenly the long absences make sense. I cringe inside, and if there were any blood going to my skin, I would have blushed. Every time I think I've caught this guy being fake, he shoves my doubts back down my throat and rubs this squeaky clean, nice guy act in my face. I'd have to be a fiend not to forgive him—and dead not to like him.

"Of course, you're going to worry. Right now, though, there's nothing you can do. They have National Guard troops in Eli trying to evacuate the city. They're hunting for the missing kids at the same time. They pull out at night and the media gets updates."

"Why do they pull out at night? That's when the ZVs are most likely to come out. Our skin is sensitive to ultra-violet rays. You should know that." I read it in the newspaper; he's probably the one that told the reporter. My new head-to-toe fashion statement isn't just to hide me from gangs when I'm in public, or keep me out of the cold, which we don't really register anyway.

"I do know. We observed that in the patients here. The ZVs in Eli stay under cover during the day. Instinct takes over as they, uh, progress through the stages of the illness. They lose the ability to reason, so instead of covering up as you do, they just stay out of the sunlight. That's what is actually causing the problem. The military has night vision and infrared for search and rescue, but the lowered body temperatures of ZVs make them unreliable. From what we've observed, the virus allows their body temperature to fluctuate towards the environment."

"Like a lizard?" Great, now I'm a reptile monster.

"Possibly. My guess is that you're just not radiating and transferring your body heat. That's part of the altered pigmentation issue. Anyway, ZV dogs are more reliable. The military isn't out to search and destroy. Contagion isn't the issue here, rescue is. Night vision can't tell you if what you're seeing is an infected person or a trapped civilian. A dog can. They're bringing in as many dogs from the schools as they can. Only problem is…"

"…ZVs eat dogs." In this context, it kind of makes me sick to admit it. "But if they leave at night, they're not going to be able to stop Greyson. That's when he operates. That's when he uses his zombie friends as decoys so he can go and murder people's families, their parents and their brothers, and steal…" I choke, as the tears start rolling down my cheek. I wipe them away.

Nicolas strides around the bed and wraps his arms around me. "They use helicopters with searchlights at night. They're going to find your family." With his hand on the back of my head, he cradles my cheek into his chest.

The comforting rhythm of its rising and falling encourages the rush of tears, the little trickle of memories, moments, and emotions condensed into tiny droplets of saltwater. "Right now, the top priority is to rescue the civilians trapped in the evacuation zone. The second one is to bring in the male mutation. The military wants him as much as the CDC, but for different reasons. I'm hoping the CDC gets him first. The two of you together could be the key to a cure." For a moment, the soft curve of his shoulder and the weight of his hand are the cushions of heaven, where all wrongs are righted, all pain is eased, and all sorrows comforted, just like they taught us in Sunday School. And then I smell him.

Before I was a vegetarian, my mom always popped a roast with potatoes and carrots in the crockpot before church. By the time we got home, the aroma had engulfed the whole house and drew us hypnotized into the kitchen. Oh, my Gosh. The way the roast just fell off the bone and melted in my mouth…mmm…Nicolas smells like those Sundays. I shove him away.

"What is wrong with you?" I demand. "Stay away from me!"

Nicolas's face contorts into something between shock and guilt. I can't look at him so I turn away with my hands on my hips. "I'm so sorry," he stammers, holding up his hands like he's being arrested. "I just wanted to…I mean, I'm so sorry for what's happened to your family. I thought I could…I thought you needed a friend." He shakes his head, apologizing. "But I shouldn't have…you're such a lovely girl, I couldn't stand to see you so sad…I guess I wasn't thinking."

I'm lovely. He's my friend. How I wish that were true. I turn on him. "You still don't get it, do you?" I shake my head, cringing that I have to explain my illness to the doctor. "I left my family; I left my home. I've been hiding out under the floorboards of an old church for months. Why do you think I did that? Because I was turning eighteen and wanted some independence? I don't think so. I left because I loved my family and I didn't want to wake up one morning and find their guts smeared all over my face and their blood dripping from my hands because I couldn't fight off the demon bug in my brain anymore!"

His hand starts to reach for me, but his eyes go hard and he pulls it back down. He really wants to make me feel better, but I won't let him.

I settle down into the depression of facing the truth. "You can't be my friend. You don't know when I'll wake up in the middle of the night and eat your heart out."

He turns and walks towards the other side of the bed. "Then we better find out when, and if, that will happen because I am your friend. And between the two of us, we're going to make damn sure you don't wake up one morning and find you've eaten my heart out."

Nicolas takes a seat in one of the chairs and motions to the other. I don't really want to sit down. "This may take a while," he assures me. As he sits, something in his lab coat pocket clanks. He looks surprised for a second and then breaks into a grin as he reaches into it. A hairbrush emerges in his hand. He hands it over to me. "Thought this might brighten your day a bit."

And that's it. I'm toast. I will always love Nicolas.

The job isn't easy. It's a delicate piece of work. I can't just yank my hair out and expect it to grow back. After days in hospital beds, jumping out of windows, and hiding in bushes, I could sell hair condos to birds.

My little sister is blessed with gobs of the most gorgeous, thick, honey-blond hair, and she won't let anyone brush it. My mom made her wear it short so it wouldn't turn into a home for wayward rodents and bugs. I brush my hair like I'm Amber and the slightest yank will end the whole hair brushing torture session. The world slows down as I brush, and untangles with the strands.

Nicolas props his elbow on the arm of his chair and leans his chin into his hand.

"What?"

He shrugs. "I'm just watching."

"I told you. It's all I have left."

He watches a while longer, 'til the whole thing falls in one smooth wave around my shoulders and the brush descends in long smooth strokes through the honey-blond silk. I feel new like I've finally got control of the chaos and it's just a matter of time and distance before everything falls into place.

Nicolas leans back in his chair. "What do you know about mummies?"

I wasn't expecting small talk. "I saw the movie."

He grins. He has the most beautiful lips. The tiniest bit of a French accent shows up in words you don't hear that often like "mummies."

"I'm not sure that's the most accurate source of information."

"Well," I stop brushing to think. "I learned they scrambled the brains with a pointy stick and then pulled them out through the nose. And then they have those five Canopic jars for the organs."

"Canopic. And there are four, actually: one for each of the sons of Horus. They tossed the brain and dried the organs and the body in sea salt. The heart went back in the body and then the dried lungs, liver, stomach, and intestines went in the jars."

"Okay, this is kind of random. Here all this time I thought you were a doctor studying the Z-Virus."

"I am. But my parents were archeologists and so were my grandparents. My father is Indian, but my mother is half-French, half-Egyptian."

"I thought there was a little French accent. But, you look Indian, so I assumed…"

He shrugs. "I grew up in France. My mother's parents were archeologists specializing in ancient Egyptian artifacts. Did you know that subject zero, the first subject known to contract the Z-Virus, a young lady named Marissa Grant, had recently returned from an internship in Egypt?"

"I think I read about her. But they couldn't find her virus partner, so they weren't sure for a while that it was a couple thing."

"Yes, well, I was able to clear that up for them. Her partner was in Egypt. My brother and I were living there. He was studying at the university; we were continuing the work my parents had begun before their accident. He met Marissa in the museum where they were both studying."

"Your brother was her virus partner?"

"Yes. The CDC was in contact with the university at Cairo and, because of my background and connections, they requested I come and consult on the investigation of the outbreak."

"And what exactly is your background? What were your parents studying? Mummies?" The brush is lying on the bed. I plant my elbows on the thin, blue blanket, expecting more than a one-minute explanation.

"In an indirect way. Have you heard of "alchemy"?

"The search for the philosopher's stone. Harry Potter. Read it while I was in hiding. Seven books. It passes the time."

He laughs. "Not exactly accredited resource material, but it will do. The Egyptians were consumed with the quest for eternal life. Alchemy is a derivative of the Egyptian study al-Kimia. The mummification process is intimately bound with the pursuit of life after death."

"I see where this is going. Life after death. Mummies. I never made the connection before, but mummies are the Egyptian version of a zombie, right? You think they actually came up with something that brought the dead back to life?"

"No. Something much worse. I was continuing my parents' research at the tomb of Zoser. Perhaps you know it?"

"Yeah, in my spare time I surf the web researching ancient Egyptian dead guys." I roll my eyes. "I just barely turned eighteen. I know the best brands of shampoo, which shoes to wear with my jeans, and what happened on last week's episode of Vampire Diaries. Oh, and I know how to prevent a stroke because I wrote a research paper on that before I became a ZV."

"Sorry, it was a long shot. I've been around it since I could carry a tool bag." He grins. "Before their accident, my parents came across evidence of an ancient dormant virus in the tomb of Zoser."

"And now another Lego piece snaps into place." I giggle at the look of surprise on Nicolas's face. "I know. You probably pegged me for a Barbie girl. I'll have you know, I have built some amazing palaces with Legos. It's impressive what a girl and a couple of little brothers can put together when they pool all their Legos."

At the mention of my brothers, a flood of snapshot memories rushes through my head. The last one, the one I only imagine, is the one where they're lying in blood and guts next to my parents. Suddenly the room shrinks, suffocating me.

Nicolas's eyebrows furrow. He tries to keep my head in the present and out of the whirlpool that surges up around me. "Not at all. There's a nice model of the Zoser step pyramid in my room back in Paris." We look at each other.

My eyes thank him for the rope. He reaches over and grabs my hand.

"It was the first one, you know. The first pyramid, built around 2500 BC. They probably fully expected Zoser to rise again."

My brain starts to emerge from the deluge of family snapshots and into ancient Egypt. I can breathe again.

"When my parents found evidence of that virus, my father began to theorize that perhaps the mummy legends might have some basis in truth. Perhaps instead of giving birth to immortality, they gave birth to a virus."

"The Zoser Virus."

"Exactly. Zombie Virus is a media misnomer. Technically, a zombie is a walking corpse."

"A mummy."

"And those of you who have been infected, have never died."

"But the virus is taking over our brains and controlling our instincts. That's why we all start to eat people...well most do, anyway." I pull my hand out from under his and we both lean back in our chairs.

"Not technically. What they're after," I notice he doesn't include me in his statement, "are the organs. The virus lives in their brain and reproduces using materials found only in organs, mainly the stomach, the liver, the intestines, the lungs and…"

"…the heart." I finish for him. He nods impressed. "I catch on quickly—3.9 GPA," I explain.

"Summa cum laude from Oxford," he replies with a cheeky grin.

I roll my eyes. "Yeah, well, personal issues messed up my college plans."

His sympathetic nod reeks with insincerity. "I'm sure with your 3.9 intellect you've come to the same conclusion my parents did. Up to now, they assumed the Egyptians dried the organs because the water in them and the body created breeding grounds for bacteria and so accelerated decay. But my parents theorized that the mummification rituals evolved to quell the virus. Think about it. The priests destroyed the brain where the virus lives, dried and removed the organs of the host which the virus consumes in order to reproduce when lacking an external supply."

"But then, why don't we know about it? Why wasn't there some huge plague or something?"

"Well, we do have the legends. But, unfortunately, that's the question we couldn't answer until my brother contracted the virus from exposure to the artifacts."

"Wait. You're saying your brother got sick from a…what?…four-thousand-year-old virus? It lives that long?" I'm horrified. Secretly I've always hoped this was like the flu. Once you run the course it's gone; you get better.

"A virus doesn't die, because technically it's not alive. It's really just dormant."

"Well, it is certainly alive and well now," I say.

"And that's the key. What was the catalyst?"

He's asking *me*. I wait. I wait a long time for the answer. Outside the door, I can hear the conversation between my soldier and my CDC guard.

"The suspense is killing me," I prod.
"Love. Love revived the virus."

Chapter 11

"Hormones," Nicolas explains. He's actually serious. "Certain hormones are more abundant in the blood during the first stages of love and fade in more mature relationships. We're researching their effect on the revitalization of the virus. But there's a whole host of other chemical responses to love that could be involved in the virus' cycle. Testosterone levels drop in men and rise in women; NGF, Nerve Growth Factor, increases. Dopamine, norepinephrine and phenylethylamine, pheromones: there's a whole soup for the virus to stew in that exists during the acute phase of falling in love and we haven't isolated the key elements."

"Just stop," I sigh. "I don't have a clue what you just said. Soup and something about testosterone, hormones, and a bunch of '—ins.' What does it mean in English?"

"Sorry. I tend to get carried away." He shrugs apologetically. "Short version: the body secretes chemicals in the early stages of falling in love that apparently provide the perfect environment for stimulating the virus. We just haven't yet narrowed down which chemicals are reacting and, more importantly, why yours are reacting differently."

I'm not sure whether to believe him or ask to see his license and diploma. Oddly though, it makes total sense—it *is* a couple's virus.

"Look, I've been studying this since before my brother got infected and my parents were researching it before that. I know more than anybody on the planet and what I know is full of holes and conjectures."

"What about Dr. Christensen. Isn't he in charge?"

"He doesn't know half what he needs to know and even less than what I know. Not that he cares. He's only here because he has seniority and no one else wanted to touch this…or enjoys cutting people up the way he does. He's in it mostly for the military funding."

"So, tell me what you do know, the short story."

"I'm actually not sure what it all means yet. The virus is complicated, highly selective, and so new that it hasn't had much time to mutate, adapt, and become significantly contagious. The instances of infection are so few, as far as we know, that we don't have the data we need to really understand what's going on."

"You mean, you need more human guinea pigs for your little science experiments."

He looks hurt but doesn't rise to the bait. "I've just barely scratched the surface of the research that needs to be done, but from samples I took from my brother and his girlfriend, it appears there are a male and a female strain of the virus. When the two combine in the right chemical environment—the environment present in the first stages of a relationship—they produce a new strain."

"You're telling me that teenagers get infected because they're falling in love. That's just twisted."

"Of course, that environment can and does exist under other circumstances, so, theoretically, others could become infected. Marissa and Smaran are our oldest victims. Of course, they were probably more thoroughly exposed to the virus. But in most instances, without the falling in love factor and the chemical environment that produces, the chances decrease of the male and female strains being exposed over a sufficiently stable period to combine and create the virulent strain that produces the…uh…odd symptoms."

"You mean the zombie effect. The urge to tear people's guts out and eat them. The nearly dead skin tones. The brain damage?"

"And, in rare cases like you, the enhanced strength and speed, as well as the resistance to the deteriorating effect of the virus. That's what the military is interested in researching and replicating in a less corrosive agent and what the CDC wants to develop into a cure. The bad news is, the virus is still mutating. It's not just couples producing it anymore. In the weekend attacks, we saw cases of people dying from exposure to the offspring strain or being infected with it."

"It's more contagious now?" I'm thinking about Amber and Cory, most likely surrounded by ZVs, if not dead. I tap the brush on the bed, waiting for him to draw the conclusion, but he doesn't. Somehow, I imagined Cory would be immune to the freaky couple's virus because he never even had a girlfriend—I don't think he's ever loved anything as much as his skateboard. Now, it doesn't matter.

"The bad news is, the age factor doesn't make people immune anymore, it makes them dead. The offspring virus can be lethal or contagious to those who don't have the right chemical/hormonal environment to sustain it, and it has grown much less selective. Sometimes, it goes straight to consuming the host's organs, doesn't bother with the brain control phase of seeking out external sources of nourishment."

Nicolas stands up and walks to the window. "Remember I mentioned we'd encountered some complications in the research?"

"Yeah. Is this one?"

"Actually, it's your friend Greyson."

"He's not my friend," I say.

"We have some reports that indicate the virus may have mutated in Greyson. A single bite from him causes infection or death. The virus has side-stepped the coupling phase in him."

It takes a minute for the full impact of what Nicolas is telling me to sink in. I feel cold like someone just turned on the air conditioning in the middle of winter. Shoving my chair back, I walk to the corner behind the door, my arms wrapped around myself, my eyes searching the blank, white wall. There aren't any answers written there.

"The virus is acting the same way in me as it is in Greyson, right?" I manage the words that rip and tear past the skin of the question into the maggot-infested meat of what it really means to me. I'm contagious…most likely. Silence rests at my back. Soft padded footsteps and the squeak of wheels creep up the hallway outside. Nicolas's chair exhales under the weight of him falling into it. The wheels creak. Everything needs oil, something to help it slide past the crust and grime. "If I bite someone, they'll be infected?" I just say it.

"I can't be sure. I need samples."

"Take them." I turn and hold out my arms.

"From Greyson."

I'm confused. "Did they bring him in? They caught him?" I'm not sure if I'm relieved or horrified.

Nicolas shakes his head. "That's the second difficulty." I nod, waiting for the worst. "This new strain, transmitted through the saliva into the blood, is bringing down some heavy pressure from the military. They want to take over the research; they're already talking of upgrading the evacuation of Eli to a quarantine.

If they get a hold of Greyson, there's no chance they'll let me near him. I don't have the security clearance. To them, he's a weapon. He represents the key to the unlocking of the super-soldier. But if I don't get some samples from him, my research is obsolete: you, my brother, everyone we care about that's been infected—we don't stand a chance of finding a cure. That's not the direction the military wants to take the research."

"And the only way we'll know if my bite is lethal is if I bite someone." The air feels stuffy like a bell jar just dropped on the top of me. I'm only half interested in what he's saying about Greyson—the half that is about me.

"I'm afraid it wouldn't be confined to your saliva. Your blood, any of your body fluids…"

I don't want to hear the rest. "So, Dr. Death and Igor Hickman could break in here any minute ready to hack me up and fry my brain to see if I have the same *superpowers* that Greyson does?"

He bows his head, and I don't know if he's thinking or praying. Maybe both. He looks back at the door. There are a couple of soldiers and a guy in a suit talking to Mitchell, my CDC bodyguard. When Nicolas turns back around, his eyes bore into mine like he's looking for something there. He reaches into his pockets like my mom rifling through her purse. Pulling out a couple syringes in sterile wrapping and a constriction band, he hands them to me. I never saw my mom pull those particular items out.

"I'm going to get you out of here. I need you to make your way back to Eli, find Greyson, and get him to give you a couple syringes of his blood, whatever you can get."

I can't help it. I laugh. "Greyson and I aren't that close."

"He's still functioning on high levels of reason. He's got to be as anxious to find a cure as you are."

"You don't know Greyson. The only thing he's anxious about is who he's going to sleep with next."

"Excuse me?"

I'm a little embarrassed that I've spiraled into crude remarks; Greyson has that effect on people. "I don't think he's interested in a cure. He thinks he's some kind of evolutionary superhuman like an X-man. He thinks the two of us are destined to create a zombie super-race. Let's just say, if he donates some of his body fluids to me, it's not going to be blood."

"But we don't even know what the long-term effects of the virus are. Wouldn't he want to know? Wouldn't anybody?"

"Greyson isn't anybody. What do you mean 'long-term effects'? Like, are you saying there's a possibility I could start falling apart? Like Bridger?"

He takes a step towards me like he's going to do it again. He's going to touch me, try to make me feel human and normal. Can't he get it through his head? He smells like Sunday to me and I've been fasting for months. I put my hand out like a policeman stopping traffic. "Never mind. It doesn't matter. Amber's in there, and so is Cory. If I go back, I can find them and get them out…or at least find them."

I hold out the sterile syringe pack. "You realize I have no idea how to use this thing. It's not standard AP Biology curriculum."

"It's pretty simple."

I snort. "For a doctor."

"Have you ever had your blood drawn?"

I display the holes in my arms for him to contemplate, lest he's forgotten. He's embarrassed, just like I wanted him to be. I feel mean.

"When you were awake, I mean, and consenting," he insists, looking through the small window at the gesticulating men outside my door.

"Yeah, when I had my tonsils out. The nurse strapped this rubber-band thingy," I wave it in front of him, "to my arm, and then she waited for the little blue vein to appear. She stabbed me over and over again because she couldn't get it in. I was actually crying by the time she called the doctor to do it. I can't stomach this crap."

Nicolas looks like I've just told him the world's going to end, and the only guy who can save us has just been hit by a car.

"Uh…well…you see…I'm sure it's just because you're so thin. The veins are sometimes more difficult to find when the patient is thin. I'm sure you'll manage."

Ha. How does he do that? He's actually making a compliment out of having been used as a practice pincushion by an inept nurse. "Yeah, well, I'll do my best." I turn to the wall and rub my arms. It's freezing in here, which is odd because I don't normally register the cold. This is so crazy.

Nicolas reaches into the cabinet that lines the side of the room next to the bathroom door. He pulls out my hoodie and offers me an empty armhole. I slip into it and he wraps it around me, waiting for the other arm. He's really close.

I slide my other arm in, and his hands rest, just a second too long, on my shoulders—bookends that keep sliding because they're not quite sturdy enough to hold together the volumes between them. My insides go all soft and warm. *Does it matter that he's like 24 and I'm only 18? Wasn't mom about four years younger than dad?* I can't help but breathe him in, so close behind my neck. His aroma assaults me and I jerk away.

"When are you going to figure out that I look like a girl, but I'm not?" I practically hiss, shuddering because I know I'm yelling at myself more than at him. "This isn't Halloween make-up that I can go home and shower off. I'm one of them. I'm infected. I'm a zombie. I eat people like you." I'm so angry that my heart feels like it's hammering nails into my chest.

"You told me you don't eat people." He stares me down until my breath tapers off into something normal. "I believe you." He steps closer, way inside my personal space. "I believe you because you're not a disease. You're brave and honest, and you love your family—," he's doing it again, "—like I do." I'm in total meltdown. What does he think? We're in an episode of *Grey's Anatomy*? Now the melted ice is seeping out of my eyes. His arm is around me. "You're beautiful, Evelyn. No virus can hide that."

And then the door swings open behind us and a nurse in scrubs and protective gear barges in with a tray of scissors and razors and a big, burly ZV Snatcher in black. I shove the syringe packages into the pocket of my sweatshirt.

"Restrain the patient, Mr. Packer," the nurse barks at the Snatcher. "Dr. Christensen wants her prepped and ready for surgery in an hour."

Nicolas gets between the Institute thug and me. Mr. Packer pulls out a gun, but Nicolas doesn't flinch.

"Let's not make this messy, Dr. Vadlamani." In the standoff silence between them, an alarm goes off in the hallway. The Snatcher frowns and glances behind him at the rectangle window in the door.

"No one touches this patient without my permission," Nicolas insists.

Mr. Packer turns back to Nicolas. "The virus has mutated. Just the bite of that mutant kid will send the shit up your veins and fry your brain. They have unconfirmed reports of secondary infection subjects infecting third tiers. We're finally going to shake Tanner's lawyers off our butts and wipe this filthy scum off the planet." A smug smile cracks his face and I can tell he and the good doctor have history.

Nicolas glares back at him. "I still have full control from the CDC over the research. It's a national security priority."

"The CDC is out of the loop. This is now a military quarantine operation and the military has reassigned command of the research to Dr. Christensen. It's a new ball game,

Dr. Vadlamani, and you're off the team. Eli is being quarantined for decontamination." He grabs my arm and yanks me to him. "This ZV is a critical contamination risk and a high-level security clearance subject. Dr. Christensen is calling the shots now."

The clatter of running and muffled screaming seeps through the door.

"What is going on out there? Those interns are useless," the nurse snaps. I remember her. She's the same woman that presided at Bridger's butchering. "You can't leave them alone for five minutes. Mr. Packer, handle this," she stabs an accusing finger at me. "I want it ready to prep by the time I get back." The Snatcher nods and the scrub nurse stomps out towards her interns.

He shoves me toward the bed. "You're going to surgery, sweetie. They're going to bring your serial killer boyfriend in and then the party's really going to start."

"He's not my boyfriend." I yank my arm out of his hand and shove him away, just enough to get him off of me, not enough to plaster his head to the cabinets. With guns in the room, I think it's best to give Nicolas and diplomacy a chance. AP History.

"You're not touching her, not if I have anything to do with it. Mitchell. Mitchell, get in here!" Nicolas yells to the door. The brown hue of his skin goes red.

"You *don't* have anything to do with it. Agent Mitchell has been reassigned." The screaming sirens make the perfect background score for his announcement as he reaches to grab my arm again.

The door opens and we expect to see the nurse with some kind of an explanation for all the commotion in the hall. It's the nurse all right, and she has an explanation. She doesn't have to say anything, though; we can see it. Half her right arm is gone and blood is gushing all over the shiny white floor. She must be in shock because she's not screaming. "Help me," she gasps, taking a few steps into the room as she pulls the door closed.

Before the latch clicks, a ZV, gashed and maimed, blood all over his face, shoves it open. He's tearing a last bite out of the nurse's severed piece of arm. Of course, that's not what the virus really wants, so he's back for the main course.

The ZV is obviously not a patient. He's wearing street clothes that are stained with blood. It only takes a second for Packer to realize that this ZV is roaming free and unsupervised. He fires. Right through the head. They know the virus controls the brain.

Suddenly, the Snatcher isn't as interested in me as what's in the hallway. The nurse has crumpled to the floor near the sink, smearing blood all over herself. Nicolas moves to help her when the door flies open again.

It's another ZV. But not just any ZV. This one hardly has any marks at all, and he's wearing street clothes. A gang of them must be invading the hospital because this ZV shouldn't be here. It doesn't take more than one glance for me to recognize my little brother. "Cory!" I yell.

Panicked, the only thing I'm thinking is that Packer is just itching to add another zombie notch to his gun. It's not going to be my brother. I dive for the Snatcher's shooting hand, shoving past Nicolas, who falls over the nurse. Packer and I scuffle. I take him by surprise, probably because despite all the facts, he can't wrap his head around the idea that I am, indeed, freakishly strong. Appearances can be deceiving.

Cory ignores me, shambling slowly towards the nurse. The smell of her blood saturates the room like fried chicken on the stove. Nicolas is hauling her to the window, away from the fray by the door. I'm struggling with Packer to keep him from blowing Cory's brains out. My brother is hell-bent on getting to the bloody nurse, or maybe Nicolas smells like Sunday to him too. The doctor and the nurse are crouched behind the head of the bed in the space below the window. Nicolas has his body draped over hers, protecting her.

I finally use my best weapon, my legs, and pin Packer to the floor. With my knee in his throat, I pivot at my waist and grab for Cory's ankle. My brother doesn't seem to register that if he keeps walking with his ankle caught in my grip, he'll fall. He hits the mattress of the bed and tumbles to the floor.

With my knee, I crush the air out of Packer's windpipe and slam his gun hand against the floor. I hear the knuckles crack. The gun is in my hand now, and I heave it out the window. Glass shatters everywhere. Nicolas ducks and covers his patient as the door opens again.

"Nice work, Evelyn."

It's Greyson.

"I figured if I sent your brother in here," he nods at Cory, who is trying to haul himself back up, "you'd come out on my side."

I'm totally stunned, and Packer takes advantage of my momentary stupor to flip me. But he's no match for Greyson. The guy is worse than a rabid animal. He's on the soldier with claws and teeth before I can even blink. Packer screams and blood flies. I shove the Snatcher off me in time to see Greyson take a bite out of his liver and toss the rest to my brother. Cory catches it and gobbles it up like it's an ice cream sandwich on a summer afternoon. I can smell it, Thanksgiving feast all laid out on the dining room table.

Greyson wipes his mouth with the back of his hand. "Don't look so surprised. You didn't think I'd sit around and let them hack up my soul mate?"

"You'd have to have a soul to have a soul mate, Greyson."

He holds out his hand to help me up. "We're a pair, Ev, whether you like it or not. I've got your back."

Now my mouth falls open and my eyes squint in disbelief. How does the guy who is chaperoning the gang of zombies that killed half my family, kidnapped my sister, and infected my brother get off talking like that to me?

"C'mon, give me a break, everybody likes me. I'm a nice guy."

"Yeah, I can see that." My gaze and my sweeping gesture take in the mayhem in the room. "What the hell do you think you're doing? The military is looking for you, and you just waltz in here and expect to pull me out?"

"Chill. You're so uptight. Unlike you, I brought backup. My buddies out there volunteered to keep them busy for a while. You should have told me you were coming after Bridger. I'd have been there for you, baby."

I shove his hand away and haul myself up on my own. Packer has stopped squirming now. The nurse is moaning.

"You want me to take care of that doctor?" he asks, glaring at Nicolas. "Bet he'll think twice now before he hooks one of us up to his machines."

A chill runs down my spine. Suddenly, the most important thing in the world is to get Greyson and my brother away from Nicolas. The good doctor has stolen a little part of me and made it his. It's hard to drag myself away without feeling I'm leaving some vital organ behind. "No. He's on our side."

"None of them are on our side." Greyson is scowling at Nicolas.

Nicolas is watching me but I can't quite read what he's thinking. There's a look on his face. Disgust. Apparently, it's finally sunk in what I am—the other half of Greyson.

"We eat their guts or they shoot us in the head. That's how it works," Greyson growls. "They think we're the monsters, but we're the future."

"He doesn't think we're monsters." I look at Nicolas to see if what I'm saying is true or not. But all I see is him working feverishly to stop the bleeding, so I cover for him. "His little brother is infected. He's trying to help us."

Greyson grabs Cory's arm and pulls the door open. "We don't need his help. We got it covered." He shoves my brother in the corridor and grabs my arm. "C'mon."

I can't help it. As I'm leaving, I look back. I have to see Nicolas's face.

"Don't forget, Evelyn!" That's all he says.

"I got it," I say, feeling oddly betrayed. I turn away, patting the bulge of syringes in my pocket as I slip through the door. He says something but it gets lost in a rattle of gunfire.

I turn my head towards the cracks just in time to watch my little brother crumple to the floor.

"No. God, no, Cory!" I rush for him. For me, the corridor has gone void. There's nothing there anymore, nothing but my little brother, shot through the head. The kid that I had to haul home from the skateboard park because he couldn't be bothered to come home to eat, is lying dead in the hallway with someone's liver smeared across his face.

My eyes blur up and my knees buckle under me. "No, no, no, no!" The wet, salty words keep bubbling from my mouth, punctuating the rattling gunshots. Greyson drags me back up. I'm surprised by how strong he is—stronger than I am.

"He's gone. He was gone before we got here. Let's go."

From the end of the corridor, a voice shouts: "It's the mutations. Use the tranqs. Doc Christensen wants those two alive."

Wrestling my arm away, I lurch back to stay with Cory. "He's my brother, you idiot. He has nobody to take care of him. I'm all that's left. You killed the rest of my family!"

"'Your family' threw you out in the street. He's dead and he doesn't need you. Your sister is the one you should be worrying about."

In one sentence, everything changes. Cory's dead. Amber's alive. "You know where she is?" I clench my teeth—and my chest, and my jaw. My shaking palms smear the tears off my face. A tranquilizer dart hits the door.

"C'mon," he yells, springing me off the floor.

We sprint down the hallway to the stairwell where Bridger and I got ambushed. Darts fly by and hit the walls around us. One grazes Greyson's jacket. I'm glad they're not bullets. The corridor is littered with bodies: zombies with their heads blown off, hospital staff bloodied and disemboweled, ZVs oblivious to the danger, crouching down to enjoy a free meal. "Get out of here," I yell at the feasters as we go by. They don't care; they're too far gone. All they want is to feed the hunger.

I'm amazed at how much faster I reach the stairwell when I'm not trying to trail Bridger along. We hear the voices from behind and above, just like last time. The window I went through is covered with plastic. "They have tranquilizers, Greyson, because they want us alive, so they can cut us up."

"They have to catch us first." He grabs my hand, the plastic in the window stretches and rips as we burst through, and then we're flying. This time the dart hits me in the shoulder. Another mark. It's not that high up, so I stick the landing. We're halfway through the parking lot when the drug starts to kick in and my head goes all woozy on me. I remember reaching for Greyson's arm to steady myself, but I don't remember whether or not I hit the ground.

Chapter 12

Pink, orange, yellow. I'm lying in a cloud of saltwater taffy—my comforter. Stars glow from my bedroom ceiling, laughing at a secret joke. "Mom!" I mumble. I slept really hard. My voice grates like sandpaper on rust. "What time is it? I'm going to be late for French. Madame is going to freak." I stumble around my room looking for my clothes, but I slept in them, so I just grab a t-shirt out of the drawer and pull it over my tank top. It's going to be a ponytail day. I head for my bathroom—the only advantage of being the oldest sister of three brothers is that I get the bedroom with its own bathroom attached.

I flip on the light and then scream.

There's a ghoul in my mirror. And then I scream again because the ghoul has my face and my green eyes. And then I remember the nightmare that won't end. I'm not back from Oz. It wasn't a dream. There's no waking up when you're the nightmare.

A figure appears behind me in the mirror. Greyson. The whole scenario is now in panoramic vision across my brain. I'm the monster they sent to get blood samples from the other monster. I sink into the corner by the door.

"Not a morning person?" Greyson asks.

"I'm not a person," I spit back at him, squeezing my face into my fingers, trying to make the reality go away and the dream come back. But the reality keeps kicking me: I have to make friends with the guy who feasted on my parents, the guy who brought my brother to the Institute and got him shot through the head.

Greyson leans in through the doorway, his hands on the frame above his head. "We're not monsters," he says. For a second, he looks different, the way his eyes are focused on me like he actually gives a shit about something besides himself. And then it all evaporates into this cheeky grin. "We're freakin' superheroes."

I stare at him, open-mouthed. "We eat people. By definition, we are monsters. If you're a little fuzzy on that issue, step outside. Note the screaming and the running. That should clear things up a bit for you."

He rolls his eyes and shakes his head; he's not buying that I can't see through the masks and disguises to the secret letters blazoned on our chests. He drops his hand and holds it out to me. "C'mon."

I swat it away. "I'm not going anywhere with you."

He leans over to take my arm and I jerk back and give him my best touch-me-and-die look. It doesn't seem to faze him, but he doesn't touch me. "Trust me, you want to see this."

"Trust you?" I can feel the syringe in my pocket; I know what I'm supposed to do. He has to trust me, and the only way that's going to happen is if I pretend to trust him. But Greyson saying those words makes a couple of nerves in my brain snap—and they're attached to my tongue. "Trust you? Are you out of your mind? You waltzed over here to my house with your drone zombies and killed my family. You want me to trust you?" I'm yelling at him from the floor, but I still kick my foot at his shin. The animal inside me controls my legs and the animal is out of control.

With not much effort, he dodges. "I get that you're mad. But that was an accident."

"Are you totally brain dead? You don't just kill someone's family 'on accident'."

"Give me a little credit here. I was trying to make you happy."

"Make me happy? By turning a bunch of starving, bloody-mouthed zombies loose on my family? Very thoughtful. I'm almost weepy." The sad truth is, just talking about it is making my eyes mist up. I'm mostly furious, but something inside my brain, not the virus, is making me twitch. There's a look on Greyson's face. Bridger used to get it. It says, "I'm sorry that boys are retarded at seeing the consequences of their actions. But I really did think this would make you happy. In my hormone-whacked head, it turned out differently." In some minute corner of my mind, I actually feel sorry for him and listen to his lame excuse. I'm turning into my mom.

"We were heading for the mortuary. I figured it grossed you out that they were eating people alive, maybe you'd feel better about us lifting the pertinent parts off of the newly dead. No harm; no foul."

Against all odds, in some sick way, this actually does make me feel better.

"I didn't think anyone would be working there in the middle of the night," he goes on because I'm buying it. "With dead bodies, that's just creepy. But there was a guy in there. I think it was Grant Porter, who works for Calder. The zombies got a whiff of him and then the frenzy got off. There's no controlling these freaks. Mrs. Calder shows up on the stairs and they're on her like a bunch of vultures. It was all I could do to grab the little girl and get her the hell out of there."

"Madi? You have Madi? Where? Is she safe? Where's her dad?"

"She's safe; I don't know where her dad is. He was gone. He must have been outside the line. That was the night they quarantined. If he was gone, they wouldn't have let him back in. Anyway, he'd be dead if he'd been there. That's what happened to most of your family." He stops to see what kind of reaction he's going to get. I force my face to go blank, put a clamp on my heart because I want to know what happened. Since I don't freak, he keeps going, "One of your brothers was outside; he heard the screaming and ran over to help. The zombies chased him back into the house. When I realized what was happening, I stuffed Madi in a tree and took off for your house. It was mostly over by the time I got here."

The "mostly" part plays itself out in my head. I can see it all because I've seen this movie before, over and over. Only this time, my parents are the actors—the minor ones that get eaten to make the movie scarier. I'm living it in my head, and in my guts, and before I know it, I'm diving for the toilet and green gruel shoots out my mouth into the bowl. Greyson grabs my hair and gathers it up while I spew. When I'm empty, I reach up and flush, and then collapse back against the cabinet. My eyes are wet—from the retching.

"I'm really sorry." He's infuriatingly sincere. "Once they get to a certain point, you can't control the ZVs anymore. The old infected ones aren't like your brother, Cory. After I bit him, even though he started going brain dead a lot sooner than the couple-infected ones, he pretty much did what I said like I was controlling him or something." He looks away to contemplate his power while the words hit me like a nuke in water. They explode underneath and shoot out the surface, shoving me to my feet.

My palms hit him in the chest and slam him into the wall by the door. His head dents the drywall and now I've gone too far. His eyes go crazy and he shoves me back. "What the hell?" he yells as I ram him a second time. He's really strong and catches me. I writhe viciously in his arms, lift up my knee, and jam it into his crotch. He groans and lets me go.

"You bit my brother on purpose. He was a boy, a real human being. I left them—my family, my little sister that needed me—lived in a hole in a church, by myself, with nothing. I left them so they wouldn't get hurt and you just go off and bite him. For what? Some sick science experiment? Does that make you feel better now, Dr. Frankenstein? You can create the monster and he does what you say?" He starts to stand up and I kick him over.

"It's not what you think…"

That just makes me angrier. How could he possibly explain biting my brother? He doesn't get to. This is his fault and I *will* hate him. No sense in keeping the animal inside caged when I'm in the jungle. My foot is on a collision course with his face. I'd like to leave a mark there. But then my ankle is trapped in his hands and my back is crashing into the cabinet. I'm sliding down. He drags me so I'm flat on my back and then straddles me. I reach up to claw at his face and he grabs my arms, pinning them to my sides.

"Get off of me!" I hiss.

"So, you can kick me again? I don't think so." My body squirms underneath him. This is humiliating. "You're going to listen to me, and then I don't care what you do. I am not the enemy. The enemies are the Institute goons in black with guns, and the pale white sickos with body parts stuck in their teeth. You and I, we're the grey in the middle. We're on the same team; we're friends."

"I am not your friend."

"Fine. We're on the same team."

I look away. The only thing I can do. "At least give me credit for saving your butt." That wins him a sour sneer and a wrench of my knees. "Cory ran up to save Amber that night." I stop struggling a bit because I believe that and more than anything, I want to know what happened to Amber. "Your family was mostly gone when I got there." It's sick, but I take that literally. "The ZVs were looking around for something fresh. It was only a matter of time before they sniffed out your brother and little sister, holed up in her room like that. I ran up to get them out, but he thought I was after them, so he takes me on with a bat. Honestly, I tried not to hurt him, but I had to get them out the window. Not even I could get through the feeding frenzy in your dining room. Your little sister was screaming and fighting me; I had to hang on with both arms. Cory wouldn't let go. All I could do was bite him and head for the window."

Now, what am I supposed to do with the fury? Swallow it? My stomach is already a boiling brew of poison.

"Can you at least give me some credit? I did risk my neck to break you out of the Chop and Fry Institute." This guy is the devil. He spins the truth in every twisted direction possible so that you have to like him. And now there's all this hate swirling around in my veins with nowhere to go. Of course, it's going to start seeping out my eyes. In about five seconds, I'm a pathetic, blubbering lump.

Greyson scoots back onto my thighs. He scoops his arms around my back and hauls me up to his chest and then I'm crying on his shoulder.

"She's safe? Amber's safe somewhere?" I hiccup through the sobs.

"She's safe." He pushes me away enough to look me in the eye as if my hair weren't matted against my face. His fingers brush through it, tuck it behind my ears so I can see his eyes like he knows I'll want to see that he's telling the truth, that the demon that's holding me is my guardian angel. "She's safe," he says again.

"Thank you." I manage to squeeze a bit of gratitude out of the almost empty tube of my soul.

Out of nowhere, his lips are on mine, they're soft and they move like they were meant to be there. His arms crush me like he's trying to fuse the two of us together. I've forgotten what it was like when Bridger kissed me, why I kept hanging out with him even though I knew we were wrong for each other months before we broke up. I craved the warmth and the wanting, and now that I'm so cold and no one wants me, I crave it even more.

My arms find their way around Greyson's neck and I soak up everything I can get from him. Bridger wasn't this good; his lips were full, but his mouth didn't swallow up my world like this. Greyson doesn't make me think of food. I think of stepping out onto the back porch on a summer's night; the warm air and quiet stillness sweep around me and I don't even need a sweater.

Now I know why so many girls lost it with this guy. He makes me feel like I'm the only one, like it's real, and nothing else in the world matters to him. I shove him away and slap him. "Don't do that again," I growl.

He shrugs, but slides off me and offers me a hand up. When I'm upright again, I turn to survey the damage in the mirror. Actually, I don't want to look him in the eye. He's watching my reflection and wipes the corner of his mouth. "Damn. You're a mess, you look like a zombie, and you're still the hottest girl in town."

"It's a small town," I snap, rifling through the drawers for a brush. That's not exactly true. About ten years ago it was a small town.

"I never could figure out why you went out with that Bridger kid."

I find a travel brush stuffed in the back of the bottom drawer and run it gingerly through my hair. "I dated Bridger because he was funny and cute. I could relax when we were together." I pause. "I think, secretly, I also liked his brother."

"Preston. Everyone liked Preston."

"What's not to like? I think he kind of liked me back." I say that just because I get the feeling it will get under Greyson's skin. A few strokes more and I add, "And I liked Bridger because he made me laugh—and he wasn't checking out other girls; he thought I was the only girl worth having."

"You are the only girl worth having." Typical Greyson. The word "having" has a totally different meaning in his mouth. I stop brushing and squint cynically at his reflection, but all I see is what I used to see on Bridger's face when he watched me put my make-up on.

"You like to laugh?" He stops the brush in my hand. "I can make you laugh." I drop the brush as he pulls me out of the bathroom, grabs my sweatshirt, and tosses it to me. "We don't want the UV rays damaging that lily-white skin of yours."

I can't help but smile as I slip into the sweatshirt. The syringes bulge a little in the pocket. I shove them in tighter. "Where are we going?"

"To jail."

That *is* funny—because it's so absurd and ironic, and laughing is the other side of crying. "Why?"

"To get your little sister." He jingles a ring of keys at me.

"You locked her up?"

He shrugs. "And about half a dozen other little kids. It was the only place I could think of where they'd be safe."

It's not so funny anymore.

Chapter 13

There are bloodstains on the tile in the kitchen. Greyson sees me wince and puts his arm around me, pulling me towards the door. "I should have cleaned that up. Housekeeping isn't really my thing. My mom made me make my bed, take out the trash, wash the car, mow the lawn, do the vegetarian crap, but she never made me do the dishes or any actual cleaning."

"Wait. Did you say you're a vegetarian?" The utter improbability of that statement distracts me from the story snarling at me from the smears on the floor. I'm stunned by the sheer awkwardness of having something so basic in common with Greyson.

"Yeah." He's kind of embarrassed. "My mom showed me all the PETA videos until it made me sick just thinking about a piece of meat. Lot of good it does me now." He opens the door, pushes on a pair of sunglasses, and then looks down at me, waiting for me to do the same.

My eyes are fixed on his face. I'm trying to see if this is some line he's feeding me. That would so be his style.

"Don't look so surprised. It's not something you advertise," he snaps. Is he actually defensive? I shove my glasses on. He's telling the truth.

I head towards the jail, but Greyson grabs my arm. "You can't go walking down Main Street in the middle of the day. They patrol all the major roads. You have to use the trails." He heads me towards the park. Eli's pretty well-known for its running and biking trails. Some of them stretch along the foothills and others zigzag through town. A few of them go all the way into downtown Salt Lake. Every girl on the track team knows them all. We spent half our lives there.

The sides of the trails are sprinkled with snow. Most of the tracks in the powder are the smeared, dragging foot, zombie kind, not the crisp, waffle kind that soldiers leave.

From certain spots, I catch a glimpse, through the trees, of houses and sections of neighborhoods. The place looks like a war zone. It is a war zone. There's trash blowing in the wind, kicked in doors, cars abandoned on the street, barricades of furniture. Some of the houses look burned out.

On the southern horizon, above the treetops, I can see the mountainside where all the construction was going on. Barbed fences and roadblocks are going up. From this distance, what looks like miniature army cars crawl along the roads. There's an explosion in one of the neighborhoods and I jump. "Geez!"

"That's new." Greyson cracks a smile in my direction. I roll my eyes. I really don't think he gets how serious things have gotten since he and his ZV buddies went on their shopping spree. "Most of us were hiding out over there on the south mountain in the basements of unfinished, repo'ed houses. The place probably reeks of ZV. They've got the dogs over there sniffing them out. It'll be a while before they get to downtown. They seem to be looking for people trapped in their houses more than ZVs. The downtown is pretty deserted."

"That's going to change. They're looking for *you*."

"I'm a popular guy." He grins.

His total refusal to note the gravity of this situation makes me squint and shake my head. "They know you're like me." He doesn't seem to be too impressed by that. "They have reports that the people you bite and infect can bite and infect other people."

"Yeah, well, that's a new development."

"Don't you get it? If that's true, and they have confirmed reports, this is no longer a rescue operation. We're not just some sick kids anymore; we're a threat, a public disaster. Once that info funnels down the command, they'll be in here to wipe us out."

He glances at me and finally decides to get serious. "We probably ought to think about getting out of town as soon as we have your sister."

A dog barks a few blocks away, and we both dive for cover in the bushes that line the trails. When the barking starts fading away from us, Greyson nods and we keep going, but he pulls me a little closer to the hedge. "That's weird. I thought they had most of the dogs up in the neighborhoods where all the houses are packed together. The fields are too wide open for hiding in." He stops and thinks about it. "Maybe they tracked an emergency call for rescue to one of these houses. Keep your eyes open."

It would be faster to cross through the Jensen's fields. There are trees for cover, but the field is a sinkhole this time of year. Brother Jensen insists on two things: being called Brother by everyone, and massively flooding his field with irrigation water before the city shuts it off for the winter. He swears an angel appeared to his grandfather in a dream and told him his fields would always prosper if he flooded them in the fall. The upside is, every year someone gets dared to drive through the Jensen swamp. Bill, down at the tow shop, pulls at least three or four teenagers out of there every December before it freezes over. Only one kid in town has ever managed to make it out—Greyson Childs. But that was in his stepdad's F-150 Raptor. I heard he got grounded for doing it.

Across the fields, I catch glimpses of the southern mountain. I point at the fences and barricades in the neighborhoods up there. "How did you get me back in?"

"I carried you."

It's kind of an "ahh, how sweet" answer, but it makes me squirm. Having to be grateful is getting on my nerves. "From downtown Salt Lake?"

"Feel free to thank me, you're not as light as you look."

Perfect. The Greyson I know and despise.

"They haven't blocked some of the mountain trails on the north side. And I have my ways of getting around."

"I was actually doing quite well on my own at the Institute. Nicolas…Dr. Vadlamani was working with me. He was going to get me out so I could find Amber." I don't mention the other reason he was going to get me out or the syringes in my sweatshirt pocket.

"Nicolas? The guy cowering on the ground when I got in the room?"

"He wasn't cowering on the ground. He was protecting the nurse. One of your little stooges made a Hot Pocket out of her arm."

"Yeah, thus the cowering."

Arguing is futile. Taking a deep breath, I swallow the words lodged in the back of my throat. It's weird how empty the trails are. Usually, I'd have passed about a dozen people by now, no matter what time of day it was. No, I have to argue.

"You can hardly blame him. The way you ripped into that soldier, I'd have been scared of you too. I just knew that I'm not your kind of meat."

He gets this stupid guy grin on his face and I know exactly what he's going to say.

"Don't even think that."

"What?"

"That I'm your kind of meat."

"I wouldn't say anything like that, it's rude."

"You so would too say it."

"You've seriously misjudged me, Evelyn. I'm hurt. And after all I've done to show you I'm a really nice guy…"

"Nice guy? Oh, that's rich. A really nice guy that bites people, steals their organs, and eats them. Real nice."

He shrugs. We pass a couple of cows feeding on the tall grass by the fence between their pasture and the trail. Greyson looks at them, and then at me, and then points his nose directly at the trail like if he can't see them, he won't smell them. I'm actually a little hungry myself.

"How many people have you bitten? Heck, how many have you eaten?" I ask, just to turn the screws.

"None. I haven't actually eaten any people. I've taken a bite out of a bunch of them."

"Before or after you knew what would happen?"

"Both."

"Seriously. You knew they'd be infected and you bit them anyway?"

"Yeah, it's not like they weren't trying to bash my skull with a baseball bat or shoot me up with tranqs so they could drag me off to the Institute of Terror. I figured they needed a taste of how the other side lives."

"Or you just like playing god with other people's lives."

"It is a little cool how I can control them."

I don't really have to try too hard to bring the true spirit of Greyson to the surface. I don't know what he's trying to prove with all this heroic, misunderstood crap he's feeding me. He's a prick and a player, and we both know it.

"You are such an egomaniac."

"I am not." He looks at me like I just kicked over his block castle.

"Do you even know what that means?"

"I sat behind you in AP Psych. I know what it means."

"What did you get in the class? A 'C'?"

He's really offended. "'B-.' I actually studied for that class."

"Excuse me!" I roll my eyes and then mutter under my breath, "'B-,' 'C,' you might as well get an 'F'."

He heard me. He glances at me from the corner of his eye and then shakes his head, flipping the hair out of his eyes. He still has really nice hair—just a little curly, and thick. "I was a little distracted in that class."

"Oh, yeah, that's right. That's about the time you were breaking up with Julie to hook up with some skank. That's gotta be pretty distracting, keeping track of your Psych notes *and* the list of dumped girlfriends."

"Actually," he leans back a little, reaches over and fondles a strand of my hair, "this is what was so distracting. It was always dangling there in front of me. I really wanted to touch it." He shrugs. "But you were Bridger's girl."

I yank my hair away. He's not going to con me the way he did Julie. "I never *belonged* to anyone." The fact that he thinks that makes me shoulder shove him towards the weeds on the side of the trail. "Girls aren't things that you collect and own. They're not like your little ZV followers that you can just toss out in front of the guns to save yourself."

He teeters, catches his balance, and then grabs my arm. I'm a little scared by the look on his face. "What do you want from me, Evelyn?"

"I don't want anything from you…except my sister." I'm wrestling him for my arm. He steps in front of me and holds me so I'm stuck there.

"When are you gonna cut mc some slack, for hell's sake! I've had a crush on you since second grade. I risked my neck and everything else—not to mention a bunch of those brain-dead zombies—to break you out of that chop shop; I pulled your little sister out of an organ-sucking mob…" He pushes me away and pulls his jean leg up. There's a white bandage wrapped around his calf. He unwraps it and displays a nasty, gaping purple-black gash. "…And got this for my trouble." He shoves the denim back down over it.

"I babysat Cory until the virus got so bad he wasn't even human anymore, so the soldiers and the gangs wouldn't tear him to pieces. I'm starving, but I don't dare feed myself what I'm craving because you wouldn't like it. What do I have to do before you figure out what's going on here? You're the Honor Student. Where do you get off being so thick?"

Now that he lays it out like that, I feel a little guilty. Second grade. We had Mrs. Smith.

"You weren't in love with me in second grade. You were going out with Laurie."

"Only because you wouldn't even look at me."

"I was shy. How was I supposed to know you liked me? You didn't even pick me for your football team."

"You weren't any good."

"I could catch."

"Yeah, but you wore dresses and you didn't have your running legs back then. If I picked you, everyone would know I liked you."

"Duh. That's the point."

"Sorry, I wasn't exactly smooth in second grade."

A dart hits the fencepost in front of Greyson and I don't have time to respond. He grabs my hand, we hop the fence, tear across the field to the cows' water trough, and crouch behind it. Greyson peeks out. Another dart hits the trough.

"You're not exactly smooth now," I quip.

"Only around you. It's the hair. And that little beauty mark on your knee. I could see it when your dresses were too short." He grins my direction before leaning around the trough. "They were always too short."

"I have long legs."

He sticks his nose around the corner for a look and snaps right back. A tranquilizer dart lands in the tree next to us.

"At least they're not using bullets," he says.

"That's not a good thing. These guys aren't part of the rescue teams. They're hunting *you*. When I was at the Institute, they were talking about 'the immune specimen.' Dr. Christensen really wants you…alive."

We exchange glances because we both know what that means. Greyson reaches behind his shirt and pulls out a gun.

I'm against guns in general, mostly because they kill people. You don't object to the slaughtering of animals and then go around shooting people. And I'm pretty sure the NRA doesn't offer a vegetarian option at their banquets. "What are you doing?" I demand.

"I'm making sure neither one of us ends up on Dr. Christensen's table."

"No. What are you doing *with a gun*?"

"I bit a cop."

My mouth is open but no words are coming out.

"I had to. He was going to shoot Cory. It's all good. I left him to guard the jail and keep the wild zombies locked up while I went after you. He showed me where all the guns were."

I still have no words for this.

"Relax. It's cool. I have the key. Unless he shoots the lock, he can't even get into the room with the holding cells."

"You gave a zombie a gun?"

"He's still in control like me and you."

"Yeah, but for how long?"

"Not very. When I bite them, the old ones go faster than the young ones."

He leans around and takes several shots—a human scream and bellowing from one of the cows.

"You hit the cow?" I can't help myself; old habits die hard. "You hit an innocent cow?" I slap his shoulder.

"I don't know who hit the cow. I hit one of the soldiers." Greyson leans around the trough and shoots. "There are only two of them and now one is injured."

"You can't shoot them. They're just soldiers doing their job. Most of them are only kids about our age."

"Wake up, Evelyn. This is war. They're the enemy. Their job is to shoot us. We shoot them or they shoot us; that's how it works." Another dart sticks in the dirt by my tennis shoe. I pull my foot in. "Can't you shoot in the air or something, and then we can run to the jail? They probably don't know the trails like we do. We'd lose them at the canal."

"Can't take the chance that they follow us to the jail. That's where I have the other ZVs, and some of them are...were...my friends. We started hiding out there and then hunting at night." He waggles his glasses. "Not all of them have sun gear."

He leans over and shoots again. The shot finds its target because I hear a grunting yell.

"That's both of them. If we're lucky, they'll leave to find a medic and we can get the hell out of here." I'm scowling. He looks down at me. "Chill. I wasn't trying to kill anyone. I'm a good shot. My real dad took me hunting when I was little. Why do you think my mom showed me all the PETA videos?" He leans around the trough again.

"They're out of here. C'mon. I'm sure they've got radios. We don't have very long before their buddies show up."

He holds out his hand. I take it.

We head towards the trail. I tug on his hand and pull him back towards the trough again.

"What are you doing? We have to get out of here."

"No sense in wasting a perfectly good cow," I say. "Besides, we might need something to feed your friends."

He smiles at me. If we ate smiles, his would be the kind with too much butter, too much cream, too much sugar, and way too many calories; homemade caramels, crème brûlée, prime rib, the stuff you only eat at Christmas when you're splurging. It's December now, isn't it?

Chapter 14

"Are any of the other ZVs vegetarians?" I ask Greyson as we come up on the Oster farm. We'll have to cut through the horse pasture to get to the jail.

"How would I know?"

"Guess. How many do you think were vegetarian before like us?"

"Most of the ones that are left were jocks, a couple skater boys, a cheerleader or two. If I had to guess, I'd say they were a bunch of carnivores even before they got infected." He slides under the wooden rails. The horses whinny and run towards the barn. "Maybe Chase."

"Chase what's-his-name that runs cross-country?"

"Yep. He's gay—just came out. Pretty sure he's vegetarian…was vegetarian. He's fast like us. He can take a gang member down and gut him before the poor slob can raise a bat. Doesn't seem to be getting any worse either."

"Well, if he's gay, and he's one of the original infected, how did he get the virus? There has to be a male and female strain." I slide under the fence and we head across the graze-trimmed grass to the parking lot in the back of the police station.

"I bit him."

I take a deep breath so I'll have plenty of air for telling him off, but he beats me to the words.

"Don't get your panties in a wad. It was an accident and I didn't know what would happen."

"How do you *accidentally* bite someone?"

"It happens."

I roll my eyes.

"Hey, you have no idea what it's like with these guys once they get in a frenzy. They'll take a bite out of anything that gets between them and meat."

That doesn't really explain how he bit Chase, but I decide to let it slide. I'm not sure I want to hear all the gory details. "But Chase is like us? He's not losing it?"

"Yeah, if he wasn't like us, he'd be dead by now. ZVs we bite go brain dead a lot faster. I usually take the ones that are really far gone out on a hunting party."

"With Snatchers and gangs all around? Aren't they easy targets?" *Is Greyson really this jaded?*

"Mercy killings." He bends down and extracts a blade of grass from its root and then stuffs it between his teeth. "They can't be lovin' life. Most of them are smashed up by then, and the virus is eating up their insides. I hear them moaning in the night. I think they feel it, but can't do anything about it."

I fold my arms across my chest and walk ahead without looking back.

"What?" he calls after me.

"Nothing." I'm looking for every excuse to be mad at him. But how can I be? Every time I think he's an idiot, he explains the method to his madness and it turns out he's actually a pretty nice guy.

I think it's going to snow. The sky is as grey as I am. Everything looks dingy. The soup of clouds, fog, and smog suits me, a thick damper that hides me from the glaring light of the sun. I feel alive in it.

"So, Chase has been around for a while," I comment absent-mindedly. I'm trying to imagine what it must be like, hiding out with friends, listening to them dying slowly in the night, being eaten alive from the inside out. My insides twisted in half when I saw Bridger strapped to that operating table.

My chest floods with pity for this kid forced to lead his friends to a gruesome death to save them from a slow, torturous one. I can't quite drown the point-blank conclusion that I might actually like Greyson. He slides up behind me and tangles his fingers in mine and then raises our hands to his mouth and blows on them.

"It's cold," he explains.

My feet stop moving. I turn around and look him in the face for a second before my hand reaches up and pushes the hair back from his forehead—the blood to my brain must have stopped. Greyson's totally as confused as I am. On my tiptoes, I let my lips touch his, just barely, without breaking eye contact, to brush his pain away. He doesn't even have time to respond. I turn back and start walking again, trailing him behind me. "Sometimes, you're kind of sweet," I whisper.

No reply. My guess is the blood isn't going to Greyson's head anymore either. A lone, gnarled oak towers over the fence that separates the sheriff's office from the farm. The leaves are gone, but it stands there waiting for better days.

"I think it might be because we're vegetarian, or we were before," I go on, ignoring the silence. "I mean, I don't have proof or anything, but the three of us that are, you know," I glance back at him because I'm still not getting any response. He grins at me like he just figured out why 2+2=4. He doesn't seem to be registering what I'm saying. "Are you okay?"

"Me. Oh, I'm good." We're just at the fence between the police station and the pasture. I shrug and pull away to swing my leg over. He tugs me back so I stumble into him. His arms around me steady the tumbling rush of our worlds colliding before his lips meet mine and we're suddenly at the center of a cyclone. For a while, my body floats in it, and then my arms push him away and the spinning stops.

"I told you not to do that again." The tingle of his mouth moving on mine, the wetness of it, dances on my lips. The back of my sleeve absorbs it all in one quick swipe.

"But, you..." he reaches for me.

"Just stop it, okay?"

He doesn't follow. "There's never been anyone but you, Evelyn. Those other girls, they were just keeping the seat warm."

He's such a creep, but at the same time, it makes me feel taller, and gorgeous like I'm all dressed up for prom and he can't take his eyes off of me. I flip my hair off my shoulders and take a deep breath, trying to clear all the grey out of my head so that I can see the black and white again. I'm looking anywhere but at him.

We hop the fence into the parking lot. Greyson grabs my sleeve. "If we can see the street, they can see us." I wish he had slapped me instead of warning me. It makes me cringe that I talk to him like I just did, but he still watches out for me. I remind myself that that's the way he plays it.

A couple of empty squad cars and a Jeep offer cover. "The jail is in the back of the sheriff's office." He points to the end of the building, at the opposite side from the door. "We have to go through the front office to get to it, though." It's one of those bowling alley buildings, long and narrow, squeezed on a lot between the new library and the utility building. When they needed more space, they pushed it out the back towards the field because there wasn't any room to make it wider.

The back entrance is a double glass door. The shards from one pane litter the sidewalk in front of it.

"Wait here." Greyson looks both ways before crossing the parking lot to the doors. *At least he follows some of the rules.* He waves me over. Staying low, I cover the open space and sprint through the broken glass. Inside the building, intercom speakers in the hallway gently blare some serious rap music.

He catches my look. "I think music is supposed to keep them calm," he explains.

"Not that kind of music."

"The cell rooms are on the other side of this wall, but we have to go through the front office to get there. Keep your head down in there. The windows are tinted, but some of them are smashed out."

The door we came in leads us through a long corridor bordered by tiny offices that runs almost the length of the whole building from back to front. At the end of the corridor is a door. I assume that's the front office, and only that part of the building is exposed to the street. We're going to have to make a long, thin U to go through the front office and into the jail area.

Greyson goes first, fishing a ring of keys out of his pocket. I've never been in the police station before. The door we open is like a back door to the front office.

Inside, around the back of the counter that faces the front windows, there's another door with a small window right next to it that leads to what looks like a control room for cell rooms back down on the other side of the wall we just came up. Stray papers on the empty reception desk flap in the breeze from the broken windows.

A fallen Christmas tree and shattered bulbs clutter the floor. Greyson strolls behind the counter and reaches for a key hanging on a board with hooks and labels. "Sweet. This one goes to the Jeep out there." He pockets the key. "Let's get the kids."

Snow is falling outside—big, fat flakes of it. Last year, I was sitting in my French class, watching the snow fall for the first time that year, tapping my knee under my desk because I had a new board and wanted to get out on the slopes.

"Wait. Did you see that?" I ask peering through the hole in the glass, out beyond the grass boardwalk, to the trimmed bushes and bike trails that line the sidewalks of Main Street.

"What?" He turns back in time to witness a couple of camouflaged soldiers scrambling for cover behind a flipped over car in the street beyond the pavement.

My head twists towards the sound of rapid stomping approaching the front door. "They found us!" I yell, running for Greyson. Any second I expect a couple more guys in camouflage to come crashing through the doors or the broken windows and shoot Greyson and me full of tranq darts.

Outside the broken window, across the street, a black Institute SUV screeches to a stop under a shiny red bell dangling from a strand of broken garland. The only thing I can think of is what will happen to my baby sister if they haul me away.

The door flies open and a body dives through it.

"Get down!" Greyson yells. Shots shatter the glass from outside and splinter the wood of the counter next to me. I duck and cover, but not before I recognize the guy coming through the door.

I dive for Greyson to stop him from shooting, even though it's already too late. My brain is moving much faster than my body can respond, so the whole thing looks like it's happening in a vat of clear Jello. The crack of Greyson's gun accompanies my descent to the floor.

The guy that he just shot at, the one we thought was here to shoot us, isn't a soldier at all. It's Chase What's-his-face.

Greyson trips forward, mortified. "Oh, God, Chase!" We stay huddled on the ground below the window line while bullets shred the place. Then I hear shouting, words like "a mutation" and "tranq guns," and the peppering stops, but the stomping and yelling doesn't.

Chase's mouth is covered in blood and his hands are full of red smeared flesh. He fell backward when the shot hit him, but he didn't let go of his death grip on the tasty little morsel in his fist. It fills the room with a spicy, fresh, hot cheese aroma that reminds me of the pizza place next to the grocery store.

"Grab his feet!" Greyson yells to me as he fumbles with the keys.

A smear of dark, adulterated blood follows me as I drag Chase through the door into the back office.

"This area is bulletproof," Greyson says, slamming the door and bolting it behind us. Now there's another door in front of us. We're in the control room and I can only assume the hallway through the back door leads to the two holding cells. Greyson kneels down to check out the damage to Chase.

"You shot him!" I grab the gun out of Greyson's hand. "Like I said, *don't give guns to zombies!*"

"He's fine."

"All except for the new hole in my shoulder," Chase moans.

"Does it hurt?" I ask.

"Kind of burns. One of the perks of being a ZV. Less pain. Did the bullet go through?"

"You're lucky," Greyson answers, pulling away the shirt. "It went right through. It didn't break any bones." He tilts him up. "Most of the wounds stop bleeding pretty quickly, but the virus doesn't let the body heal the wound over," he tells me like I'm some sort of med student.

"Yeah, I know. The virus uses the blood," I explain to Chase, "so, it stops the bleeding. Nicolas—Dr. Vadlamani—told me how it works." My eyes shift to Greyson when I say Nicolas's name. Greyson catches the flinch. His eyes go hard. He knows there's something there. Or is it just that I know there's something there?

Chase creaks to his feet, rotating his shoulder. "Everything seems to move okay," he observes. His pale, purplish-grey complexion matches Greyson's and mine. He's totally normal—the tall, thin, picture-perfect cross-country addict that I remember—except for a drying, blood-smeared piece of intestine still stuck in his fingers. He rips it in half with his teeth like beef jerky, and then sighs and nods, the way the guys working at the 7-Eleven do when they step outside to light up.

His eyes dart around the floor and then give us the once over like he's lost something and we're the most likely suspects. "Didn't I have a liver in my other hand?" I grimace. He reaches for the door like he's going after it. "I'm sure I got like a lung or something…maybe liver too. The intestines are okay, but they're kind of gamey."

"Sorry," Greyson intercepts him and hauls him away from the door. "You can't go out there; you'll get shot."

"He's already shot," I point out.

"In the head. They'll blow your head off, dude."

He looks disappointed but shrugs it off. "More where that came from," he grins. Greyson laughs. "Hey, Evelyn Cross!" I feel a little guilty because Chase knows my last name and I can't remember his. Of course, there are only five letters in mine. "Greyson got you out. Nice work, dude. What's it like in there? As bad as the stories?"

"Worse. They killed Bridger," I tell him.

"Sorry, girl. He was a good guy." Pause. We all look somewhere else so the others won't see that we're not just sad, we're scared that it might be us one day, and wondering what's so special about us that it's not us right now. "So…I'm a zombie now," Chase says.

"Yeah, uh, I could kind of tell."

"What a trip. It's not bad enough I make my mom cry because I'm gay…you knew I was gay, right?"

"Everyone knew you were gay, Chase."

"Oh. Thought maybe I came out after you left…anyway, now I've got to make my mom scared I'm going to go all Hannibal Lecter on her brains. Don't even know how I got the virus. I thought you had to have a girlfriend. Fate sucks."

Greyson shakes his head at me. I figure it's better not to upset the current order of things by establishing the true origins of Chase's infection.

"A gay zombie—in Utah," Chase sighs. "Strike three. All I need is a redneck with a bat and I'm out. Dead." We all nod sympathetically. Chase was in AP Sociology with Greyson and me. "At least, I still got my legs," he says grinning. He was always a happy kind of guy. Must be the endorphins. I wonder if that still applies.

"I wanted to ask you about that, Chase. You're like Greyson and me, right? You don't get any sicker. Are you faster?"

"Hell, yes. And stronger. Biceps weren't my thing, before, but I'd take on this pansy any day." He postures towards Greyson.

"Save it for the Snatchers." Greyson grins. "You're still a wuss." The biceps Greyson displays for us bulge out in sexy lines and curves. "Someone, call the vet. These puppies are sick," he announces. They both laugh and shove each other back and forth.

"You realize he just shot you, right?" I ask, just to see if Chase is really still with us.

"It happens."

I'm not sure if the idiocy is a symptom of the boy gene or the Z-Virus. Doesn't matter. "Chase, were you a vegetarian?"

"And proud of it. No soda either. Slows you down." He nods appreciatively and then looks a little perplexed. "Course, I'm a lot faster now, and I'm pretty much more of a carnivore."

"You're an organ junky," Greyson chimes in. Chase grins. "He and I stuck to dogs and cats for a while. Chase is one of the reasons we tried the funeral house that night. He got caught up in the feeding frenzy the night the Institute took Bridger, and ever since then, it's like he can't help himself."

Chase looks mortified, shaking his head. "It's like running. Gotta do it." His fist shoots into the air above his head, dangling leftovers. "Obey your thirst!"

"Hunger," I correct him dryly. "About that, Chase." I step a little closer so he can see how serious I am. His head towers above mine. The bite marks on his shoulder, I assume from Greyson, glare back at me in tones of purple and red. "You need to watch out, keep a low profile. They're looking for ZVs like us. They'll haul you away to the Institute, cut you up alive, and then fry you in an electric chair."

He swallows and backs away from me like I'm going to bash his head and eat his brains. Good. I want him to be scared. I pat him on the back. "Stick with Greyson. He'll take care of you." My eyes meet Greyson's. The sound of the words turns solid and slides back under our skin. It's true. He will.

We all jump when a gun goes off in the holding cells behind the wall.

Chapter 15

Shit!" Greyson jangles the keys in the door. It swings open and he's through it with his hand finding nothing in his back pocket. "The gun. Give me the gun!"

Against my better judgment, but from a newly acquired reflex of trusting Greyson in a high-stress situation, I pass him the gun and sprint behind him down the hallway. The sound of little girls screaming competes in syncopated beat with the rock lyrics spewing out of the intercom speakers.

"Donny. What the hell are you doing, man?" Greyson yells, slamming open the first door. The shot we heard was the zombie deputy blowing through the lock. He's shambling towards the bars that separate him from a cell of about half a dozen terrified little girls.

"Amber!" My little sister's face is the first one that processes.

"Evelyn!" she screams, holding out her arms and bursting into tears.

"Evelyn. Evelyn!" They all join in, a chorus of caged baby birds.

I know most of them. Little Madi Calder starts bawling. "Make it go away. The dead people are getting me. Make it go away, Evy!"

"He's popped!" Greyson lifts the gun and points it at the deputy's head. The deputy's expression doesn't change; he just points his gun through the bars at the huddle of squealing six-year-olds. "Don't make me do this, Donny!" Greyson hisses through gritted teeth. His arm is shaking. He's not as steady at point-blank as he is at long range.

"Just do it!" Chase yells. "He's brain-dead. He's not listening to you, man, the virus has him by the balls."

The deputy's thumb slides over the hammer and it clicks into place. *Too much shooting; too much dying.* I'm not going to stand here and let Amber watch Greyson blow Donny's brains out. My leg shoots around, just like I learned in Karate class, and connects with the deputy's chest. The gun clatters to the floor, discharging on impact. One of the little girls screams, her leg pierced by the stray bullet. The smell of fresh blood explodes into the cell.

"What the hell, Evelyn!" Greyson goes after Deputy Don and pulls out the cuffs dangling from his pocket. The zombie objects vigorously.

"Give me the key to the cell," I yell.

"I'm kind of busy here." The sheriff gnashes and struggles, grasping to get at the tender, baby-girl blood smell. Greyson wrestles him to the far side of the cell and then lands a fist to his jaw. The deputy's head cracks to the side and his body tumbles to the floor. Greyson locks his limp wrist to the bar that's bolted into the wall.

Chase is standing at the other end of the cell, mesmerized, his nose through the bars. "She's bleeding," he murmurs. The brunette I don't recognize is crying, holding her leg. Blood streams out from between her fingers. The other girls cling to each other and cry. Chase's arm reaches out for the injured one through the bars, but I'm worried that it's not because he wants to help her. I'm worried that he's still hungry.

"It's okay, baby," I say to Amber. "I'm here to get you. I'll take you someplace safe. You too, Madi. Don't cry, sweetie. We'll find your daddy and take you to him. We'll get you all somewhere safe." Amber reaches for me wriggling away from Madi's death grip on her neck. I glance at Chase. He's watching my baby sister, the way my cat used to watch Cory's gerbil in its cage. "Stay there with Madi, baby. Greyson is getting me the key. I'll come get you." Deputy Donny moans and gurgles but doesn't move.

Greyson slides over to me and digs through his pocket for the key. "What were you thinking?" he demands, turning his head away so the girls won't see us arguing. "I had him covered."

"I didn't want a bunch of little first graders to watch you blow a man's brains out."

"So, you got one of them shot instead? Much less traumatic."

"How was I supposed to know the gun would go off like that?" The guilt makes me turn it on him. "You're the one that gave a zombie a gun. You didn't want to shoot him any more than I wanted to watch you shoot him." Greyson's not buying it. He's ready to argue and I cut him off. "Look, it doesn't matter now. It happened. We have to deal with it." I step closer and whisper, "I don't trust Chase—especially not around a kid that's bleeding. Can't you smell it? Little kids smell sweeter than grown-ups."

"That's sick, Ev," he takes in a whiff, "but true."

"You have to get Chase out of here. I don't want him to know where we take them."

"Hey, Chase. Evelyn thinks you're interested in snacking on one of those little girls. Is that right?"

"What are you doing?" I mumble through my teeth.

"You got it under control, right, buddy?" Greyson is looking at me but talking to Chase. "Done enough pretending and hiding. Time we just lay everything out the way it is, be who we are, and deal with it."

Chase backs away from the cell, looking like he just woke up from a really good dream, and nods at Greyson. "Yeah, I'm good. I got this. I just ate; I'm not even hungry."

"Remember that." Greyson waits for a nod from Chase before he glances at me and winks like we're talking an honor code snack box and not the lives of first graders. "At least he didn't shoot her," he quips.

The lock clicks, the door swings open, and suddenly the little girls are stuck to me like we're all wrapped in Velcro. I recognize most of them: Madi Calder, Katie the little ginger I babysit, and another friend of Amber's from school. There are actually five of them, including the one I don't know that got shot. I'm a little nervous that Chase is heading into the cell, straight for her, but can't do anything because I've been taken over by clinging girls.

"Why just the little girls?" I ask, trying to sift through the sobbing mass. I find Amber and lift her up.

"They hide—not very well, but they hide," Greyson replies. "I had to fish most of them out of their closets or out from under their beds. The boys run or fight. They were gone before I got there most of the time." He doesn't define the word "gone."

Amber finally loosens her death grip around my neck so she can look at me. My lips cover her little face with kisses. There are soldiers outside the bulletproof walls and a zombie deputy handcuffed to the bars three feet behind me; most of my family is dead; I'm hooked up with the sweetest douche bag on the planet and a gay ZV. But with my baby sister clinging to my neck, for the first time in a long, long time, I feel like life might still be worth living.

I lean down to kiss Madi and maneuver our little girl party farther into the cell with Greyson and Chase who are kneeling over our shooting victim. I don't recognize her. "Hey, sweetie, what's your name?"

"Crystal," Chase answers for her; Crystal seems to be in shock. Maybe it's just the deep black curly hair against the stark paleness of her skin that makes her look that way. She's whimpering quietly into Chase's arm as he pets her hair. "She's my niece."

Oh...my bad. I guess he wasn't hungry. Zombies can be hard to read.

"I want mommy," she murmurs into his sleeve.

"Greyson," my First Aid skills are kicking in. "There's a First Aid cabinet out there in that control room, next to the intercom. Go get stuff—bandages, gauze, tape, antibacterial—whatever they've got."

I set Amber down. "I'm going to help Crystal. You stay right here by me, okay?" She nods. There's not much chance she'll be wandering off.

"Can I see the owie?" I ask, keeping my distance from Crystal. I don't want to intimidate our patient by invading her space. AP Psych. I can smell the sweet, fresh meat aroma. I glance at Chase, just to make sure he's still with us.

Crystal shakes her head. "The grey man did it." She points at the deputy. At least she's not blaming me. "You're grey too."

"I know I am. But your Uncle Chase is grey." She looks up from his arm to his face as if she hadn't noticed. "See. He's grey, but he still takes care of you. And he loves you too. Right, Uncle Chase?"

"You betcha." He kisses the top of her head.

"Some grey people are nice, especially the ones that love you. Isn't that right, Amber?" My baby sister doesn't answer; with a big grin, she throws her arms around my neck and nearly knocks me over kissing me. Crystal smiles. "Can I see?" I ask again.

The blaring of the music shuts off abruptly and everyone relaxes. Greyson saunters back toting a wad of First Aid supplies.

"Maybe we can make it better," I dangle the roll of gauze and a Sponge Bob bandage that might be tempting but totally inadequate, "but only if we can see it."

She's not too sure. Chase gives her a nudge. Her lips pout a little, but then slowly her fingers lift off of the sticky red splotch. A year ago, in First Aid class, the sight of blood would have churned up my stomach like a half-eaten, moldy, maggot-infested sandwich. Now, looking at blood is like eyeing a plate of frosted brownies on the dessert table—a time and a place for everything, I guess. At the sight of the bloody gash, all the other girls back away en masse, grimacing like Crystal *is* the moldy, maggot-infested sandwich. I lean in for a closer look.

"They're out there," Greyson whispers in my ear and nods towards the front office. The bulletproof walls are soundproof, but there's a window in the control-room door.

The wound is not as bad as I thought. Looks like the bullet just grazed her skin. The relief collapses the tension built up in my chest. I exhale deeply, the air puffing my hair. "It's not too bad, Crystal. We can fix you right up." My hands are sifting through the medical supplies for some kind of antibiotic. Chase scoots behind me and lifts Crystal onto his lap. His stretched-out legs push the clump of little girls behind me farther away so that I can actually breathe and think. "How are we going to get out of here?" I whisper back to Greyson. Before I dab the antibiotic around the wound, I warn Chase and Crystal, "This might sting a little." Chase holds his niece tighter as she scrunches up her face.

"I'm working on that," Greyson answers, standing up just as I apply the cream. Crystal squeals, all the little girls squeal with her, and Madi's voice rings out above them in a blood-curdling scream. I swing around in time to catch the blur of Greyson diving to grab her.

The backward motion of the clump of little girls behind me has shoved Madi too close to the front of the cell. The zombie sheriff has his free hand a couple feet inside the bars; her arm is locked in his fist. She's squealing her head off, yanking at her arm, but he gets it in his teeth before Greyson can get to him. Even I scream, "Oh, my God. Madi!"

With one good kick, Greyson breaks the deputy's jaw. The little girl flies over and throws herself at my neck. Greyson pulls out his gun and shoots the snarling zombie right through the temple. He collapses limp to the floor, his arm dangling from the handcuff. Now all the little girls are in a frenzy, piled on my head.

"It's okay, sweetie." I manage to wriggle free of the muddle of girls so I can pull Madi closer. The poor kid is hysterical. Her whole body shudders and shakes in sobs. "Let me see your arm, baby." She won't let go of her stranglehold around my neck. "C'mon, Madi, the dead guy isn't going to get up again. Greyson stopped him. Let me see your arm." Once I pry Madi's arm loose, I can see the bloody red bite mark. The sheriff got a chunk out of her.

Greyson peeks his head into the corridor to survey the siege through the small window in the doors while I patch up the wounds to a chorus of sobbing, and whining, and "I want my mommy." The really sad part is most of these girls don't have a mommy anymore.

At least Crystal is pleased with the Sponge Bob bandage I tape over the top of the white gauze I've wrapped around her pajama pants. Red is slowly seeping around it. We have to get her somewhere where she can get real help soon.

When Greyson comes back, the little ginger is clinging to his chest like a baby monkey.

Madi is still plastered to mine. She's starting to feel hot against my shirt, and I don't normally register most temperature changes. She must be really hot. This is not good. The couples that get infected usually register a steep drop in temperature first. It must be different for the bite victims.

Crystal is draped around her uncle now. She sobs, and then her eyes close, and then they startle open again, and she sobs, and her eyes flutter closed again. I'm not sure how we're going to manage an escape and a nursery at the same time.

Greyson is watching Crystal too. "Do you think we can make a run for it, to the Jeep in the back, with all these kids?"

"Back through the front office? Are you crazy? They'll all end up shot. I don't think you get it, Greyson. I'm surprised they switched to tranquilizer guns. The last thing Nic…Dr. Vadlamani," I feel the prick of tension between us, and glide over it, "the last thing he told me was that your bite…our bite…is infectious. And even worse, they think that people you bite are infectious."

"Well, that's good then," Chase inserts, glancing from Greyson to me. "They're still trying to take you alive. They won't be shooting bullets."

I give him the "you're-such-a-baby-because-you-don't-know-anything-but-I'll-help-you" look I learned from my mother. "That is definitely not good. You don't want to get taken alive, Chase. Trust me. I've been in the Institute. You'd be better off taking a bullet to the head."

"Bullets or tranquilizers, we don't have to go through the front office," Greyson says. "At the end of the hallway, around the corner, there's a thick metal door. It's on the back corner on the right side of the building. If I remember right, the Jeep is closer to that door than the back entrance we came through."

"I want my mommy," Madi whimpers.

I pat her and push her head up against my chest, bowing my head down over hers. She snivels a bit and then goes quiet.

"What makes you think they're not covering that door? You saw it out there. They've evacuated the town. For all I know, they could be planning to blow the whole thing up just to get rid of the virus. If they haven't done it already, it's because they've been told to make sure they get us," I look Greyson in the eyes, "—or you—first."

"They're not going to bomb a whole town to kill the virus," Chase sneers.

"Are you kidding?" I say over Madi's head. "Don't you go to the movies? If they think just a bite spreads this thing, we're toast."

"But there aren't that many like us." Greyson was never really a dummy. He's working it out in his head, but I can see by the way he keeps taking stock of the room and glancing out into the corridor, he's also calculating an escape plan.

"As far as we know. And what if the virus changes again?" I nod at the dead sheriff zombie and then glance down at Madi in my arms. "You bit him; he bit her." I rub my hand across her forehead, but it's just a formality, the heat radiating off of her is soaking us both. "She's got a nasty fever."

"That's how it started with Chase when I..." Greyson starts and then changes his wording, "when Chase...uh...got infected."

Madi half cries, half groans. "Mommy, JoJo's in my head; he's hopping and scratching in my brain," she murmurs.

"Then disorientation?" My eyebrows arch meaningfully. "JoJo is her bunny."

Chase backs away a little with his niece. The bandage shifts. The scent of sweet and sour pork mists the room. "That's what happened to me," he reports.

"And the deputy," Greyson adds.

Greyson and I exchange glances. It's pretty much proof enough that the people Greyson bites are as infectious as he is. There's only one hope for Madi now: she's vegetarian.

"I think we need to get these girls out of town," I say. "The best way to do that is to send them out to those soldiers. They'll find their parents, or take them somewhere safe. They're not safe with us."

"I don't want to go with the soldiers, Evy. I want to stay with you." Amber clamps onto my neck again.

"I know, baby. You can stay with me. And we'll keep Madi."

Greyson looks like he's ready to object. "She's my sister," I say. He doesn't get the significance of that. "We have similar DNA?" Still not with me. "They wanted to find out why I react to the virus the way you and I do?" It looks like he's following now. If they knew she was my sister, she'd be as screwed as a rat in a poison testing lab.

"Why Madi?" he asks. "They'll get her to the hospital."

"Not the hospital. The Institute. She's infected. I'm taking her to her dad."

He's hissing now, trying not to wake her up. "If she's infected, you can't set her loose on her dad."

"Madi is a vegetarian—comes with growing up above a funeral home."

"Are you sure?"

"I babysat her for five years. I think I know what she won't eat."

"Okay, but are you sure about the vegetarian thing and the virus?"

"No, but I'm not handing her over to the Institute for them to make sure. We need to keep her with us. If she's like us, her dad is the best person to take care of her. I know Mr. Calder. He's really nice—and he's not afraid of dead people."

"And," Chase adds, nodding appreciatively, "he has a decent supply of 'meat'."

I try to ignore that, but Greyson finds it a convincing argument. "What about Crystal?" I ask Chase.

He has to think about it. "A ZV got my sister…Crystal's mom…in the raid—and her dad. I'm pretty sure her grandma wants her out. She probably thinks she's dead." He shrugs. "My mom thinks I'm dead. She has for a while."

It looks painful to be Chase, and not just painful but really confusing. I know how he feels. I can't think about doing what ZVs do once they've lost control—tear apart the people they love—without feeling disgusted with them and myself. It makes it hard to feel for them. But if I stop feeling for them, I'll become one of them, or even worse, I'll turn into some deranged ZV gang killer. At least I always knew my mom loved...no, I can't go there right now. I let Chase work through it. "Greyson, didn't you say you have friends here too? Don't we need to get them out?"

With the little redhead still clinging to him, he's salvaging a few items off the deputy. "Deputy Don took care of that. Set them all loose. Shot through the lock on the cell in the next room." Whether this is good news or not remains to be seen. The upside is, we don't have to sneak out of here with a bunch of invalids in various stages of brain decay. Greyson flips the radio on and static crackles out of it.

The downside is... "How many of 'your friends' did you actually bite, Greyson? Accidentally or otherwise."

Guilt. All over his face. Just like when I asked Bridger how many girls he'd made out with over summer vacation when I was in Dallas with my family. "A few. Maybe...five."

Chase snorts. "At least ten, more if you count the girls." He turns to me. "He had this idea of making a gang of his own."

"Hey, dude, you bit Lori Parker," Greyson deflects.

"She deserved it, man. She's the one that outed me...on Facebook. You're the one that told me to do it." He turns to me. "He said she owed me a little zombie servitude."

"Nobody deserves this," I mutter.

Crystal startles in her sleep and Chase starts cooing at her and brushing back her hair. She nestles her nose into his chest. I'm having trouble processing how guys that can be so incredibly sweet, can also be so unbelievably shallow.

Chase looks up from watching Crystal's face. "If I send the rest of the girls out the front, you could sneak out the back during all the drama. I could tell them the little girls are coming out and send them one at a time."

"And then what?" I sneer. This goes way beyond stupid. "They haul you off to the Institute and dissect you like a worm. I don't think so."

"No way. You get Madi and Amber into the Jeep, swing around, and pick me up as soon as Crystal is safe. You pull up onto the sidewalk and I come through the broken window. Easy."

"Are you kidding me? Did you see the way they shot up the front office?" I'm totally stunned he'd even come up with this. "The Jeep isn't bulletproof. I don't need any more holes in my head, thank you very much!"

"You heard them. They're not using bullets," Chase argues. "They saw you guys and switched to tranq darts. Besides, there'll be a bunch of little six-year-old girls. Who's gonna use bullets?"

This is the dumbest plan ever. "So, what if something goes wrong? They hit you with a dart and drag you off to the ZV Institute of Torture. No way."

"Maybe. But Greyson got *you* out."

"He has a point there." Greyson grins.

"You're not helping," I snap. "You had surprise on your side. They weren't expecting you. You can bet they've got themselves some military boys for backup now. Don't you see how crazy this is, or are you both going all zombie on me?"

"Really, Ev," Greyson shrugs, "seems like a pretty good plan to me. I mean, who's going to shoot up the place with a bunch of kindergarten girls between us and them?"

My brain has to stretch and bend to imagine any scenario where he's wrong, and my jaw and stomach revolt at the idea of actually agreeing to this, but I can't let the Institute get a hold of Amber or Madi, not after what I saw there. Those doctors are twisted and sick.

Madi's starting to get fidgety and making funny gurgling sounds. Frankly, the thought of having to take care of a little ZV terrifies me. I look Greyson over. If anyone can manage a superhero escape, it's him—his sheer strength of ego could pull it off. If I'm going to be totally honest with myself— which is not always the best policy—I have to admit that I can't think of a single time he's let me down. And what's worse, the last time I interfered, a little girl got shot.

I cave. "Okay, fine. Let's just do it."

Chapter 16

How are you going to get them out of the front office?" I ask after we have all the little girls on board with the plan. That part was easier than I thought. The other two friends of Amber just want to go home. Too bad the best they can hope for is a good foster home until someone figures out if they have any surviving relatives close by.

"No problem." Chase hoists Crystal up to his shoulder so he can stand up. She stirs but doesn't wake up. "You saw the intercom in the control room for the soundproof walls."

I manage to get to my feet without disturbing Madi, although an 18-wheeler busting through the wall would probably not disturb her at this point.

"I want to go with you," Amber whines in her tiny, spoil-me voice, pouting and raising her arms. Even though I'd much rather be in charge of my baby sister, I feel like I can't abandon Madi. She only has me and she needs me.

"Amber, baby, Madi is so sick. Can you go with Greyson?"

The frown on her face isn't promising. But when she looks him over skeptically, Greyson winks at her. Her mouth cracks into this embarrassed little smile, and her cheeks go red. Amber is such a sucker for a cute, older boy. She spent more time on Bridger's lap than I did.

Greyson is familiar with the look of the vanquished. He hoists her up. "C'mon, baby, it's you and me." As we file field-trip style towards the door, he whispers to her just loud enough for me to hear, "I'm faster than Evy. We'll be first."

Amber grins back at me, the secret bubbling out of her eyes…and damn if I don't really like Greyson—again.

"There's some little kindergarten girls in here." Chase is speaking into a mic on a twisting phone cord. "We just want to get them back to their families." He holds Crystal up to the little window. "We've been keeping them in a cell so the other ZVs wouldn't get to them." I can only assume a couple of Snatchers or Guardsmen are in there. "Clear out. I don't want to see anyone closer than that flipped over car in the street. No one wants any of these kids to get hurt." Chase pantomimes that the soldiers are communicating and then he nods and grins. "They're leaving."

"This is it, dude," Greyson says. "We'll see you in five." They do a man hug.

I squeeze Chase's neck with my free arm and kiss him on the cheek. "Be careful," I say. "We're the unknown. People are afraid of what they don't know, and they don't know what they're doing when they're afraid."

"Hey, that's what Mr. Kaufman said in Sociology." Like I said, Chase is a bright kid. I shake my head. I have nothing but bad feelings about this, but these two act like it's a run through the park in May. Don't they realize it's December and it's snowing? There should always be a plan B.

"Chase!" I burst out at the last minute. "If something goes wrong—I mean if we get separated somehow—do you know the old Methodist church on Main Street?"

"Yeah, is that where you've been hiding out?" He nudges Greyson. "I thought you checked that place and didn't find her."

"He didn't know where to look," I say. "Listen. Third pew from the front, on the left—under the floorboards. They used to hide polygamists in there."

"Sounds fun," Greyson muses.

"Don't even—" I start.

"Chill!" Chase stops the fight before it gains any steam. "You better get to the Jeep. And don't bother to stop," he quips with a sly grin, "just slow down and leave the door open." He checks the small window again. "Wait until I send Katie out. They'll be distracted. It'll be your best chance."

I give Crystal a peck on the cheek. "You're very brave, sweetie." She snuggles her uncle. "Tell them the grey people are nice, okay?"

She nods and pops her thumb in her mouth. "I'm going to see grandma," she mumbles sleepily around it.

Hiking Madi a little higher on my hip, I follow Greyson out of the control room, past the two holding cells, and around a corner into a small entryway. The door requires a key even from the inside. Greyson pulls out a ring and finds the right one. I watch behind us as Chase opens the door and Katie steps out. Total silence when he shuts the door again.

"Who's driving?" I ask when Greyson has the key in the lock.

He glances back at me like I've lost all ability to reason. "Me!"

"Good, 'cause I have to hold Madi. Amber, you crawl in the back. We have to hurry. Put your seatbelt on right away when we get in, okay?" Greyson cracks the door open, slowly. "I'll drive next time," I say.

"We'll see," he says and then pokes his head out the opening. "It looks clear. I can see the Jeep. It's only a few yards away, but there's this air-conditioning unit about twenty feet down the wall towards the street. I can't see what's behind it."

"We have to take our chances. Chase is screwed if we don't show up."

"I'll go first." He sets Amber down. "You and Amber stand a better chance locked in here with Chase where it's bulletproof if there's trouble."

By trouble, he means if he gets shot and killed, or shot and caught. I put my free hand on his cheek. Dear God! Do I like him? My life is such a freakin' mess. "Thank you!" It comes out desperately like I might not get the chance to say it. "I know you don't have to do any of this. It doesn't mean anything to you. It's all about me."

He pulls my hand off his cheek and kisses the palm. "I told you before, it's always been all about you." His lips are on mine. His hand grabs the back of my neck and pulls me closer. If he keeps kissing me like this, I won't be able to let him go out the door. When he finally pulls away, my lips cling to his like they belong together. Amber giggles.

"Sorry, I know you said…" he apologizes.

"I'm a ZV. I can't be responsible for what I say."

He eases the door open with the key. I peak back around the corner. Chase is bent over giving Amber's blonde friend a pep talk. That means Katie got out without trouble.

"Wait!"

"It was good for me too, but this isn't really the time."

"Shut up!" He can be such a jerk. "Look. I know this is going to sound weird. But maybe Amber should go first. You guys were right." I never thought those words would come out of my mouth. "They're not going to shoot at little girls. If they spot you, they might start shooting and Amber could get caught in the fire. Let her go first. If someone's watching, she'll be safe in the car. If she's in there with you, you're both safe. You can pull the Jeep up here on the sidewalk and I'll hop in."

He scrunches up his eyes and shakes his head. "I don't know…"

I bend down. "Amber, baby, can you go get in the Jeep?"

"Is Greyson coming?"

"He'll be right behind you." I turn to Greyson. He's not liking my plan. "Does the key have an automatic door lock?"

Greyson points the key at the Jeep. We hear the faint click.

"This is a bad idea," he says. "I should go with her."

"No!" I put my arm in front of him and nudge Amber. "She should go alone. It's safer."

Amber trots out across the three feet of pavement. She has no idea there's a small posse just up the street, around the corner. The air is trapped in my lungs. Greyson isn't breathing either. We hear birds and faint radio talk. Amber has to reach up to open the back door and climb up onto the running board to get in. The air-conditioning unit makes a creaking noise and Greyson puts his hand on his gun. A breeze shoots up the alley. Snow flurries and Amber's scent whistle through the crack in the door. We breathe in deeper…and then she's in. We both exhale.

"Maybe there's no one out there," Greyson whispers. "It's totally possible the Snatchers don't know about this door. There's only a couple of camouflage boys out there, and most of the people that work here…" I wait for him to finish, but he doesn't.

"What?"

"Well, they're gone now."

I don't even want to know. "Let's just go together. C'mon. One, two, three."

Greyson's out the door, and I'm on his tail. Two steps down the sidewalk, a stride away from the curb, and the faint click of metal on metal stops us in our tracks.

"Hold it. Right there!" The words barrel out from behind the air-conditioner unit. I know there's a gun behind me. I can smell it. Greyson reaches for my hand as he turns around. A soldier with some kind of automatic murdering weapon is staring down his sights at us.

"Please," I beg, turning so that Madi is out of the line of fire. *We are so freakin' lucky Amber isn't anywhere near the end of that gun.* "That's my little sister in the car. Our parents were killed by the ZVs; we're all she has."

"Evelyn? Evelyn Cross?" It's hard to see through all the military paraphernalia and the fat snowflakes, but I recognize the voice. Some great power in the universe loves me, or maybe it just feels sorry for me. Either way, the soldier holding the gun on us is Preston Green—Bridger's older brother.

"Oh my gosh. Preston. Preston!" I'm so happy to see him, I don't even notice, not much anyway, how good he smells even though he's upwind. He adjusts his gun, but he's not looking at us through the scope anymore. "Preston, please. You have to help me. They don't understand. We're not hurting anyone." He doesn't move and the gun is still pointing at Greyson. "We're different. We don't eat people. I swear it. You and Bridger know me. I don't tell lies; I can't."

The gun relaxes but I can see he's breathing rapidly. "I heard what you did for Bridger," he barks out. "Poor kid, he never hurt anyone. They should have helped him. He shouldn't have ended up that way." His voice cracks under the weight of an older brother's guilt.

"But they don't help," I say. "They're sadistic monsters, Preston. I was in there. I saw what they do. But there's one doctor, Dr. Vadlamani. His little brother is sick too, but he's like me and…" I'm not sure if I should bring Greyson into the conversation or not. I know what they think about him out there. If Preston doesn't recognize him, maybe it's because he's part of the search-and-rescue team and not the seek-and-destroy one. "Dr. Vadlamani is trying to find a cure. He tried to help Bridger and took care of me in the Institute. I'm helping him." Pulling my hand free from Greyson's, I fish in my pocket and pull out a sterile syringe packet. "See. I'm gathering blood samples so he can find a cure. I'm the only one who can do this—obviously."

The point of the gun drops, but not far enough. "Please, Preston. Amber's only six. I'm her big sister, the only family she has left… Please, I'm just trying to help. We're not hurting anyone."

"What about that little girl?" He points at Madi with his gun. The white bandage on her arm stands out against the bright pink Dora the Explorer pajamas she's wearing. "What's the matter with her?"

Greyson speaks up and I hold my breath. He knows that Preston and I have history. "There's a dead zombie deputy in there. He tried to take a bite out of her. I shot him."

This has to be a confusing piece of info. Why would a zombie be shooting another zombie?

I step in and try to spin it in our favor. "The virus has mutated. A bite spreads it now. She could be sick. They'll take her to the Institute, and you know what will happen there. She's just a little girl."

"Shit!" Preston swears, glancing back towards the street. I'm praying he doesn't want to let what happened to his little brother happen to an innocent six-year-old.

"Greyson and I can take care of her. I think she's like us. You know I'm different. If I weren't, I'd be falling apart by now—like Bridger. I don't want to hurt anyone. She won't hurt anyone either. Please, Preston. I'm just trying to get my little sister out of here."

Total silence in the alley. From around the corner, we hear shouts. They have the second little girl. Preston looks back and forth from us to the street, which is nearly hidden behind a line of trees and bushes. He stares at me for a long time. Then, he slings his gun back on his shoulder and starts walking past us towards the parking lot. He passes right by me, brushes my arm. "I didn't see anything here, but this town has its burn notice. The brass gave the Guard 72 hours to find and evacuate trapped civilians and deliver some classified package they're looking for. After that, this place is toast— package or not. Nothing is getting out alive."

Greyson and I don't need to be told exactly what package they're after. Preston evidently doesn't have clearance. We don't have to be told twice to get the hell out of here either. I want to hold Madi on my lap, but it's safer to buckle her between Amber and me. The Jeep is creeping around the corner to the alley between the police station and the library before I click my belt. The passenger door is open and the window is down. Preston is crouched behind a squad car, watching the back door.

Halfway down the alley to the front of the building, I modify the plan. "Wait. We have to time this just right. We don't want any of those little girls getting shot in the crossfire when Chase comes running out and we fly through there."

A couple years ago, the mayor decided State Street needed a face-lift and they put in a big, wide park and sidewalk area with separate access for runners, bikers, and walkers, complete with drinking fountains and benches. The mini-parks run all up and down Main and State and make shady little pit stops for practice 5Ks in the summer, and also serve quite conveniently for camouflaged patrol cars stalking speeders.

"Pull over there," I say, pointing to a well-hidden spot. "I'll crawl in behind those bushes and watch. When I see Crystal has made it, I'll run for the car."

Greyson shakes his head, doubtfully. He doesn't want me to do it, but we both know timing is everything. I know what the problem is. Whoever goes to the bushes is exposed, but if Greyson takes the dangerous job, that leaves me driving.

"I got this." I pat my sensitive chauvinist on the shoulder and slide out of the car. Hiding in the bushes reminds me of going after Bridger. They have the same prickly shrubbery here. Apparently, no one wants to encourage hiding in the bushes, and I get why: it's usually the bad guys in there.

My heart is jumping like a frog in a hot tin can. Around the corner, I can see the flipped car with a handful of Snatchers and a couple soldiers mostly hidden behind it. There are more out there now than there were when we first dragged Chase into the back office, at least I think so.

I spot Katie and the little blond in a Humvee that pulled up next to the Institute SUV after we holed up. I'm relieved that the military has them and not the Snatchers. The soldiers in camouflage and the Snatchers in black are all focused on the building. When I lean my head around far enough to see the front of it, Crystal is climbing out of the broken window. She's having a hard time of it because her leg still isn't completely mobile. She finally maneuvers it out and starts hobbling across the sidewalk. She stops and looks back through the window. I can only imagine Chase is waving her on.

Seconds after she's out of the window, I watch some of the Snatchers disappear from behind the SUV. I can hear the rumblings of radio communications. The little girl hobbles across the grass and pavement, and then sidesteps the curb so she can keep her bandaged leg straight. She's only a few yards away from the Humvee and the SUV parked across the four-lane highway. I rise up off my heels, ready to run for the car, and signal our pick-up.

Crystal stops, turns around, and nods towards the window, waving and smiling. She blows a little kiss.

As her hand drops back to her side, before she can even turn back around, a black-suited Institute thug jumps out from behind the SUV with his automatic killing machine and points it right at Crystal—tiny, fragile, little Crystal—standing alone in the middle of the street.

My mouth drops open and my heart stops when I hear him yell, "Fresh wound. She's infected. Decontamination protocol!"

Bullets rip through the air, crumble the brick, shatter the glass that's left in the windows, and tear through the curly-haired girl, Crystal, who loves her uncle and didn't notice he was grey until we told her. She jerks and wrenches as little balls of lead crunch her bones, pierce her head, and toss her to the ground like a scarecrow in an angry wind.

I don't even realize I'm screaming until the bullets stop. I tear away from the bushes and race towards the car, stumbling. The picture of Crystal falling is burning itself into my brain; my eyes are brimming and I can't see. I hit the vinyl seat as the Jeep squeals around the corner.

"What the hell happened?" Greyson screams at me.

But I can't answer because my brain can't process into words what I just saw. "Dead," is all I manage, and it comes out in a wail. "She's dead!" I can't breathe well enough to say anymore.

The firing has stopped by the time the police Jeep tumbles into the street. And then Greyson sees it. "Oh, my God. Oh, my God. She's just a baby."

A Snatcher runs out to the bloody, baby-doll body with a massive gun in his hand. "What's he doing?" Greyson yells.

The black-suited goon points it right at the soft little shell that was Crystal. Flames shoot from the mouth of the gun at the same time that Chase leaps through the office window. We screech and bump onto the sidewalk just as his foot hits the pavement, but he doesn't duck into the open door. He hurdles onto the hood of the Jeep, screaming, "No. No. No!"

Greyson flies out his door and wrestles Chase back to the Jeep. The only possible reason we're not being showered with lead is that we're in a police car, but, once Greyson makes his appearance, the veil falls and fear's fury descends on us. Greyson literally throws Chase onto the front bench and dives in after him.

Chase is writhing on the front seat, pulling on his hair with one hand and holding his stomach like some alien is in there gnawing on his guts. "No. No. No. Mom. No!" He's rolling back and forth. I try to reach over the seat and hold him.

The army transports are after us. I'm sobbing. Bullets pepper the back of our car, shattering windows, piercing the metal, ripping through the vinyl. It's all I can do to keep the little girls' heads down and one arm over the seat on Chase's head.

The Jeep fishtails and weaves. Greyson takes a hard right and breaks through one of the swinging fences that keep motor vehicles off the trails. Right on our tail, the SUV skids to make the turn, rolls, bounces, tosses the Snatchers into the ditch at the side of the trail, and then lands on top of them.

Madi flops around with the jerking of the car, too fevered to wake up. Amber crawls over her to get to me. She didn't see anything but just watching the people that saw the horror is scaring her. She whimpers and I pull my arm away from Chase to hold her. I hug her, our hearts beating double time. It could have been her, so I hold her like she's Crystal that no one can hold anymore. My tears fall in her hair.

The Jeep breaks through a flimsy barbed-wire fence into a field that can't be seen from the road. Suddenly Chase is dead silent. We bump and tumble over the plowed mounds. Without any warning, he shoots up from his fetal position, opens the door, and rolls out.

"What the hell!" Greyson yells out the empty open door.

"Stop!" I yell at him.

"I can't!" Without breaking he leans over and slams the door shut again.

Chase stops rolling, jumps to his feet and runs, runs like I've never seen a kid run. The Humvee is still following us. They fire at Chase and us before Chase disappears into the ditch that runs alongside the canal trail. Bullets whistle through the back windshield and shatter the front. I duck and cover the little girls.

"Are we gonna die, Evelyn?" Amber whimpers.

I pet her head. "No, baby, Greyson will get us away from the soldiers. Won't you Greyson?"

"We're coming up on Brother Jensen's field," he says, and I know what he's thinking.

"You're not seriously thinking of taking us into the mud. We'd be trapped like flies on flypaper."

"No, we're not going in, but you'd have to be from Eli to know anything about the mud swamp. I'm guessing those guys…" he nods at the Humvee bouncing behind us, "…aren't. This Jeep is built for speed. If I can get far enough ahead of them on the road that goes around the field, they might be tempted to cut through it."

The Jeep plows through a stick and wire fence, bobs over the irrigation ditch, and bangs onto the road. Greyson hits the gas and we fly down the street. He's right. The Jeep outruns the Humvee, and by the time we turn the corner on the other side of Brother Jensen's field, the soldiers are just crossing the intersection on the opposite end. They aren't from here. They're not ten yards up the street when they tear through the fencing and squelch into the mud.

"They're not getting stuck," I report.

"Just wait. They haven't hit the pond yet. It gets soggier and deeper."

"You better go faster. That's an army car. It's probably built for this."

"Nothing's built for this."

"Your stepdad's truck got out."

"Because I was driving."

I wonder if he's enjoying this, and then Crystal's innocent face flashes in front of my mind. I see her pouting eyes and lips, the glassy tears because she doesn't want to show me her leg, and then it all goes up in flames and I realize no one is enjoying this; we're all just trying to survive.

The Humvee hits the low point in the field where the water is about a foot deep. "It's stopped. They're backing up."

"That just digs it in deeper."

I'm looking through the back windshield now. We'll never know how long it took them to get out, and maybe they never did, but it slowed them down enough for Greyson to get us away. After we abandon the Jeep, we sneak through backyards, lifting Amber and Madi over fences until we get to the old Methodist church. We all snuggle into the hiding space until the images of Crystal have faded from our minds into our nightmares and Madi's fever has broken.

Chapter 17

Madi is a ZV.

After three days, it's pretty obvious—not that I'm surprised. We expected this. It's more that she never got to hold hands with a boy, or dance in her first recital, or run in her first track meet, or flaunt her first 4.0. There are just so many photos of things-that-will-never-be, snapshots that have been wiped off her profile page before she even had a chance to paste them there. I don't care who she is; every girl has her moments waiting to get snapped into someone's phone. But all Madi's photos burned up in her fever before the light could ever hit the lens, and Crystal's burned up in the flames…

I'm glad I have two little girls to take care of now. The job keeps my mind from wandering into dark, flaming streets. We gobbled up what we had left from the cow in the first hour. Of course, Amber won't eat meat, especially not raw meat. Greyson is pretty decent at slipping around, picking up supplies from McKee's Corner Market. He avoids the grocery store, though. It's too obvious. To pass the time while he's gone, we read Amber's favorite stories that she left in the tree, and try to ignore the fact that we're holed up like trapped mice.

Going out with the girls is out of the question. Other than the occasional muted spray of gunfire and muffled barking of dogs in the distance, downtown is still and quiet. But the military and the Snatchers are definitely hunting down the zombies; we couldn't ignore what's going on out there even if we wanted to because we can smell so well. They're not catching them and taking them in; they're not bashing their heads. They're shooting them and then burning them. The film of tainted smoke hovers around us. Madi's senses grow keener and she asks me what the smell is.

How do you explain to a six-year-old that she's become her worst nightmare without making her feel like a monster? My only advantage is that Madi has always loved me. I detail the positives, things we have in common: she'll be faster.

"Will I get a letterman jacket like you, Evy?"

At this point, team and spectator sports are pretty much out of the picture. At a track meet, they'll be running *from* her, not *with* her—and she won't understand why—because she's a little grey now? Because they're convinced the grey ones want to slurp their insides? They won't wait to see who she really is. They won't listen if she tells them she's different. They'll only see the grey and be afraid.

I've spent so much of my life winning prizes and competing; I have no idea how to measure up in a world with no applause. How do you know who you are if you can't see yourself in everyone else's eyes? How will I know if I'm good enough? How will Madi know?

"Evelyn?" Madi asks when Amber drifts off to sleep. My little sister has been conditioned, by years of bedtime stories, to fall asleep to the sound of my voice.

"Yeah, baby?" Before she can whisper in my ear, I pick up the faint sound of mud squishing and dead leaves cracking outside the building. It's a sound I've trained my ears to hear. My hiding place is super safe, but if anyone bothers to look really closely, they might notice the glow from the flashlight through the cracks of the floorboards. Greyson has been gone for a long time—almost too long.

Every time we hear shots or dogs barking, I start chewing on my lip and twisting Amber's honey hair in my fingers. I see visions of Greyson, holes spattered all through his jacket and torn through his head, and I imagine the flames. My throat seizes up and I have to close my eyes, breathe deep, and make my mind go black. I can't face Greyson dead. I can't face Greyson gone. I'd forgotten what it was like to have other people, people to argue with and laugh with, to talk to and lean on. I was starving for it for so long that now that I have it again, and I know how warm and full it feels, I want to horde it. "Just a minute, Madi. Listen. Do you remember I said you could hear like Superman now? Listen."

The sloshing is slow and hesitant, irregular. A big smile lights up Madi's face. "I can hear it." Then she looks worried. "Who is it, Evelyn. More dead guys?"

I pat her hand. "Sweetie, the dead people aren't ever going to come after you again." I don't have the heart to tell her she's one of the dead people now. "But we do need to worry about the Snatchers and the soldiers. They might take you away from Greyson and me, and then you wouldn't get back to your daddy. Greyson and I are going to get you back to your daddy." We both listen carefully. I'm pretty sure it's Greyson coming back from his supply run. I can feel the calm radiating down to my toes. "The bad guys wear big boots. You can hear them clomping."

"Like the Big Billy Goat Gruff. Clip-clop, clip-clop?"

"Yeah, like the Big Billy Goat Gruff." There's a little whistle, maybe a small bird. "The chirping is Greyson." We both enjoy the tunes of our super hearing until Madi tugs on my sleeve again.

"Evelyn. Something smells yummy. I want a taste of it." My eyes flutter to Amber's head in my lap. Madi nods. I don't say anything, but we both look at each other's faces, skewed by shadows in the dwindling beam of the flashlight—I hope Greyson scavenged some batteries.

Suddenly, I feel for my mother...and my father. I love Madi, but the risk is horrifying. It must be to her too, just like it is to me. Madi and Amber have been friends since they could both pull a toy puppy on a string. It's one thing to be ripping people open and devouring their important parts when you're mostly brain dead and don't know what you're doing. It's another thing to be totally lucid and imagine your hands bloody and warm inside your best friend. How do you not be afraid of yourself when you're a monster?

The trap door opens up above us. Fresh air and Greyson slide in. "Hey, beautiful," he says and kisses me on the cheek. Amber wakes up to the rustle of grocery sacks. The two girls crawl over him to get to the bags. Greyson hides them behind his back. "You don't think I'm going to just give this to you for free, do you? I had to sneak by all those nasty Institute Snatchers. No way. You have to earn this kind of stuff." He leans closer to them, grabs the flashlight and shines it in his face. "Who is the best-looking guy, you know?" he asks like he's their second-grade teacher reciting times tables with them.

"Greyson!" they both yell.

"And who is the strongest," he flexes for them, "and the fastest?"

"Greyson!" They jump on his arm and swing from it.

He nods and grins at me. "Very smart girls." I just shake my head, smiling. He's so full of himself but in such a cute way. And then it dawns on me. Greyson knows. He knows who he is. He knows what he's worth, and no one has to tell him.

He takes a deep breath, thinking of some other way to swell his already monolithic ego. "And who's the smartest?" He asks, one eyebrow inching slyly above the other.

Pause. The little girls look at me; I shrug, raise my eyebrows. It's like we know something that all girls know. They look back at Greyson. They're clearly torn between their prize and the truth.

Only Amber speaks up. "Evelyn is smartest, Greyson," she apologizes. I bust up laughing. But she's not done. Her little eyes scrunch up, cushions to the blow she's about to deliver. "You're a little stinky too." She waves her hand in front of her crinkled nose. "But boys are stinkier than girls. My mom always says so."

Mock indignation. "That is such a stereotype." He's talking to me now. "You're all racist against boys."

"Yeah, well," I stifle my laughter, "stereotypes are wrong," and then I can't hold it back anymore, "but mostly true." I break into a fit of giggles.

He snorts and then frowns at the girls. "Well, you got two out of three. So, I guess you win."

"Yeah!" they spout in unison, wriggling from side to side. He pulls from the bag a bottle of milk, Cheerios, a couple of apples, and some other random stuff.

"Cheerios? You have the whole store and you bring Cheerios?"

"That's what little kids eat. They're all over the benches after church."

"Yeah, when they're like one or two. Amber has teeth."

"I love Cheerios," Amber hugs him around the neck.

He nods smugly in my direction. "I got batteries."

Okay, he gets points.

Madi is on Greyson's knee, trying to get to the other bag. "Something smells good."

"Yes, it does. There's a fine little butcher shop in McKee's market. It escaped the looting and most of the zombies hit the grocery store on East Street." He unveils his catch. "Liver!" He announces, pulling it from the plastic sack.

Madi claps and grabs it. I don't think she's vegetarian anymore. She rips off the plastic and tears into it. She looks like Amber did when my mom first let me drop a tiny sliver of chocolate on her baby tongue. Her whole face is enjoying the flavor.

"And to top it off, a little delicacy—tripe." That should be totally disgusting—cow's stomach. But it smells heavenly.

The quiet content of munching follows. The three carnivores share, passing around chunks of raw meat; Amber slurps her milk out of the plastic bowl that Greyson so thoughtfully provided. The rest of us don't bother with plasticware.

After our late dinner, the girls are exhausted. There's just enough room in this hidden cellar for all four of us to lie next to each other. Obviously, Greyson and I sleep between the two girls, just in case Madi's not herself when she wakes up in the night.

Amber's breathing turns regular and deep, a soft metronome to the shallow notes of *On Ira Tous au Paradis*. My French teacher was pretty gutsy to teach us a song that means *We'll all go to Paradise* in a state where most kids are convinced only a select few are going. Amber doesn't know what it means, but she likes the sound of the French words. Not many people know this, but I have lungs that can power a jet. I can hit high C at will, just not when I'm supposed to in the song.

"Is yours asleep?" I whisper.

"Yep," he whispers back. I already knew she was; I could hear her breathing as well. I just wanted a reason to let Greyson know I was still awake. "You have a nice voice," he says. "I almost fell asleep myself."

"I'm sorry. I didn't mean to wake you up."

"I said, 'almost'." He turns and smiles at me. In the fading light of the flashlight that we leave on until the girls fall asleep, actually until I fall asleep, Greyson's smile is as sexy as he's been accused of being. It's like a high school dance, where, in the shades of darkness everyone looks good, but when the lights come up, the make-up is smeared, the wild hairs appear, our sun-starved complexions blare; we all look like we've been dead for a week.

"It took you a while. I was worried about you," I say.

"It's nice to be missed."

I reach over and shove his shoulder playfully. "You know what I mean. How bad is it out there?"

"Well, they're keeping busy." He's avoiding telling me something. "Oh!" He rumples all the blankets reaching for his pockets. "I got you something. That's what took me so long." He hands me a cell phone. I open it up. The screen light strikes my eyes and a picture of my mom and dad laughing hits me in the face. I don't say anything. I'm trying to suck it up. Suck it up the way my dad always told me to when there wasn't time for little girl tears and drama. "I had to wait for it to charge," he says, filling up the silence that can't really be filled. "We need to call Madi's dad. We have to get these two out of Eli. It's not safe for either of them—or us."

"My mom and Penny Calder, Madi's mom, were friends," I say flatly, flipping through the contact list. It's best not to let any emotions through; one emotion has a funny way of leading to another, and the next thing you know you're just an oozing pile of tears and guts.

"I checked," he says. He can obviously feel the tension because I can feel that he's as uncomfortable as I am. "The number is in there."

I snap the phone shut. "Thanks." He puts his hand on my shoulder. I turn onto my back so that his hand falls away. He turns onto his back and folds his arms across his chest. That's exactly what I wanted, but my head is screaming at me that what I want is someone to cuddle up to on a cold night. I don't want this stiffness, but I can't seem to make it go away and I can't stop myself from teasing it along.

He pulls the blankets farther over to cover Madi—habit, I guess. Then he rolls back on his side and props himself up on his elbow. One thing you have to say for Greyson: he's tenacious. There's no shutting him down. I'm actually glad. "I'm worried about what Preston said," he finally says. I nod. "Obviously it's not safe here for Madi anymore. I checked a few of my old haunts to see who was still shambling around and who was still lucid. Nothing but charred remains. They're hunting them down and 'decontaminating'."

Just the word brings the flames back to my eyes. I have to cover them with my hands to make the images of Crystal go away.

"This place is safe," he continues, "but I keep thinking about old Brother Jensen's place. Were you here a couple summers ago when it got infested?

"No, I was in Texas visiting my aunt."

"Well, they tried spraying and trapping, and finally they just gave up. They evacuated everybody, put a big plastic sheet over the place, and fumigated."

"You think that's what they're going to do here?"

He shrugs.

"I think the CDC and the army want to get a hold of you," I say, shrinking a little into the curve of his body. "That's why they're hunting. They want to know what it is that makes you stronger and faster when everyone else is dying or going zombie and then dying. And they want to know if they can make it into a cure—or a soldier."

"But what if the risks start to outweigh the benefits?" he asks.

"You mean like if anybody can get infected by a bite?"

"Pretty much." This is the first time that I've actually seen Greyson look afraid or worried—or both.

"What did you see out there?" I reach up and tangle my fingers in his hair and rest my hand on the back of his neck.

He shakes his head.

"Tell me. It's just you and me, Greyson. You can't have secrets. If you have secrets, then it's just you."

"I saw it at your house when I went to get the phone. The place is crawling with ZVs—new ones, most of them in camouflage. Some of them have guns and knives. It's like a ZV army. If they're all together like that, and not wandering around aimlessly ripping the livestock apart and raiding the grocery stores, it's because someone is keeping them there. Someone's putting together their own personal mini-army."

Chapter 18

This is bad. The last thing we need is to be stuck in the middle of an all-out war. What side could we be on? I can't let my little sister anywhere near a mob of rabid zombies, and the uninfected won't let the other three of us anywhere near them. We both think the same thing at once. "Chase?" I say it, and Greyson nods.

"It's the only thing that makes sense," he says. "Madi is proof that the bite of someone who has been bitten is infectious. What did it take? Only a few hours? But if the ones I've bitten were going around just biting people and not bothering to eat them, we'd be crawling with zombies. He's working on a plan."

I shiver and he wraps his arm over my waist. Amber snuggles up to my back. His lips fluttering against my skin, Greyson whispers. "It takes some brains to keep them all locked up and under control. Your house is perfect. The whole neighborhood was searched and barricaded at the beginning of the evacuation. It's on the golf course, and the golf course is a dead end. There's no way out of the valley from your house except across wide-open greens. The military doesn't patrol it as much."

It's true. At one time, Eli was just a little farming town, mostly corn and hay fields with a bunch of cows and horses. Much to the local's dismay, the city bled south and east. The mountainsides, that locked Eli into a hidden valley, attracted a bunch of construction. They built a golf course in the valley behind the bluff where my house is, and never finished the east bench road because the golf course was there and the owners of the mini-mansions on the benches didn't want the traffic. So, all the roads from around the bluff feed onto one main street that goes down to the highway. The morning traffic is a pain because Eli isn't big enough to have its own high school and there's only one road out of the valley.

"You think they might give up and just torch the place?" I ask, letting my fingertips toy with the stray curls around his brow.

"They may not even know these new ZVs exist. They may have the soldiers listed as missing or killed. If they're being dragged off during the patrols, I don't know how they handle that. They have to suspect something. Once they realize how potent Chase is, it'll be a freakin' domino effect."

"Some of his victims must have had time to get back after they were infected before they started changing. They have to know by now how quickly it spreads."

"Yeah, but the question is do they think it's random infections roaming the city now or part of an organized plan. I'm not sure they know that once we infect someone, they're kind of…obedient."

"And you think Chase…?" I ask, not really wanting to finish the question.

"Could you blame him?"

Even after what I saw, I couldn't actually say I didn't blame him. I mean these soldiers aren't the guys that killed his niece; they have families somewhere too. They're not the ones that came up with "decontamination" or who made the call about a little girl with a bandage. But I absolutely understand. "I think he's lost it," I say. The look on Chase's face before he jumped out of the car is still branded on my brain.

That day sits between us, heavy. Greyson slides his other arm underneath me and pulls me into his chest, squeezing the unthinkable horror away. I have no words for the feel of arms like his around me—bandages on a cut, maybe. I huddle up to the soft cotton of his sweatshirt and try to heal.

"Tomorrow, you should call Madi's dad."

I nod. He can't see me because my face is cuddled into his chest, but he can feel me. "We could meet him at the golf course clubhouse. Since the golf course is across the ravine and the entrance to the club is in another city, it's probably not part of the quarantine."

"I doubt they're letting anybody play," Greyson says.

"No one golfs in December, anyway. Not after it's snowed. They're probably watching it, but it's not like he'd be breaking the quarantine by going in there."

"We just have to figure out a way to get us in there without getting shot and flame-broiled."

"Not we," I correct him. His head bends down and mine turns up. "I'm going to take Madi by myself."

"Yeah, right. Like that's going to happen." He sits up and rips off his sweatshirt. "Is it really hot in here?" He starts unbuttoning his shirt. We both know neither one of us reacts to changes in external temperature.

"We can't leave Amber here alone, and you can't take Madi because her dad doesn't know you. I'm sure he's heard what the military says about you. They think you're a sadistic pack hunter."

I don't tell him what I told Nicolas about him—that he's a power junkie, egomaniac. "Even if Mr. Calder's only heard what I know about you from before we were ZVs, he's not going to want you anywhere near his daughter." Greyson's about to object with some half-brain plan, so I cut him off.

"I'm the only one Madi's dad will trust enough to meet; I'm the one that has to take Madi. And you're the only one I trust with Amber." I sit up and cup my hands around his face so he knows I mean it, that I'm not just trying to get my way. "I'd know she was safe with you."

"Fine." He slides down onto his back and I snuggle into the soft dent between his shoulder and his chest. "You can call her dad in the morning and set it up for the night. We need to get out of here before they get desperate and burn us out before Chase lets that army loose." I can feel the tension in his arms and drop my hand onto his bare chest. It's nice to have someone worry about me again.

"Where can we go?" I ask, trailing the tip of my index nail in little circles around the curves of his abs.

"Somewhere where the locals won't think it's strange that we walk around all covered up the whole year? Alaska?"

"How would we live? It's not like you and I can get jobs and take care of Amber. And this is the only place where the grocery store has been conveniently abandoned. Amber needs to go to school."

"You could home school her," he suggests. "You have to face reality. We're outside the box now. We're not going to follow 'the plan'."

I raise myself up on my elbow so I can see his face. "Doesn't it bother you? Doesn't it make you mad that some microscopic bug climbed into your brain and changed everything, destroyed your whole life, took away everything you'd been working for?"

He pulls one arm out from underneath his head and tangles his fingers in my hair. "Not really. Things change all the time. I lost some stuff and I got some new stuff. It's not all bad." He flashes his cheeky grin at me. "Some of it is pretty damn good."

I can't help myself; I smile down at him. "Oh yeah. Like what?" My voice has gone deep and the words flow off my tongue like hot fudge off a spoon.

His eyes narrow, a half-smirk plays on his lips. He knows what game I'm playing, and he's not sure he wants to play. That's when I know for sure he means it. If he just said that I was the best thing in his world without thinking about it, I'd know he was playing me. I'd know he had nothing to lose, no risk. But he's protecting himself because he's already lost something and he's not sure how much more he's willing to put on the line. "Like you," he finally says.

His palm is on the back of my head. He nudges me down towards his mouth. He wants to kiss me, but he doesn't take what he wants. He waits for me to come to him. I close the gap between us, just enough to brush our lips together, barely. And it's over.

I want to see his face. Is he just winning? No, there's no smug victory there, just deep wanting. I'm the one who's winning; he's totally mine. I let him share in my spoils. Our lips press together and our bodies move in rhythm with them. No, it's both of us. We're both winning.

"You're not going to slap me now, are you?" he asks when his lips are far enough away from mine to make words.

"Should I? Are you already thinking of cheating on me?"

He grabs me and pulls me on top of him. There's a general tossing of the blankets. Amber and Madi stir and mumble. "I told you," he whispers. "You and I are soul mates. There's nothing but you. They could turn me into a worm and I wouldn't care, as long as you were under the rock with me."

"Ew! I don't want to be a worm," I grimace.

"What does it matter? Live in the present. Embrace what you are; make it work." He pushes my hair out of my face. "This works." He wraps me up in his arms and in his whole world. Oddly enough, in the middle of this quarantined town, hiding like a rat, I feel normal, strong, and beautiful— just not the way I felt normal, strong, and beautiful before.

Greyson holds his arms around me like I might slip away any minute. "It's like when my mom died," he says. "She was the only one that I could ever count on. I mean, she made me do all this vegetarian crap and she was always on my case about something: forgetting to make my bed, driving too fast, not wearing my seatbelt, staying out too late, sloughing church; but she was there for me, man. After she died, I thought, 'Well, this is it. I'm on my own.' But then Ray," that's his step-dad, the one whose truck he *borrowed* to plow through old Brother Jensen's field, "he really stepped up. I lost a mom, but I got a dad. Hell, I got two dads: Ray and JC, my stepdad and my real dad."

He glances down at me like I don't already know that, like the whole town doesn't already know that. Connie Childs was not a quiet woman. The fights between her and JC were not the behind-closed-doors kind. They played out in the street, at the grocery store, and sometimes with the police. "They got along really well once my mom was gone."

"Why do you suppose your mom and dad fought the way they did? I mean, they were married; they must have been in love sometime."

"Yeah, they loved each other; they just didn't like each other. JC was a screw-up—at least she thought he was. She was always yelling at him; he couldn't do anything right. And he drank. I don't blame him, though. What guy wouldn't drink if he lived with someone who treated him like some kind of disease?"

I put my hand up to Greyson's face. "That's so sad. The person you live with every day should make you feel powerful, don't you think? Like you could be anybody or do anything you set your mind to."

"That's why I thought it wasn't such a bad thing when they got divorced. At least the fighting stopped. I never really got along that well with Ray, not until my mom died. I guess he didn't want to squeeze into my dad's spot. My mom wasn't perfect, but when she was gone, I really missed her, and Ray knew how to step in. My new life wasn't bad, it was just different."

He stops and thinks about it for a while.

His life hasn't been anything like my suburban cliché.

"Then I got the virus. My stepdad, he would have kept me at home, but I didn't want to end up...." He doesn't have to tell me what he was afraid of. "I had to run. For a while, I thought my life pretty much sucked, but a lot of the other ZVs I bumped into weren't that far gone yet, and I made some friends."

"Where'd you hide out?"

"Before the jail? You know that huge mansion on the mountain?"

"That castle place they didn't finish 'cause the guy went bankrupt. You were living there?"

"Yep. The bank owns it. No one ever goes there. We stuck to the basement, but we were living in style." He grins at me. "And then I was stronger and faster, and I wasn't dying slowly, losing my brain and body parts like all my friends were." He sounds a little sad now. There's a moment of silence when I realize that Greyson's seen a lot more than I have. He had to watch his friends turn into monsters and die. No wonder he took them out where it would be quicker. "And then, one night you showed up. I didn't think life could get any better."

I can't help myself. I push myself up so that my lips are on level with his. My mouth is there in the moment and he lives it for all it's worth until I can't breathe anymore. His hands find their way inside my tank top and past the elastic of my PINK bra to the bare skin of my back. My fingers slide in through his open shirt. I can feel the definition there and it sends little waves of warm up my arms to meet the shivers from my body where he's touching it. I roll away to my side. He lets me go but keeps his arms wrapped around me.

He's right about everything. My life is totally screwed up, and just now, I really don't mind. We both soak up the moment. I'm as happy as anyone could possibly be in a 10x10 polygamist's hideout. "But don't you want to be normal again?" I ask him. "Have things back the way they were? Fit in?"

He snorts. "Fit in? You? You never fit in, Ev. You were always a class of your own. Besides, normal's not all it's cracked up to be. When I was normal, you wouldn't even look at me."

"You weren't normal. I didn't even look at you because you were the biggest player on the planet. Everyone said you got the virus because God was punishing you for sleeping around."

"Really?" I almost believe he's shocked. "People thought that?" I nod. "Then what was he punishing you for?"

I laugh because that's the funny part. If something bad happens to someone who's "bad," they're being punished; but when the same thing happens to someone who's "good," they're being tested. "He wasn't," I reply as gravely as possible. "Bridger and I never got past making out. I got sick because God was helping me build character." I don't really believe that. I think it's just a good theory for people who want to be happy that life punched someone else in the face. In the end, stuff just happens to everyone sooner or later.

Greyson appreciates the sarcasm. "Well, then, God is really unfair or badly informed, because I never got to have sex with anyone. I think if you get punished for doing something, you really should at least get to enjoy doing it."

We're teasing, but that's a bit of a stretch. "Liar. Julie told me what happened."

"She told you that her mom came home early and I went out the window in nothing but my shorts?"

"No way. Get out!" I shove him over, so that I'm on top again, looking into his eyes.

"Seriously. Her mom thought she was smoking weed out the window because it was open in the middle of winter. Searched her whole room. Made it a lot easier for Julie to play innocent, though. She wasn't even thinking about *smoking*."

"Well, see?" I lay my head on his chest and let the rhythm lull me. It's late. "You didn't deserve your punishment—unless you count that whole 'it's the thought that counts' issue. Maybe you got sick so you could get cured. That's the other option."

"They have a cure?"

"No. That's what Nicolas...Dr. Vadlamani is working on."

"Hmm." Greyson tenses a little underneath me. His expression is forcefully blank when I lean up to see. I drop my legs around his waist and straddle him so my hair tickles his nose.

I start babbling nervously while he pulls my hair back out of his face. I take the bundle from him and tuck it into a messy knot. "Nicolas is the only one in the Institute that really cares about us. I told you his little brother Smaran is infected. He's like us because the virus isn't progressing, but he's not like us because he's weaker, not stronger. Nicolas took some of my blood to compare, but there's a male virus and a female. He needs samples of the male."

"That's what those syringes you flashed at Preston were for? Too bad they're burning all the corpses. You could have filled those up no problem. Most of the poor S.O.Bs wouldn't have even noticed another hole or two."

"Actually, it's not just any infected blood he needs." I feel oddly self-conscious and I don't know why exactly. Of course, Greyson will help me—he's done everything else for me, why not give me his blood? It's just that when I agreed to find him and try to get some blood out of him, it was kind of out of spite, and I've been hiding the syringes. Now that I've found him and I realize how wrong about him I was, it feels kind of awkward. "He needs your blood, the male that matches mine."

Greyson pushes up onto his elbows. I draw one leg back over him so I'm off his stomach and on my knees next to him. The blankets are a mess again. Amber whimpers and I pet her hair until she stops. Greyson is staring at me when I look back. I can't quite read his look, or maybe I don't want to.

"Dr. Vadlamani asked you to get some of my blood. Before I even came to get you out?"

"He was going to get me out himself, so I could find you and see if you would help us." *Why do I feel so guilty about this?*

"But you barely knew me. What made you think I'd help? You didn't really keep it a secret that you thought I was a total jack-off S.O.B."

"I didn't...I mean, I did. But I don't now." I reach out a hand to touch his cheek, but he leans away. "You've been really sweet." I look down, maybe to see if there's somewhere soft to land, but there's not. "I really like you." He doesn't respond. He's just watching me with hard eyes. "But I thought if you got to know me, and we talked about it...well, maybe you'd want to help."

He nods, looks away at the dark wall, and then back at me. "Sex me up a little and get my blood. I gotta tell you, Ev, I never saw that coming."

My mouth is open but I can't get any words to come out. He's taking this all wrong. That's not really how it is...it's how it was, but not how it is.

"So, you went along with me at the hospital because I gave your plan a short cut, played right into it. Bravo." He shakes his head. "The little girls were right. You are the smart one."

I reach out, but he stops me with the flat of his palm. "It's not that way, Greyson. Even if I didn't have these syringes in my pocket, I'd have still fallen for you. Even if we had a cure, you and I, we'd still be together."

"Would we?" He holds out his hand. "Just give me the syringes."

I dig them out of my pocket but can't quite bring myself to hand them to him.

"Don't worry, my mom was diabetic, I know how to handle a needle." He grabs them from me, flips off the flashlight, and turns over towards Madi. I'm still wondering how this happened, when he mumbles, "I guess someday I'll thank you; someone had to teach me what it feels like to be used."

I turn my back on Greyson and cuddle Amber. The words between him and me wring my brain like the inside of a spin cycle, round and round until tears start spilling onto my pillow. The thoughts in my head are so loud that I'm not aware of anything else but Greyson's back against mine.

In the dark, thrashing, sleeplessness, Madi stirs and crawls over Greyson. My survival instincts clear my brain. My first thought is she doesn't know what she's doing and she's coming after Amber. We can't live like this.

But then she stops before I have to restrain her. "Did you hear that, Evelyn?" she whispers in my ear.

I couldn't have heard air raid sirens through the yelling in my brain. "What, baby?"

"Clip-clop; Clip-clop—Big Billy Goat Gruff."

Chapter 19

"The Snatchers have searched here before," I hiss to Greyson, who pulls his gun out. All words are dead now; there's only staying alive. "If we're quiet, they won't find us."

He takes the safety off.

The boots squelching in the mud are tentative, sneaking. "It sounds like only one," Greyson says. "I don't hear any dogs."

Amber snores happily. Ignorance is bliss.

Madi cuddles up in my lap. "Is he going to shoot me or eat me, Evelyn?"

"He's not going to do either one if we're very quiet. Remember the troll under the bridge. What did he do?"

"He ate the goats when they crossed his bridge."

"Greyson is the troll, baby, and this is just a little Billy goat."

She leans toward Greyson and whispers with her hands cupped around his ear, "Don't wait for his big brother."

"Shhh." I put my finger on her lips because the sloshing has been replaced by clomping on cement. At least we don't hear the pitter-patter of paws.

My breathing sounds loud to me, everything sounds loud to me. I can feel Madi's heart pounding through her pajamas. Her lungs are jumping up and down in her chest. Barely a breeze seeps from her lips.

The door opens—no creek, I oiled it. I expect to hear the wandering and searching, footfalls on entry carpets, the click of doors and cabinets opening and closing. It's a decent-sized building. It'll be a while before they make it into the main service hall—there's a basement. They always check there first.

The double doors to the main chapel open. Suddenly I feel very warm. Why would someone start looking in *here*? I listen hard for the pauses to look under pews, but the steps are slow and steady, right up the middle aisle. Greyson and I exchange glances. He searched this building before himself. I'd be willing to bet he didn't head straight for the third pew on the left from the front. I shrug and shake my head. I don't know how anyone else could know about this place.

Preston. It was Preston who ratted Bridger out for showing it to me. Would he really let me get away from the police station and then hunt me down and shoot me?

The floorboards bend and moan a few yards in front of us. Amber stirs. I put my hand on her. The footsteps stop. Maybe Preston knows who Greyson is now. Maybe he found out that he let their main target slip out of his hands, and now he's trying to make up for it. I think I'm shivering.

The steps turn down our row. *Oh, dear God, it can't end like this. We have two baby girls with us.* Would Preston shoot them? Greyson points the gun at the slat where the light will come through if someone lifts the board out. Can I let him shoot Preston?

I squint through the slat, but I can't see anything. The board wobbles. The intruder is right on top of it. Greyson steadies his hand. The board starts to slide, Madi gasps. And then it hits me.

"Don't shoot!" I yell grabbing Greyson's hand. "Smell. He's one of us."

"Yeah, p-please don't sh-shoot me—again. I've already got one more bullet hole th-th-than I need." The voice is Chase; when the board is free, his face appears.

"Shit!" Greyson relaxes. "You scared the shit out of us. Glad to see you, dude!"

He grins down on Greyson. "Nice s-s-set up you got here." An army duffle bag drops onto the ground between us before army boots, and then all of Chase, descend through the opening. Greyson throws an arm around Chase's shoulder. He's all decked out in black. "S-s-something smells good d-d-down h-here," he says. I glance at Greyson before I scoot casually between Amber and Chase. Slurred speech: that's where the downward slide starts. For several minutes the cramped little hideout oozes with reunion man-hugs and little girl kisses. Amber wakes up and joins the general festivities. I keep a close watch on her.

Chase won't look at me. He hasn't even said "hi." I know what that's all about. The friendliest kid at school doesn't suddenly go all ice boy on you for no reason. The reason haunts me. He thinks it's my fault, what happened to Crystal.

It wasn't my fault. I wasn't the one who bit the deputy. I wasn't the one who gave him a gun. I wasn't the one who started a zombie feeding fest that freaked out of control so that little six-year-old girls had to be locked up while their families got gutted. I was just trying to keep the whole ugly mess from getting up close and personal. Those little girls had already witnessed enough to fill a decade's worth of therapy sessions.

I want to make him understand. I want him to know that part of me died when I watched them burn that tiny piece of innocence, that I see her every time I close my eyes. But I can't bring myself to talk to him, to break open the scabs.

Greyson hefts the bag. "So, what you been up to?"

"Gathered up a few s-s-supplies from some of the abandoned…Institute v-v-vans and army trucks."

"And how exactly did these vehicles come to be abandoned?" Greyson asks.

"D-d-drivers got out and n-n-never came back. Must have got l-l-lost." He gives Greyson a close proximity to a cheeky grin.

"Or maybe they got an invitation they couldn't refuse?" Greyson asks, unzipping the bag. "What the hell?" It's full of guns and grenades and stuff I've only seen in Matrix movies. "What are you up to, Chase? I've been to Evelyn's house. I know what's going on there."

"S-s-surprise," Chase says.

"For whom?" I ask, and then regret it because I really like Chase, and I feel sick about what he saw happen to his niece. But when he looks my direction, where Amber is cuddled up behind me, I can see the animal come out in his face. He's got it bad, or maybe that look is all about me. Bottom line is, I don't want to have to protect Amber from Chase.

If he's running wild, infecting soldiers and Snatchers, I don't exactly agree with it, but I'm not going to judge. They did away with doing the right thing when they torched an innocent little girl. They can suffer the consequences. But I'm a little scared because I thought Chase was like Greyson and me...and Madi, I hope. I thought our bodies would fight it, forever, and maybe win. Chase is losing.

He's not looking pretty. A shallow, putrid-purple gash furrows his jaw like maybe a bullet grazed him. Bruises and scrapes distort his face and hands. There's a chunk of his hair missing from the side of his head. And the smell...the infected with serious wounds start to get a rotten smell, the ZV version of BO. Chase has that big time. Amber has her nose covered and Madi's is scrunched up too.

"I'm t-t-takin' it to 'em," he stutters. "I've been hunting the s-s-Snatchers, ripping their guts out, and feeding them to my soldiers. I'm gonna b-b-blow up the Institute. Got everything I n-n-need."

"You can't do that!" It's my gut reaction. Nicolas is at the Institute, and so is his brother Smaran. After I say it, I realize how stupid it sounds to them. Chase looks at me like I'm a cockroach in his soup. I've lost all credibility. Greyson looks like he sort of likes the plan. After what just happened between us, I don't want to bring Nicolas up again. "There's no way you can get in there."

"G-G-Greyson did."

"That's what I mean. They weren't expecting Greyson when he showed up; it was a surprise. But the military was taking over the place. They'll be waiting for you."

"Maybe not," Greyson says quietly. "They're here hunting us. They've got the roads quarantined. They may think we can't get out the way we used to."

"We can't," I say.

Greyson wags his brows at Chase.

"How?" I ask.

"The same way we got you in," Greyson replies.

Amber lies down and looks grumpy. "Stop talking, Evy. You're keeping me awake."

Greyson hoists himself out of the cache. "Come up here, Chase, my man. Let's have a little talk.

I want to go with them, hear what they say, but Greyson doesn't want me there, and there's no way I'd leave Amber alone with Madi. I tuck them back in, shove the guns over by my books and suitcase and leave a space for Greyson between us. The only thing I can do at this point is figure out a way to warn Nicolas, but how do I do that without setting Chase up? As much as anyone here, I'd like to see the Institute go up in flames, but we can't lose Nicolas; he is our best hope. I fall asleep wishing I'd gotten his number, and drowning my worries in a sea of Crystal nightmares.

* * *

Greyson never comes back, at least not to sleep. When I wake up, there's a note on top of the two syringes full of purple-tainted blood, a small bag of groceries, and clothes from Amber's room:

> *You got what you came for*
> *Call Madi's Dad*
> *I'll be back for Amber before you leave*
> *Grey*

It's the wrong term to use in this context, but I feel like he's got his teeth in my heart.

Everything is numb. When you're infected, there's always this slight sensation of numbness, but you get used to it. This is numb like someone cut off half of me and I can still feel it there, but it's gone. How did he make himself part of me like that? I try to tell myself that if he's going to get mad and write me off for something as little as asking for a couple syringes of his blood, he didn't really care that much anyway. But I can't fool myself. I know there's more involved in that couple of syringes than just blood. And anyway, it's not "just" blood. We need the stuff to live.

I wait for a decent hour and then flip open my mom's old phone. Her face smiles back at me and I want to cry and tell her how my heart hurts, but she just smiles that silent, paper smile.

"Why are you sad, Evelyn?" Madi looks over my shoulder into the phone.

"I miss my mom," I say.

"I miss my mom too." Madi's whole face falls, and she squints like she doesn't want to see the images that are in front of her eyes but she can still see the scene when she closes them, so she doesn't know where to look.

"I miss mommy," Amber chimes in.

The tears billow up at the edge of her big, brown eyes. I wrap my arms around them and hug them tight and hard because their moms never will again.

"I'm going to call your dad, Madi. We'll see if he can come and get you now."

I dial the number from my mom's phone. When Mr. Calder himself answers, he sounds all freaked out, and then it dawns on me that he's getting a phone call from a dead woman.

"This is Evelyn Cross," I say.

"Daddy, daddy!" Madi's jumping all over me. I hand her the phone. "Hi, Daddy. It's me, it's me!"

I can hear the strain and crack in his voice as he answers.

"It's me. Madi." She's very quiet now. "I'm with Evelyn. She's keeping me safe from the dead guys. They came alive, Daddy."

She starts nodding instead of saying things.

"Let me talk to your daddy, sweetie."

I have to breathe deep before I talk to Mr. Calder. Madi is listening. I don't want her to hear how he reacts to the news that she's infected. She's convinced that she's going to be the Last Airbender with her new superpowers. I cover the receiver, "Madi, go put on some of Amber's clothes from that bag."

163

When she's on the other side of the hide, I turn towards the back wall and put my hand up to the speaker. "Mr. Calder. Listen. I want to get Madi back to you, but it's dangerous. I need you to meet me."

"I can't get in. They've quarantined the city, blocked the roads."

"I know. But the entrance to the golf club isn't in the city." Thank goodness for the smugness of the one percent. They're convinced a disease would never walk into their private golf club and they have enough pull to keep it from getting shut down. "You're a member. Go to the clubhouse and I can get her there. Can you meet me tonight? Around 6:00? It's easier for us to move at night."

"Yes, of course. Whenever you can be there. Is she okay? She must have seen…"

He can't even say it. The line goes quiet while I work up the courage to tell him the truth. "Madi's doing great, Mr. Calder. You heard her. She's excited for you to come and get her."

He babbles on some more.

"Mr. Calder?" He stops. "She's infected."

"Oh, my God."

"I know how you feel. Believe me. I know. But it's not as bad as you think. Madi was vegetarian like me. I don't know if you've been reading the papers, but a few of us, we don't die, we don't get worse, we resist eating people. I think it's because we were vegetarian. I think Madi is one of us." I only hope I'm right. After seeing Chase last night, my optimism is fading.

Mr. Calder isn't making much sense and I'm not sure he gets what I'm saying. "I need you to listen carefully. There's a doctor up at the ZV Institute, Nicolas Vadlamani. His brother is infected. He's working on a cure. I need you to talk to him. Tell him about Madi. He'll help you. Tell him…" I'm not sure he's stable enough to handle this, but Mr. Calder's my only option. It's not like I've got Internet and can look up Nicolas's contact info. If only my mom had got herself an iPhone. Why do moms insist on carrying around these cheap flip phones? "Tell Dr. Vadlamani that Evelyn says he needs to get his brother out of the Institute. Now. Tonight. Do you understand me? Can you do that?"

He repeats the info. I can only hope he comes through and doesn't screw this up for me...or for Chase.

I try to ignore the fact that the rest of the day I spend getting the little girls ready for the night, but don't really know what I'm doing because all I'm really thinking about is where Greyson is and why he's not with me.

Now I'm as pathetic as all those other girls that he conned into thinking that they belonged with him, that they were the only girl in the world that meant anything to him. I'm too smart for that. I don't need this kind of crap to bring me down. Freakin' *merde*! I should have just told him what I wanted when I first got here and still thought he was a messed up, zombie freak job with a power complex.

By the time I've convinced myself I'm better off without him, that it's a good thing this happened before I really like, fell in love or something, the light in the church windows is dim and I'm picking through Chase's army bag full of tricks with my flashlight for something that looks manageable.

Madi tugs on my sleeve and my whole insides smile when I hear the sound of feet on the steps. I'm a moron. What am I thinking? A couple hours of fresh air have cleared everything up and now he's back and all ready to dive into the warm blood of my heart?

Amber jumps on him when he drops into the cache. "Greyson!" She holds her chest out so he can see her shirt. "You brought my Kitty shirt!"

"Of course, I did. You said it was your favorite."

Madi flings herself into his arms. "Look at me!" She's got on one of Amber's Avatar sweatshirts. "I'm the last Airbender."

He stumbles a little. "Go easy with those powers, girl. You nearly knocked me over."

Madi motions in large wide circles. "Don't worry, Greyson. My powers will hold you up. Do you think the Airbenders can win the Firebenders?"

I manage to find a gun that doesn't make me look ridiculous.

He nods at the weapon hanging in my hand. "Do you want me to leave?"

I shrug. What I really want is to be six, jump up in his arms, hug the air out of him, and demand that he look at me. I'm pathetic, so instead of my dripping, shredded guts, I hold the gun up for him to see. "I thought I should bring something. Just in case."

"Probably a good idea."

"Where have you been all day?" I ask.

"Helping Chase. You ready? Can Calder meet you?"

"We're going to meet my dad at the golf club," Madi chimes in. She's all bubbly about it. *Please, God, let her dad see grey*!

He smiles at her and then looks at me. "Did you tell him?"

At first, I think he means did I tell Mr. Calder about Chase and blowing up the Institute, and then I remember he doesn't know about me wanting to warn Dr. Vadlamani. He doesn't know I'm keeping more secrets. I nod. "He knows she's infected. I think he can handle it."

"Give Greyson a big, old kiss goodbye, Madi. You're going home," he says. She plants one right on his lips. "You be good and do what Evelyn says." She nods and hops down. He lifts her out of the hole and into the chapel.

He looks at me. My heart feels like it's been scrunched into the wrong body. Walking away from him like this, with things between us the way they are, without fixing it, is withering me.

"Be careful," he says. "I checked the canal trail on my way back. It's clear." That doesn't surprise me. By now, I'm pretty sure we're the only free-range ZVs left. Well, besides Chase and his zombies. "The soldiers are working the other side of town. You shouldn't run into too much trouble now that it's dark." He offers to help me up.

I take his hand, just to feel him once more before I go. "Take care of Amber for me."

"Like the little sister I never had."

He starts to lift me up, stops, and turns me around to him. He looks at me deep, the golden-brown of his eyes swallowing me up. He wants to say something, but he can't. And then the words force themselves off his tongue. "Just come back. I don't give a damn if you're only using me, Ev. I can live with that." His head goes down.

"I'm not just using you, Greyson."

Before he lifts me out into the church, he kisses me like this is the end of the movie.

Chapter 20

A few hours ago, I would have sworn this night was doomed to failure. I wouldn't have been surprised if some prehistoric monster from the molten masses of the earth opened up a rift in Jensen's field and swallowed up Madi and me. Now, I totally expect Santa Claus to show up and hand us a miracle. It *is* almost Christmas.

We're supposed to be covert, but Madi is humming a little carol to herself, and I don't shush her. On the canal trail, we're hidden from the streets. It dead-ends, like all the roads, at the ravine in front of the golf course. I can't smell any dogs and the barking is far away on the other side of town. The roadblocks and fences are sweeping our direction from the southern mountains. I'm not totally throwing caution to the wind, though. After a couple of blocks, we stop and crouch near the bushes, listening. No engines, no electric buzz, no babble of voices—only the distant roar of the helicopter at the other end of town. The searchlights are combing the mountainside. It's too cold for bugs to be twittering; they're all frozen now. Little patches of snow, shade sheltered by day, sparkle at the moon.

From the ravine below the bluff, I can see my backyard and wonder what Chase is up to. Whether Greyson likes the idea or not, which I think he does, he's bound to help him. They're not just friends from the track team. Greyson's dad, JC, worked as the foreman for the construction company that Chase's dad owns. Chase and Greyson have been working together every summer since junior high.

Everyone knows Chase's uncle on his mom's side is kind of high up in the church and hands a lot of contracts to the company, thus the crying mother when Chase announced he was gay. Must be hard for a mom to have to love her kid through the black and white lenses of how other people see him. I just hope Mr. Calder isn't stuck with the same glasses that can't see grey.

About halfway to the course, I grab Madi's sweatshirt, put my fingers over my lips, and stick my nose in the air. We wait. Madi presses her lips tight between her teeth. In all the excitement of going to meet her dad, she's forgotten how dangerous the world became the moment she got superpowers. And then I see it again—the flash of a searchlight—but I don't smell dogs. Greyson says the military are using the dogs; the Snatchers are setting traps. These must be Snatchers.

I know where I am. The overflow pipe I dove into when they came to pick me up that first night is only a few houses down. Normally, I'd never even think about taking a six-year-old in there, but I don't think Madi has to worry about snakes.

"It's dark in there, Evelyn," she whimpers. "What if there are dead guys?"

"Remember, sweetie. You have superpowers now. You don't have to be afraid of the dead guys. They're afraid of you. I know it's dark, but your daddy's at the other end. You want me to go first?"

She nods. We sit in the middle for a while. At one point, a splash of light plays around the opening. Madi gasps and holds her breath. I squeeze her tight. It's a catch-22. I don't know which side to put her on. I don't want her running right into them and I don't want her behind me if we're running from them. I'm counting on the Snatchers not knowing that you can't actually see the ends of the runoff pipe unless you come off the road and walk into the trees. But if they're that brave, the only choice I have is to play decoy while Madi runs.

"Madi. Do you know the soccer field at the end of this pipe?"

"Where Amber and I play on Saturday?"

"That's it." I take her face in my hands. We're both going to have to do stuff that's not really in our age bracket to do. I don't want to start killing Snatchers, but, if they force me into it, I'll be what they think I am to save Madi. She and I are both going to have to step up. "You know where Katie lives?"

She nods.

"If the Snatchers find us, I'm going to run out that way." I point to the way we came in. "You have to sneak out into the soccer field, across the playground, where the swings and the slide are, and go to Katie's house. You can get to the golf course from there. Your daddy's waiting at the pool. You've been to the pool, right?"

She just nods, her eyes wide. "I want you to take me, Evy."

"Shhh." The searchlights are on the soccer field now, and they've stopped.

I slide down the pipe so I can see what's going on. When I peak out the end, the air catches in my throat. There's a massive oak tree near the edge of the fields down inside the sunken runoff area that doubles as a soccer park. Under cover of the tree, a soldier is kneeling with the sights of his gun trained on one of the backyards that borders the fields beyond the tree line. His back is to me, but I can see the end of his automatic sticking out from his silhouette.

The Snatchers have their lights trained on him. The SUV stops at the curb above, and then the light snaps off. Now I can only see silhouettes in the eerie yellow glow of the streetlamps. The Snatcher in the passenger seat jumps out.

"Hey, soldier!" he shouts. "You got a live one?"

The soldier doesn't move. The Snatcher starts walking towards him, over the curb and down the slope. Something is all wrong here. The vague ZV smell isn't just Madi and me. From out there in the open breeze, I pick it up.

"Buddy. You think we can take him alive? Out here, by himself, he's probably a talker!" He sounds excited like maybe they'll be hunting tonight. The Snatcher has a tranq gun. I know what he's looking for. I only hope he's too excited by the prospect of bagging a talker to notice the storm drain.

The other Snatcher gets out of the driver's seat. "What's he got, Bill?" He heads around to the back of the car, opens the hatch, pulls out a gun, and slams the door shut.

The driver is heading past the tree line onto the field when I see the dark movement above the soldier in the maple tree. The next thing I know, a shadow swoops down on Bill. He screams and his gun goes flying. The driver swings around and heads for tree cover to the tune of a blood-curdling massacre. The streetlamp lights the whole bloody mess. I've seen some pretty gruesome wildcat attacks on Animal Planet, but they're kitty play compared to this. Before the driver can get to cover, the snarling shadow looks up from his kill.

"Sh-sh-shoot. Shoot now, you bl-bl-bloody zombie!" It's Chase. Whatever else he's losing, it's not his hunting skills.

The soldier turns mechanically like he's voice-controlled, and opens fire on the driver, who has only managed to get one tranq dart off. Chase runs towards the slope to finish off the soldier's prey. He's hauling the limp driver to the back of the SUV when I can't stomach anymore. I guess the Snatchers aren't the only ones setting traps.

I slide into the center of the pipe and wrap Madi in my arms. She's shaking, but she knows better than to whimper.

Chase whistles and the soldier walks by the front of the pipe dragging Bill by the foot. I cover Madi's eyes and don't speak until I hear the sound of the SUV driving away. I don't trust zombies with guns.

"We're good, baby." I grab her hand and lead her out onto the shadowed green on the other side. All the possibilities of what might have happened run through my head and keep the adrenaline rushing. I feel like I should hunt something. I stop and hug Madi to me, long enough for the feeling to pass and for me to start worrying that the gunfire is going to spark some interest in this place.

It's actually not that hard sneaking into the clubhouse from this side since trees surround the course. There's really only one tense moment when we have to cross an open green before we hit the landscaping around the pro shop, but even that comes off without a hitch.

It's the dinner hour, and there are a few cars in the lot. I recognize Mr. Calder's black Cadillac. "There's your daddy's car, Madi," I whisper.

Her face blooms into a grin. "Where is he?"

"He's meeting us at the pool cabana. There won't be anyone out there this time of year."

We're crouching in the shadows when I see the tall, slightly balding figure of Mr. Calder slide in through the gate from the clubhouse. He looks around nervously and I whistle. He hesitates before coming our direction. When he's about ten feet away, I can't hold Madi anymore. "Daddy!" She's out of my arms and running to him. He doesn't close the gap, but freezes. I hold my breath. She's around his neck, kissing him. He pries her back, pushes the hair away from her forehead. "It's me, Daddy." His lips land on her head and I can hear the tears in his mumbling. I figure it's okay to stand up.

He doesn't see me for a minute. His head is buried in her shoulder. When he does look up, he reaches his hand towards me. I hazard a few steps closer and he pulls me into a shoulder hug. "Thank you. Thank you so much. You don't know…"

"I do know," I say, but pull away because my eyes are getting hot.

"You smell good, daddy," Madi chirps, sniffing him.

We exchange glances. He reaches in his coat pocket. I know what he's fishing out before it appears. "I brought you something."

"Liver!" Madi claps her hands and unwraps it like a sucker.

"Are you okay?" I ask him. "You can do this?"

He nods.

"She can't be seen," I warn him. "They can't find her. You don't know what they do, even to a baby like her. I've seen it."

He nods again. "Dr. Vadlamani told me. We'll keep in touch. I told him I could help with his research."

I nod. Madi's going to be okay.

"I'm an Airbender now, Daddy. I have powers like Evelyn."

"I bet you do, sweetie." There's more than just a thank you in his eyes when he looks back at me. He can see grey. "Nicolas told me to thank you for the heads up. He's leaving. He wanted you to know you could go with him. He'll wait until tomorrow night. I could take you now."

"Thanks, that's very nice, considering…" We both know what I mean. "I don't want you to take the risk. I have my little sister to look after."

"Is she infected?"

"No."

"Well, then…thank you again. You have my number. Oh. Nicolas gave me his cell number to pass on to you." He waits for me to fish my phone out of my pocket and reads me the number. "You know you can call me. Any time."

"Take care of Madi." I reach up and touch her cheek. "Bye, baby. Be good."

"Bye, Evelyn. I'll come see you with my powers as soon as I learn how to fly."

I wait until Mr. Calder has Madi belted in the car and drives away before I sprint for the trees. In the cover, I flip open my phone, scroll to the new number, and hit dial.

"This is Dr. Vadlamani."

"It's Evelyn."

"God. Evelyn. Are you okay? Where are you? Do you need help? I can come and get you. Just tell me where."

"No, I'm fine. I'm fine. I just gave Madi back to her dad. Thanks for helping him."

"Of course. But what I really want is to help you. Where are you?"

"I'm in Eli."

"You can't stay there. Once they get their hands on that kid, they're going to decon…"

"Decontaminate. Yeah, I know. I've seen the process."

"Let me help you, Evelyn. I've been worrying about you ever since you left. I thought you and I…I thought we…I thought I could help you. We could work together."

"We can. I have what you need."

"You found him? Greyson? He gave you the blood?"

"Yeah, I've got a couple syringes full."

I can hear the excitement in his voice. "Is he still…?"

"Alive. Yes. But we have to get out of here."

"We?"

"Greyson had Amber. He was keeping her safe for me."

"Is she…infected?" It's the hesitation that nags at me. Yes, he's on our side. Yes, he thinks I'm beautiful despite the disease. And yes, he can see past it, but no, not through it.

"She's fine. He kept her locked up so the zombies couldn't go after her. Greyson's like me. He doesn't eat people."

"But you and I both saw…I've seen the reports."

"Yeah, well, what you see isn't always what it looks like. Greyson has issues with Snatchers. Can you blame him?"

"Is it true? That the bite of his victims…"

"Yes. Madi Calder is proof. I watched it happen. But he's not the only one. It gets worse; once they start to go zombie, they're kind of obedient. It's spreading out of control."

There's a long pause.

"Are you sure?"

"Of course, I'm sure." I sound a little exasperated. I need to hang up, but Nicolas put himself on the line to watch out for me in the Institute; I owe him. "Greyson has seen it."

"I'll come get you, you and Amber. You have to get out of there. I can help you both. We can fight this together, Evelyn."

I can feel my insides going soft. The thought of Nicolas showing up and taking over lets me breathe inside. It makes me feel like I could maybe be a teenager again. But I can't explain to him about Greyson. He won't get it. He won't understand what I've just figured out myself. When I'm talking to Nicolas, I need somebody; I need fixing. When I'm with Greyson, I don't need anyone; people need me.

"Greyson's not what you think he is. I can't leave without him."

"I see." I wonder how much he really sees.

"It's too dangerous for you to come here. But you can do something for me. We need a car. I could get my dad's car, but there's no way I could drive it out of here." I'm wondering how Chase plans on transporting his little zombie squad.

"You can use Smaran's Mercedes."

"A Mercedes?" I pause, picturing the scene. It doesn't play out all that well. "Do you have anything less conspicuous? A Honda or a pick-up or something?"

"Uh, no that's about it. The Mercedes is black though, hard to see at night. I could maybe come up with something. How can I get it to you? Where will you go?"

"Don't worry about it. I'll figure that out later. If you can get Smaran's car parked in the golf course lot, that will be great." A Mercedes won't stand out in that parking lot. "I can get to it and get out. The entrance is across the ravine and outside of Eli. Can you leave the key in the ashtray?"

"I can do whatever you need, just let me help you."

"You are helping me. You need to worry about getting yourself and Smaran out of the Institute for the next couple of days. Call in sick or something. It's heating up in here and it's about to boil over."

"Look, I'm already transferring out to Atlanta. There are people there that I trust who will help us; they'll look after you and Smaran."

"I'll think about it," I say it, but I know I won't. "Get the car over here tonight, if you can. I'll meet you in the parking lot outside the Institute—the far end, away from the building. What are you driving?"

"BMW. Blue."

Of course. "I'll pick up the Mercedes just after dark. And Nicolas?"

"Yeah?"

"Thank you. I really appreciate what you did for me in the Institute."

"No, Evelyn. If you have those samples, I'm the one who needs to thank you. Knowing you're out there gives me hope for my brother. I think we can beat this." Pause. "We could do it together."

What he means by "this" is me; he just doesn't realize it.

"I'll make sure you get the samples. I hope you find what you're looking for." I flip the phone closed and turn towards the church.

The night is still. Dead leaves make a ruckus under my feet as I tromp through the trees that line the edge of the ravine.

My conversation with Nicolas plays over and over in my head. I know he likes me. He wants me with him. Obviously, that sends little impulses of smiling electrons flitting about my brain. I'm not wavering; being with Greyson has become a choice, not a lack of options.

There's some noise coming from the direction of my street and the faint smell of burning hangs on the air. I wonder if the military and the Snatchers have started patrolling at night. The little scene with Chase and his zombie soldier plays through my mind. I almost feel sorry for the soldiers he's trapping and infecting. But I'm also a little worried because, even though the deputy was mostly brain dead when we got to the jail, he still had some deputy left in him. He could still use his gun, almost like a reflex. It's got to be the same with the Snatchers and the soldiers—only with the way Chase feels about Snatchers, I'm sure there are more soldiers than Snatchers in his little club.

I realize I've started running. I really want to get back to Greyson and Amber. I want to be home.

Halfway across Calder's field, I see the uniforms. If they were sneaking up on the place, that would be one thing. But they're not; they're walking towards it, all around it, mechanically, drawn on some kind of string that they're reeling in. This is not a military squad. These are Chase's zombie troops. They can only be here for one thing. They're hunting, and they've sniffed out Amber. I have to force myself to breathe.

I crouch behind the big maple that separates the horse pasture from the churchyard while my brain files through my options and pulls up an assortment of blank cards. I reach for the gun in my back pocket. I don't really want to kill any of them, but they're going to die anyway and Amber is still alive and well. If I only hit them, it definitely won't stop them—didn't faze Chase—but it might distract them.

The real kicker is that I don't know what the heck I'm doing with a gun, and the chances of me hitting anything I'm actually aiming at are slimmer than an anorexic Cosmo model.

Greyson has to know they're here. The question is, does he realize he's dealing with zombies that won't need to search around for hideouts because they'll be following their noses? Amber's dead meat if they corner them in that hole.

The only thing that makes sense—or even if it doesn't, the only thing I can do—is fire a shot. One of the ZV soldiers is standing beneath the main stained-glass window, framed by the angels in the Gothic arch above him. The moon is out full and vibrates the colors in the darkness. I pull the trigger, the gun cracks and jolts. I've never shot a gun before, and the violent force of it knocks me on my butt. I end up squeezing the handle and firing again as I hit the ground. My shots don't get anywhere near the closest soldier, but I hear glass shatter and the heavy *ping* of metal on metal.

The zombie reels around like a robot. Staring at my corner of the lot, he fires off round after automatic round in a line down the length of the fence. Splinters fly. I dive for cover behind the tree. He's not even aiming. I guess you don't really need to aim when you're firing about 600 bullets a minute.

When he gets to the end of the fence, he doesn't even bother checking to see if he got me. He just turns around, puts his nose into the air, and starts walking again.

I'm too close to the church now to see more than the one zombie soldier on this side. There were about five of them milling around when I first spotted them from across the field. Glass shatters and bullets fly on the front side where the doors are. The crack of shattering wood splinters the night. They're inside.

I have to figure out a way to clear my side of the building. I wonder if Greyson's already out. Maybe he and Amber went somewhere and they're not even here. Of course, that's just wishful thinking. Why else would the zombies be sniffing around unless they'd caught the sweet scent of my baby sister? I sneak up behind the soldier. Even if he can smell me, he's probably gotten used to the smell of other ZVs and won't even notice.

Shots from inside the building blast through the night. The soldier has found the lower entrance and doesn't even bother to look back when I kick a rock and it smacks into the bushes right by his feet. I don't have a choice. I'm close enough to fire point-blank through his head. I have to close my eyes—my heart, my mind—so I can pull the trigger.

This time I'm ready for the kick, but I wonder what the hell is happening because at the same time the bullet blows a purple hole in the zombie's temple, the big glass angels above my head explode. A man flies out with the shards, lands back first on the pavement next to me, and rolls. Tucked in his arms is a thick bundle of coats with some little strands of honey-colored baby hair peeping out the top.

Chapter 21

"Amber!" I detangle the bundle from Greyson's arms and give him a hand up.

"The dead guys are here again," Amber whimpers.

"Are you okay?" I look her over for bite marks.

"She's fine." Greyson is shaking off the impact.

"You cut your head." I wipe away the purple-black ooze.

"Battle scars," he smiles. Is it so totally inappropriate that I want him to kiss me right now? "Madi?" he asks, but he's looking back up at the window. A couple of soldier ZVs are jostling for the privilege of being the first to climb out.

"With her dad."

He nods. "Let's get Amber the hell away from these guys."

"They'll follow us as long as they can smell her; doesn't matter where we go," I say, knowing what that means, because even if we outrun them, there's only one way they'll give up.

"I heard shots. You have the gun still?" he asks, pulling a much bigger one out of his pocket.

"Yes, but I only have a few bullets left and I can't hit anything that's not standing in front of me. Do they all have guns like him?" I nod at the guy on the ground with a hole in his head.

"You did that?" he asks, surprised.

"Sorry."

"No, I'm impressed. After that incident with the deputy, I didn't think you had it in you. I only have a few shots left myself. I had to use a couple of them to get Amber out the window, but there are more zombies than I have shots for. Not all of them have guns, though."

The first soldier ZV drops to the ground from the window. He's got his eyes on Amber like the rest of the world is a black hole and she's a twinkling star. "Get Amber up in that tree." Greyson waves his gun at the big maple. "I stashed Madi in a tree the night I found her. These guys are the ones Chase has lost control of. They're not coordinated enough to climb."

The second ZV stumbles out the window. Amber is light and some of the branches of the maple are low enough for me to hoist her up. I hear the shot behind me, and then the thud when the ZV falls. Then the second shot. It has to be in the brain.

"Get up as high as you can." I wave my sister up into the higher limbs and wish there were leaves, but then remember a wolf doesn't need to see the rabbit to find it.

"I'm scared. It's high!" she whines.

"You choose, baby. High or zombies?" We don't have time for sugar coating.

She grimaces at me, and then reaches for a branch. Underneath her, my arms are waiting outstretched. I glance towards the church. Two more zombies, a Snatcher, and a soldier shamble around the corner. If Amber falls, I don't think I'll have time to get her back up before they get to us. I fire a shot, hoping to slow them down, but they're oblivious. I try to aim a couple times, maybe cripple one with an injury, but miss totally. And now I'm out of bullets. I lob the gun and hit one of them. He wobbles but keeps coming.

Amber's coat catches on a branch. She teeters. I slide to the left underneath her. She tumbles into my arms. With no time to even catch my balance, I shove her back up to the lowest branch. The zombies are close enough to reach for her. They don't pay any attention to me; they probably think I'm after the same thing.

I crane my neck around to see if Greyson might be coming to the rescue, but the broken stained-glass window has vomited another zombie onto the ground. Grey has his hands full with the two coming at us from that direction. "Go. Go. As high as you can!" I yell, stretching my arms out of their sockets.

"I'm trying. I'm trying!" Amber is crying because her legs are low enough for the ZVs' fingers to reach her. The soldier actually grabs her sock at the ankle. She squeals and kicks like an angry bunny and I use the leverage of the branch she's on to haul myself into a rounding kick that sweeps his legs out from under him and knocks him on his butt. Amber scrambles up the branch away from my arms in time for me to take on the second comer.

The Snatcher is a big boy. He's totally focused on Amber and walks right over the top of the soldier. I take a jab at him with my fist, but it doesn't do much other than make him look at me, which is an improvement, I guess. Forget the fists, this guy is definitely a leg man.

"I can't use any more bullets except to finish them off," Greyson yells. "We're going to have to take them down first to make the shot count." I would blanch at the gruesome bluntness of the idea, but my skin doesn't color like that anymore. Like I said before, they started this when they shot a little girl. Right now, the only thing that matters is getting them off Amber's trail. She's the innocent one here.

I have to jump. Maybe the ballet classes weren't a total waste. My foot clips the Snatcher hard, but he barely wobbles. I do manage to make him angry with me, though. He's completely sidetracked from hunting my little sister. I have to be careful because this guy looks like he could leave marks if he weren't so slow. He grabs at me, growling, and I dodge under his arm and come from behind with both feet, dropping him to the ground and landing on my side. There's barely time to catch my breath and see where Greyson is before the smaller soldier is back on his feet and heading towards the tree.

Greyson got the worst half of the bunch. One of them is big, slow, and stupid like the huge guy I just planted on his butt. The other one, he's smaller but with really ripped arms. I can see the bulges of his pecs through his green t-shirt. That's not the big problem though—he's still coordinated and obviously trained to fight. My guess is he's the one who orchestrated this little mutiny and led the hunting party. He and Greyson are going at it like lions and hyenas over a kill. I figured Greyson could handle himself, but I had no idea how well. No wonder he thinks he's some kind of Batman knock-off.

As much as I'd love to watch, I have my own henchmen to deal with. The soldier that I had to kick off of Amber has hauled himself up to the tree again and she's screaming. It's not really fair though. This one is so brain dead, he keeps running into the tree like a rabid wind-up toy. When I pull him away, he snarls and growls like a wolf, snapping at my arms. I avoid his teeth. I know I'm infected, but who knows if his strain of the virus is mine. My best option is to lay him out on top of the other guy. Then they'll have to struggle with each other to get up.

I'm heaping him, thrashing, on top of his buddy, when I hear the shot behind me. Amber screams. The Ninja ZV is flat out on the ground with a bullet in his head. Greyson grabs the other one by the legs and hauls him writhing and growling over to the pile.

"Do we have to shoot them?" I ask.

"The 'decontamination' option is a lousy way to go, but I'm out of bullets." He nods towards the one still twitching, "He was my last shot."

"We have to get out of here: you, me, and Amber. I've got a car at the golf club. Nicolas sent it. He said we could go with him and his brother. They have family that can help us."

"Help us what? You've been talking to Nicolas?" His tone goes acrid. "Oh, yeah, I guess you had to arrange to get the blood samples to him. But maybe, better yet, you can just bring me in!"

I can't believe it's going this way, but I don't get a chance for rebuttal. Headlights flood the street in front of the church.

"Shit!" Greyson swears. "I knew gunshots at night were a bad idea." He turns around and reaches for Amber. "Come on, baby, we're going back to the hole. These guys can't sniff you out." She dives into his arms like he's me, only better. He nods at the snarling mass of camouflaged limbs struggling to detangle themselves. "We'll let the Snatchers deal with them."

We're already through the back entrance and into the hide when we hear the scuffle and roar of the Snatchers finding the zombie soldiers. The next attack on our senses is the scent of burning, putrid flesh. Amber covers her nose.

There's silence surrounding the squelch and pound of boots scouring the churchyard. Amber huddles close to Greyson. I want to sit by him, with his arm around my shoulders, but I don't dare. He has the same look on his face that Bridger had when I told him I didn't see the point in us going out anymore.

Muffled voices from outside begin to filter into our range of hearing. My hand reaches over to graze Greyson's knee. Our eyes meet. He knows before I mouth the word to him. "Preston."

"I didn't think of it before now, Sarge." Preston's voice floats through the wall and up underneath my skin, making little goosebumps. "It was a long time ago. My grandpa showed it to my little brother and me. Evelyn knew where it was. Bridger caught hell when my dad found out he took her there."

"Doc Christensen doesn't give a shit about her." The other voice is deeper and grittier. "He has what he needs. He said to burn her if we find her. It's that prick pack hunter Greyson, the one we're stuck here looking for. We bring him in and we can burn the place—finish this shit. One of those ZVs we just decontaminated over there went through basic with me."

"They were together," Preston insists. "If she knew about this place, chances are he does too. Why else wouldn't we have found him yet? We've been over the whole damn town."

"Are they bringing the dog?" the other guy asks. "If there's something hiding in that hole, I want to know what it is before we open it up."

Greyson and I look at each other first and then down at Amber. The two of us could maybe make it out alone, through the window, before they got inside. We could cut out through the fields. But we don't stand a chance with Amber. We both know we can't leave her here for them to find. They know she's been with us. They don't take chances, not even for innocent six-year-old girls. And even if they did, she'd end up as a specimen at the Institute.

Greyson shuttles Amber over to my lap. I shake my head at him. But what else can I do? Amber is everything; Greyson's the target. If he bolts, they'll chase him and I can get out with my sister. If I go, they'll burn me or capture me, but they'll still come looking for Greyson.

I can't let him do this—she's not even his sister. He thinks I'm only here because I'm working with Nicolas. Why the hell is he doing this? My eyes mist up. Tears dribble down my face, as he crouches under the trap door, ready to make his move. There's barely enough light to see tears, but his fingers find my face and wipe them away. "I'll meet you at the car," he says.

Like hell, he will. Why doesn't he just stab a knife in my chest? There are at least six totally lucid gun-toting Snatchers and professional soldiers out there with only one purpose in life.

I grab his arm. "I can't let you go." My voice catches on the last word. Amber reaches up and touches my cheek.

Greyson wraps his arm around my neck and pulls me to his mouth, squishing Amber between us. Life burns through his lips into mine. He pulls away and Amber wraps her arms around his neck and kisses his cheek. He doesn't look at her though. His eyes are memorizing the shadows of my face. "I swear, Evelyn, you are the punishment for all the sins I never committed." And then he swings the boards away and slides out.

Amber and I sob silently in the hole until we hear the furor of the soldiers finding him and the chase explodes: glass breaking, bullets shattering through walls, a dog barking, stomping, yelling, "It's him. It's the mutation!"

When all the sound is out in front, Amber and I creep out the back and into the fields around the irrigation canals where the deer hide in winter.

After ten minutes of creeping, I'm surprised by how far we've gotten. I'm getting used to Greyson exceeding my expectations. Maybe he *will* meet us at the car. Maybe I underestimated his superpowers. I've underestimated him before.

Beyond the church, a helicopter roars through the night sky, flashing up the darkness with searchlights. A volley of muted shots—the dart guns don't sound the same as the bullet guns—yelling, a dog barking, whoops of celebration, and then silence. Amber and I hug each other, alone in the darkness.

Chapter 22

I leave Amber bundled up in the black Mercedes parked in the country club parking lot. The key is in the ashtray under pennies. Who would bother with pennies?

Now I know what it feels like to be a zombie: no emotion, no worry, no pain, and no thought—just a single, driving need. I need to find Chase. Whatever he has planned, he has to do it now. I move through open fields and don't even look for soldiers and Snatchers. They have what they want, as far as they're concerned, this town is already ashes.

When I sneak through my back gate into the yard, I'm almost too late. The door to the garage is open. Chase is ushering the last of his soldiers into the back of an Institute van that looks like it should have been put out to pasture.

"Ev'lyn!"

He looks bad. He's not happy to see me. Even the gashes on his face can't hide the surprise. "D-d-on't eat people...bad."

I'm not sure what he means. Wrong or not healthy? Maybe both. The conversation is rough but, in the end, I gather that he's on his way to the Institute. He proudly displays stashes of recovered ammunition and other interestingly murderous weapons. I'm not horrified because my heart is breaking to see how difficult it is for him to speak. Chase and I have both been on the honor roll every semester since ninth grade. He's not just a kick-ass runner; he's a really bright kid—and the nicest guy you've ever met. Sometimes I used to think he ran to escape all the disapproving faces that he just couldn't do enough to win over.

"The Snatchers got Greyson," I say, to make it as simple as possible, and because I don't think I can manage much more without lapsing into a full emotional meltdown. I'm not sure how much is still computing for him. I don't know if he even remembers what happened to his niece. It seems like this idea of blowing up the Institute is what drives him. "I'm going to the Institute. I'm going to break Greyson out. You can't blow it up until he's out. Do you understand?"

"Un-un-der-der-der-stand. Hurry."

Hurry. Him or me? That could go both ways. I'm not going to fuss. I know how I'm getting out of here, but I'm not sure he understands that at this point, nothing living, or nearly living, is going to get across the quarantine line and nothing living is going to survive once they move to decontaminate this town. "How are you getting out of here? You can't drive out."

It takes a lot longer than I really have time for, but the gist of his answer is that he's going out the same way Greyson got me in. It seems his uncle's crowd of church VIPs are not fond of sitting in traffic. Chase and Greyson have worked every summer on a network of underground passages that lead downtown. Not many people know about them.

"I'm in a black Mercedes, Chase. If you can, wait until it leaves the parking lot. I'm going to get Greyson out, whatever it takes."

"Gr-Greyson," he repeats. I don't think he cares too much about anyone else at this point, but there's something in the way he looks at me, the tilt of his head. Past the torn scalp, the purple gashes, the bloodshot eyes, and the grey skin, I can still see the boy that took me to prom.

My heart melts. I want to throw my arms around him, convince him that it wasn't my fault. Every time I see him, I see pictures of Crystal waving good-bye and Chase's mom crying. I wonder who dealt him these flimsy cards and expected him to build a house with them. I may not get another chance.

"Chase!" He doesn't turn around. I follow him to the van and put my hand on his arm. He pulls it back like I've got cooties or something. "I'm sorry. I'm so, so sorry." My eyes well up and my throat swells closed on the words.

"No!" There's no stuttering for that second. His hand goes up to stop me. It's shaking. "Don't." He's deadly serious.

"Be careful," I whisper.

He shakes his head. "Not c-c-careful." He limps off to the driver's seat, dragging one leg a little; his pants are gashed and stained.

* * *

Amber's asleep in the back of the Mercedes when I get back. It's a European model, a stick, and it's really fast. Luckily, my dad let me drive his car a few times. I'm careful, really careful. I stop at all the stop signs and obey the speed limit. I slow down even more through the construction zones. I don't want to attract any more attention than I already do.

The drive takes about thirty minutes when there's no traffic. Every so often my heart starts pounding and my head feels like it's going to pop right off. I start thinking that I'm heading for the snake pit. The monsters that shot a six-year-old and burned her body are roaming free in there. I start breathing too fast and my foot hits the pedal too hard. I have to slow down, think of Greyson, think of everything he's done for me and for Amber. And then I wonder what will happen to Amber if I don't manage… I really can't go there.

Exhaling deeply, I remind myself that I know the set-up this time. I'm on familiar territory. I make myself inhale slowly, hold it, and exhale. And, if I'm lucky, I'll get some backup from Chase and his zombie crew, for a distraction, at just the right moment. This is the right thing. It has to be because, without Greyson, everything is wrong.

The Institute parking lot is guard-protected now; construction on the fence is in full swing. Like every construction project in Salt Lake, it's still in progress. The easy parts are up and they've added some barbed wire to the top. But there's another building to the south of the Institute with just a sidewalk that separates their adjoining parking lots. The fence isn't finished between them; there are gaps where the cement has been torn up but the new posts haven't been dropped in. I spot a blue Beamer in the Institute lot and park at the edge of the connecting lot facing it. I can't see anyone in the driver's seat, but there's a passenger—a well bundled-up kid, a little older than I am, who must be Smaran, Nicolas's brother.

From my car (well, Smaran's car), I watch the grounds around the Institute. There are two soldiers on patrol. They pass at staggered intervals a couple of times while I'm watching. One's taller than the other, and the tall one seems to be gaining on the shorter guy with his longer steps. He's going to lap his buddy at some point. Apparently, they care about keeping people out now. It's nice to know I've made a mark on the world—it's made enough of them on me.

While I'm watching, about half a dozen combat-ready soldiers stroll up from the guarded parking lot on the other side of the building. They chat with the tall patrolman as he passes the entrance, which is on the west end of the building, and then go inside. I wonder if I've arrived just in time for the changing of the guard.

I hit the remote to lock the doors around Amber and knock at the window of the BMW.

"Evelyn?"

"Yeah. Smaran, right?" I drop my bag and lean into the window.

He nods. "Nice to meet you."

"Where is he?" We both know whom I mean.

"He heard they brought in the mutation male."

"His name is Greyson. He's like us. He doesn't get worse."

"Like you, maybe. Not like me." He wraps his blanket closer and coughs, covering his mouth with the blanket. When he pulls his hand away, there's blood. "Nicolas went to see what he could do. He thought you were rather fond of Greyson." My insides go cold. That's an understatement.

"He saved my little sister—and me. I owe him. I'm going in after him. My little sister is asleep in the car. She's not infected. If I…if I don't come out, ask Nicolas to look after her for me." I would have moved her into the BMW just to be safe, but Smaran's a ZV and I don't know his eating habits. I dig in my sweatshirt pocket and hand him the two syringes. "This is what Nicolas sent me after." The kid takes them and stashes them in the cubby between the seats.

"It won't be like when Greyson broke in to get you," he warns me. "The security is tighter. There are soldiers on every floor and all the patients are in lockdown. You'd need a small army of your own to get in."

"Well, I'll see what I can do. I know you've been living in there. You have any idea where I might find him?"

"Definitely second-floor pre-op. Christensen won't be able to wait to cut into this guy." My insides freeze again; better not to think or feel. Just go.

"Here," he turns and leans over the seat, rifling through an overnight bag. He pulls out some scrubs and a mask and hands them to me. "These might help. We're about the same size."

"Thanks," I turn away. I can change in the bushes outside the institute.

"I have to tell you though," he says. I stop. "They'll pick you out right away. It's the hair. It's a dead give away. That's how I knew who you were, and I've never even seen you. You won't get past the first person in the hallway."

I pull the hood of my sweatshirt over my hair as he rolls up the window. My all-black ensemble suits the occasion perfectly. "Hey. Wait." I tap on the glass. "You don't have any scissors in there, do you?" I'll do whatever it takes to get Greyson out.

"My brother's a doctor." He opens a small First Aid kit and pulls out a pair of scissors that look like David's sling next to my Goliath hair.

"Thanks." I pick up the soldier trick-or-treat bag that Chase brought and head for the bushes. I spend a lot of time crouching in the bushes these days. Does that mean I'm the bad guy?

There's a bit of new security. A guard at the entrance to the parking lot asks for ID. But there's not much more outside, other than the two soldiers I've already noticed. My guess is they're still feeling smugly secure, especially now that most of the ZVs have been hunted down and "decontaminated." There weren't that many of us to begin with or, at least, not that I knew about. Wait until they get a look at Chase's new friends.

While I'm crouching in the bushes of a lovely kidney-shaped flowerbed, I start to wish I'd put in more hours playing Call of Duty with Cory. I'd be better equipped to deal with this. But like I said, I'm better with my legs than my hands.

The building is a big rectangle, so there's quite a bit of time between guards. The stairwell at the back of the west end of the building is not too far away from where I'm stashed in the bushes. Last time I left, I came out through the window. The glass is all shiny and new in the moonlight. This time, to get inside, I'll have to kick the outside door in. I'm good at that. But I think I'm going to have to do something about the guards, and that worries me a little.

They're not the brain-dead zombie soldiers I fought off outside the church. I'm not sure I can handle them. Their guns don't scare me much. Chase took a shot to the chest, stood up, and walked away. I'm willing to live with a few holes if it gets Greyson out of here. Besides, I'll definitely be a fast-moving target, and I don't plan to give anyone a clear shot at my head.

In the movies, they have silencers and stuff for this kind of work. I'm a low-budget operation. Tonight, it's just me and my elementary school Karate.

There are a few seconds of blank time when one soldier rounds the corner just past the stairs and the other hasn't come around yet. I make a break with my duffle for the nice little prickle hedge that lines the buildings.

By the time the tall soldier makes his way in front of my new hiding place, my heart is pumping gallons of ZV blood to my legs. I spring on him like a panther on a stray deer. The kick to his head sends his gun clattering. He goes down and hits the sidewalk hard, but not hard enough. He's not out. I'm going to have to drag him to the bushes before his little buddy comes around the bend, but he's not going to go willingly.

Of course, it crosses my mind, but there's no way I'm going to kill him. I feel the snarling head of the virus rising with the adrenaline my body is pumping. I have this ghastly urge to forget about whatever I came here for, sit down, and enjoy a little soldier snack. He's like only a year or two older than me. I grab his gun and smash the butt of it against his jaw. I saw that in the movies too. It works.

I've made some noise now, so I have to hurry. I don't need more guns, so I toss this one down the hedge. I really don't like guns anyway. The little guy comes around the corner at a trot just as his buddy's boots disappear into the bushes with me.

"Tyler?" he yells. Now he has his automatic thing off his shoulder, dangling from his arm. Better to pounce from behind. I handle this one a bit like the guy who tried to grab Bridger. I body-slam him and then pick him up and toss him. He's tough and struggles back up. My first agenda is to get rid of his gun. Once it's safely on the grass between the sidewalk and the hedge, I turn back to the soldier. But he's had his Karate classes too and knocks me off balance with a direct kick to my chest.

He's going for his handgun while he comes after me. I can't let that happen; not because of the holes it'll leave if he gets a shot off, but because of the alarm. The last thing I need is to announce my arrival with a gunshot. Before he can draw the gun, I've flipped him again and stomped on his femur. The crack is fairly disgusting. I'm just glad he's wearing a bandanna because I can use it to stuff in his mouth. "Sorry, buddy. You're working for the bad guys. You can thank me later for taking you out before the real party gets here." He doesn't respond. He's holding his leg, moaning through the wad of fabric, and he's definitely not going anywhere. The virus is raging now. I'm starting to think I won't make it through the night without taking a bite out of someone.

Disgusted with myself, I shove the soldier away, grab my duffel out of the bushes, and strip. I pull the scrubs on underneath my hoodie before I tackle my next hurdle.

The door into the stairwell is locked. It looks pretty sturdy like it'll take a couple good kicks to go in. I test it once or twice, back up a bit for a running start, and then fortune smiles on me—Santa Claus opens the door from the inside. No, seriously. A student in a Santa ensemble is standing inside the back doorway.

"Geez, where's Casey?" he demands. "She was supposed to be here twenty minutes ago."

This kid is obviously confused and pissed. "She got a hot date," I improvise.

He's really disgusted. "Typical. We've had this planned for a month now." Casey's obviously let him down before. "We had to get clearance for this. Where's the elf costume?" He's so ticked off at Casey that he lets me in without even waiting for an answer.

I stride past him with my head down like I'm sorry; the black hood shadows my face.

"Have you been standing out here the whole time? We can't use this door anymore. Everything is all locked up now. I had to have an armed escort down the patient wing. There's a guard outside the stairs."

That gets my attention. Through the small window in the door, I can see a soldier walking away down the hall, talking with another coming this direction. And now the kid has gotten a good look at my face. "Geez. What the...."

I feel really bad about mugging Santa. It was quick—and quiet. Apparently, they don't offer afterschool Karate at the North Pole. But now I won't have to use the scissors; he has the wig, the beard, the costume, a pass, everything. When I look at the pass, I see that Santa is from the Bennion Community Service Center. Inside the big, red bag he was carrying are candy canes and little cellophane Christmas bags full of beef jerky.

I'm such a sap. I get all misty and have to stop and breathe deeply. Enemies have surrounded me on all sides for so long that I've forgotten there are people who care, even about deranged zombie patients. For a few seconds, I'm stunned that a whole bunch of students actually put time into making sure the patients at the Z-V Institute weren't forgotten for the holidays. The guy I've stashed under the stairs will probably wake up thinking he's been kicked in the teeth for caring, and he'll never know just how helpful he was—or how much I appreciated him showing up. I hope this doesn't land me on the naughty list for life.

I stuff a couple guns in my oversized fur-lined pockets and don my red velour jacket.

When I get to the second floor, I take a deep breath, open the door, and peek out. As far as I can see down the hallway, there's only one guard, a Snatcher—at least for the moment. Looks like the night patrol hasn't made it upstairs yet. The Snatcher is stationed outside the door to pre-op where they had Bridger when I tried to break him out.

Memories of my epic failure to break my ex out bring me to a hyperventilating halt in the stairwell. There wasn't even an armed Snatcher at the door the last time I tried this, and Bridger still ended up fried. This has disaster written all over it. But the other option is that I walk away, and Greyson...

No. My fingers resolutely grip the bar that opens the door. I can't even think that without my insides caving in on each other.

I remind myself that, since the last time I was here, I've spent a pretty decent amount of time hanging out with Greyson. That's like a field course in survival and self-preservation with guest lectures on heroism, isn't it? *I am the other half of Greyson*, I remind myself. And then, I'm a zombie. As long as I don't take a shot to the head, how does the saying go? *Whatever doesn't kill me makes me stronger...* or just leaves another mark.

I transfer some guns from my duffle into Santa's bag.

"Come on, Evelyn," I say to myself, "you can play this right."

From the look on the Snatcher's face, it's obvious that he thinks the idea of a girl Santa is hilarious. I'm a little relieved because he could have just seen the other Santa Claus. My guess is, the guy under the stairs never made it up here. I dig past the guns and beef jerky and pull out a candy cane.

Sauntering down the hallway, twisting on the balls of my feet, I hold out the candy like a gun. The Snatcher's eyes are all over me.

"Ho, ho, ho. Merry Christmas," I drawl.

Both his hands are tied up. One is running through his hair and the other is reaching for the candy. "How 'bout *you* come sit on *my* lap, Santa. My place?"

I play along to get closer. "You are definitely on the naughty list." I wag my gloved finger at him.

"Sure you don't want to come on by tonight, Santa?" He wraps his fingers around the candy cane. "I've got a little something to slip in your stocking."

What a prick. When my foot connects with his jaw, he has no idea what hit him; Santa wears combat boots. Before I got the Z-Virus, there was no way I could have taken this guy out and dragged him into the small prep room outside pre-op before the patrolling guard returned—or the new shift arrived upstairs. Things are different now.

Embrace what you are.

Chapter 23

Pulling off the Santa hat and wig, I peek through the corner of the observation window of the operating room. The scene framed in the glass sends a nasty rush of déjà-vu tingling down my spine. Dr. Christensen and Dr. Hickman hover like vultures over the prep process. Just looking at them unleashes a whole rush of chemicals that seem to poke the beast in me. I have this urge to run into the room, rip out their guts, and eat them while they watch. I take a deep breath and look away. At least, they're both bandaged up. I did do some damage the last time I was here.

The nurse has just finished shaving Greyson's head. There are clumps of blond hair all over the floor—horrifying. He's lying there, strapped in like Bridger was before, but this time, there's a faceguard—Greyson's bite is lethal. I can only hope there's at least one more similarity to when they did Bridger: no anesthesia. It'll be much easier to get out of this place if Greyson is running than if I'm carrying him.

Nicolas is in there, like last time, arguing with Dr. Christensen. I'm irritated because I told him to stay out of the hospital, but totally relieved because it's probably because of him that Greyson's brain isn't already exposed. After the way I painted Greyson to Nicolas, I would have expected him to stand by and let the oversexed, pack-hunting animal get what he deserved. Nicolas is a saint, a very good-looking, slightly brown one.

One thing in the room is different from last time: there's another armed Snatcher at the side of the bed. Since I can't risk Nicolas and Greyson getting shot if I burst in there firing, I'm trying to figure out a way to get the Snatcher out here, when Dr. Christensen takes care of it for me.

He gets fed up with Nicolas, shoves him away, and yells for the guy whose gun I just confiscated after I kicked him in the jaw. "Davis! Get in here and get this idiot out of my hospital. Find out who let him back in here." Nicolas keeps pestering him so he gestures to the other Snatcher. "Get out there and find out if Davis has gone deaf or if he's found something better to do than his job."

Positioning myself strategically on the other side of the door, I wait until the door shuts behind the Snatcher and he's bent over Davis. The butt of Davis's gun smacks his head with a sickening crunch. Both unconscious bodies have a pair of handcuffs hanging from their belts. How convenient.

Shoving the door open, I step inside pointing the gun directly at Dr. Death. Part of me is snarling, hungry to shoot him and put the world out of its misery. I tell myself the gunshot would bring every soldier in the Institute swarming up here. "Nicolas, would you be kind enough to undo the restraints on my friend Greyson?"

"Friend?" Greyson asks at the same time that Nicolas realizes it's me inside the Santa suit.

"Evelyn?" Nicolas jumps to the bed and begins ripping away at the facemask. The nurse shrinks into the corner under the small window.

Dr. Death has gone purple. He looks like he's just swallowed turpentine. He shoves Dr. Hickman. "Her again! This is your fault. How does she keep getting into my O.R?"

"She's not going to shoot that thing," Dr. Hickman scowls, but he doesn't move.

"There are soldiers on every floor. You stupid girl! We could have helped you here," Dr. Christiansen blurts out.

"Helped me? The way you helped Bridger? You're an animal." I point my gun at Christensen's head. Nicolas starts unhooking Greyson's arms.

The doctor sneers at me. "The only animal here is strapped to that bed. You think you're some kind of hero breaking in here and letting him loose? He's the beginning of the end. There are already reports of infections in Dallas and L.A. This thing is out of control. You have no idea what you're unleashing on the world."

"Maybe not. But I do know I should do the world a favor and just shoot you. You don't belong anywhere near these people." I need to control myself, but the white tile walls bring up what feels like eons of stored up anger, too many awful scenes. "You're less human than the worst of your patients. You rip people apart to feed your greed for power and money. For you, it's a choice, not an illness." Now I've really worked myself up and I can feel the virus churning in my veins. The meatiness of the doctors fills my nose and makes me angrier. "You could have used this place to help everyone. But you're too clueless and vicious to do the right thing. You're the stupid one here."

The "stupid" comment hits a nerve. Christensen loses his head, growls, and dives for the gun in my hand. He was right. I wouldn't shoot. He's lucky Greyson is still half restrained. The only time I've ever actually seen Greyson rip the guts out of someone was when that someone was attacking me. I'm fast enough to jerk the gun away, but it clatters to the floor. The doctor grabs a handful of my hair; it rips out from the roots. I snap and snarl, taking a bite out of his arm. He falls away, screaming.

Dr. Hickman comes after me and I catch his arm, flip him onto the ground, and then stomp on the bone in his leg. The crack leaves him howling.

Dr. Christensen's blood in my mouth is tangy, but I feel the bitterness of it and spit it out. I'm angry with myself for biting a human being, and even angrier with him for releasing the animal in me.

"There! Now you can do some research. You can find out if the female bite is contagious. Or maybe they won't let you live that long. Maybe they'll shoot you and torch your body on the suspicion you *might* be contaminated. I don't know, Dr. Hickman," he's rolling around holding his broken leg, "what do you think? They don't make exceptions for six-year-old girls with bandages on their legs that haven't even been bitten, so do you think they'll make an exception for a homicidal doctor with teeth marks?"

Nicolas opens the last of Greyson's restraints. His hands are shaking. "I might be able to get us out of here," the good doctor offers, "but your outfit is a little conspicuous."

Closing my eyes and breathing deeply to subdue the monster raging inside, I shed my costume. The guns clatter out when the coat hits the floor. Greyson and Nicolas exchange looks when they see what was in there. Freed from his restraints, Greyson sits up. "Santa Claus?"

"What? You don't believe?" I ask, tossing the beard away with a huge smile. I nod at his bare scalp. "That's a good look for you. Very smooth."

He runs a hand across his head, a look of regret flickering across his face.

"Kind of *Prison Break*-ish," I add.

Only Greyson could manage flippant under the circumstances. "You know me; I'll make it work."

Greyson picks up one of the guns I dropped and hands it to Nicolas while Dr. Christensen cowers for cover, blubbering over what he's about to become. Maybe now he'll change his position on unsedated brain surgery for Z-Virus victims.

"Thanks," Greyson says to the slightly anxious-looking research assistant. "I'll take Evelyn's word for it that you're on our side."

Nicolas takes the gun and apologizes, "I'm afraid I don't know how to use this. Not part of the standard Bio-Chem curriculum."

Greyson sighs and leans over to show him.

Nicolas looks uncertain but game. He drops the gun into one of his lab coat pockets. Those pockets are reminding me less and less of my mom's purse. "Before we shoot our way out, let's try just walking," Nicolas suggests. "Greyson looks like a patient and you've got scrubs. I'll play doctor and you be nurse."

Greyson's okay with the plan but shoots me a look about the 'play doctor' part. I give him my best don't-even-go-there frown. We pull a wheelchair out of the prep room for him. I push the chair and Nicolas grabs a clipboard. "It's better if I look preoccupied."

"You won't get away with this, Vadlamani," Dr. Christensen whines. "They'll pick you up. You aren't even a US citizen."

"That's right. I'm not. But, around here, that doesn't seem to be doing any good for anyone who *is*."

To accommodate the wheelchair plot, we have to take the elevator, which is fairly close to the front of the building, away from the stairs I came up. The clipboard seems to do its job when we pass a soldier on patrol. I keep my head down, but my hands are shaking. Nicolas doesn't pay any attention. The soldier just keeps walking. I step up the pace. The elevator is still several yards away. The tension gets to me and I glance back. The soldier is coming up on the door to pre-op. He stops and looks around. He's got to be wondering where the Snatcher is. I nudge Nicolas.

"Hey, did you just come out of here?" the soldier yells to us down the hall.

We pretend like we can't hear and walk faster.

The door in front of the soldier creaks open. "What the…" the soldier says and disappears into the prep room.

We break into a run and pounce on the down button, expecting a pleasant little ding. Instead, an enormous crash rocks the building, shaking the whole front end of it as gunfire rattles up through the shaft.

Chapter 24

"Chase," I mutter to Greyson as the elevator door starts to open. "He must have driven right through the front doors."

"Hey, stop!" the soldier yells.

I push Greyson into the elevator and the soldier opens fire on us. He runs down the hallway, spraying bullets and shattering tiles. Nicolas jumps in and I lean on the close button. A couple of bullets ricochet off the doors before they shut.

It's strange listening quietly to the muted cacophony of what sounds like a minor war below.

"Don't get me wrong, Nicolas," I mutter, "I'm really glad you were here to help, but this is why I wanted you out of the Institute." I stop to catch my breath, leaning on the handles of the wheelchair. "There's another one like us—at least I thought he was. They *decontaminated* his little niece right in front of him. He made himself an army of zombie soldiers and brought them here. He's going to trash this place."

The scent of Nicolas overwhelms the whole tiny elevator space. "With you in the mix, we won't just have the army on our tails, we're going to smell like Christmas dinner to those soldier ZVs."

The elevator dings to announce our imminent arrival, but instead of slowing to a gentle halt, the whole place shakes like the room next to us was hit by a bomb, and the elevator jerks to a stop.

"Chase has, like, a dozen grenades," Greyson explains.

We pry the doors open: Greyson on one side, me on the other. The building is under siege, we're trapped in an elevator, and still, I can't help but notice that Greyson looks hot even in a hospital gown with his head shaved.

When the door starts to open, the sound of mass destruction rushes in: machine guns rattling, half-eaten hospital staff screaming, ZVs growling, soldiers yelling, fire alarms squealing. The sound alone could knock you out.

Pulling the door open far enough, Greyson and I poke our heads out cautiously, covering our ears, to survey the damage.

We're about four feet above ground. The elevators are in a small passageway between the reception desk and the hospital rooms. Down the wing directly to our right, the electric shock therapy room door has been blown off its hinges—mystery of the recent explosion solved. The mangled door is lying in the middle of the floor. The walls are pockmarked with bullet holes; glass and tile shards litter the floor.

Zombie soldiers roam the halls, mechanically shooting anything that moves. A few of them have thrown over their orders of total annihilation in favor of crouching down to feast on easy prey: Snatchers and Institute personnel squirming in the hallways.

To the left, the large metal doors that guard the ward from the reception room are lying mangled on the floor. The old Z-V Institute van sits abandoned—all its doors thrown open, and the windows shot out—in the middle of the wreck of the reception desk. A zombie soldier has deserted to pillage the spoils of war in the reception area. The white tiles and walls are mostly splotched red with the occasional pool and smear of dark purple.

Greyson pulls his head in. "It doesn't look good," he yells over the din.

"I know the elevator seems like the safest place, but we can't stay here," I reply. "Chase is not going to be happy until there's nothing left but a pile of rubble." I lean my head back out, come face to face with a zombie displaying a grenade in his fist, and jump back, grabbing for my gun.

"Easy, baby, it's Chase!" Greyson touches my arm.

"B-B-Booom!" Chase grins and waggles his grenade at us. At least I thought he was grinning—then it hits me like a shot to the chest that the grin is smeared guts.

"You were supposed to wait until I got Greyson out," I yell. Bullets pepper the outside elevator wall and we jump back. Chase ducks and covers, disappearing from view behind the small table and chair that sit between the elevators.

When he appears again, he yells out halting orders to a soldier down the hall. "Up th-the stairs!" He turns back to us. "Z-z-zombies," he complains disgusted. But he's one of them now. I don't think he's grey anymore.

Unfortunately, Nicolas speaks up. "Does he understand that the room just behind him is the oxygen supply room? If he sets a grenade off in there, the explosion will bring down most of the building."

I see the plan dawn on Chase's face before it even reaches his fogged-up brain. He pivots slowly and looks at the door with the big red oxygen logo on it and flammable gas warnings. There are at least three different signs with words and pictures in different colors in case you don't get it the first time. Chase looks back at us with a crazy smile on his face. The kid doesn't even notice the bullets flying everywhere and pieces of tile shattering off the walls.

"You can't get out in time. Those things only give you about five seconds," I yell.

Chase looks at Greyson. Greyson shakes his head. Chase doesn't flinch.

"Chase, you can't do this," I plead. I still want things to work out for him. I want to see him catch a break. I want him to touch the silver lining on the grey.

Greyson man-hugs him. "You run like hell, dude."

Chase just pats his back.

"What's going on?" Nicolas demands.

"We're leaving." Greyson crouches in the doorway and nods at Chase who disappears again. "C'mon, Dr. T-bone, you better go between Ev and me. We can try to protect you from both sides." He's talking to Nicolas but looks right at me when he adds, "You're the most fragile one here." And then he hoists an automatic gun and jumps out of the elevator pulling Nicolas behind him.

It's insane. ZV soldiers and recently liberated patients crouching on the floor—totally oblivious to the volley Greyson fires to clear the way—turn and grab for Nicolas. Only the living soldiers and Snatchers take cover. Greyson hauls Nicolas away from the clawing hands, shooting his way to the cover of the desk. It's my job to beat off the pursuers who see Nicolas as the new definition of fast food. I'm just lucky most of these guys left the fight because they were out of ammo. It's now down to mano y mano—well, sort of. I'm more of a leg girl and they seem to prefer teeth.

I slip in the blood. A Snatcher cowering behind a wall of boxes grabs my foot and yanks. Nicolas slips out of my grasp. A ZV soldier snarls and dives for him.

The red-slimed tile won't give me any traction to break free. The Snatcher's face is only inches from my foot. He strikes at my trapped leg with a very manly looking knife, burying the blade a couple inches into my thigh.

The virus hasn't killed all the sensation. The tip burns as it rips into the muscle, spreading a deep purple stain across my light blue scrubs.

Virus angry and screaming, I slam my combat boot into his nose. The impact shoves him back behind the boxes, blood streaming all over his face.

By the time I'm back on my feet, the ZV soldier has Nicolas up against a pillar. The doctor handles himself better than I imagined he would, but he's fumbling in those huge, white pockets of his for the gun Greyson gave him, and he's not going to make it.

Throwing myself on the ZV's back, I wrestle him away long enough for Nicolas to find his gun. "Shoot him, Nicolas! Shoot him in the head!"

The bullet plows a neat little hole through the ZV's forehead, dropping him to the floor. But it's not from Nicolas's gun.

Greyson pulls his gun in from the driver's seat window and yells, "Quit dancin' around out there! Get the hell in the van!"

It's taken longer than I think Chase is willing to wait for us to hustle and batter through the mayhem. Tossing Nicolas in the back, I dive in on top of him. Greyson slams his door, grinds the key, and shoves the van into reverse.

The tires squeal and every still-living, undevoured soldier pelts us with bullets. A couple make an assault on the van as it passes and I have to leave Nicolas unprotected to pry them off. We lurch to a stop when Greyson slams into the flagpole.

I grab Nicolas to keep him from flying out the back as Greyson shifts into drive and makes a screeching U-turn.

Through the flapping back doors, I watch the gaping hole of what once was the Institute entrance.

Was there a second or two of actual silence and slow-motion? Or did I just will time to stop in my mind so that the kid who never seemed to be able to catch a break might, in the end, come shambling through the jagged hole ahead of the flames?

Five, four, three, two, one. The deafening crack, the smoke and flames—but no Chase. Stinging tears, heart imploding, no justice—well, some maybe. I bury my face in my hand, not sure if the wet is blood or tears.

Nicolas directs Greyson to the blue BMW. I retrieve Amber, who has already seen so much that the sight of the building exploding interests her more as a fireworks display than a tragedy. Nicolas's car bumps over the curb into the adjacent parking lot and revs into the streets.

When we're safely up the canyon on the highway to Cheyenne, Smaran introduces himself to Greyson and tosses him a pair of Nicolas's scrubs. I try not to watch when he slips out of his gown and slides into the pants, but he's not too shy about it. Amber's all eyes.

We're near the summit when the radio starts to carry reports of the hospital blowing up. Less than half an hour later, they're talking about Eli being "decontaminated." By then, Amber is asleep, cuddled up under Greyson's arm, probably drooling on those well-chiseled abs. I'm not sure if she snuggled up to him before or after he fell asleep.

Smaran's breath comes rough when he sleeps. He's really sick. Every now and again, Nicolas looks over at him, the way I look at Amber when I'm wondering how we're going to make life work and wishing I took that class where you have to carry the baby around and play mommy for six weeks. When Nicolas looks at his little brother, I can see in his face what drives his research.

In the semi-dark, I'm surveying my own damage the best I can. The bloody hole in my scrubs has dried already. The pain is gone. I wonder how long before the wound starts to reek.

With my blood-crusted fingers, I explore the bald spot Dr. Death left me. It's easier to cry about that because it's harder to hide, so I do a little.

Nicolas glimpses me in the rearview mirror. "I'm really sorry I wasn't there to stop him, Evelyn. I know…I know what that means…maybe…maybe we'll find something. I just need a lab…"

I'm so embarrassed that he thinks out of all the horrible things that have happened tonight, I'm crying about my hair. I'm mortified that he always speaks to me in broken sentences because he's afraid of damaging me with something he says. "It doesn't matter," I say, shrugging it off and assuming my best prom queen voice. "I'll just part it on the other side." I feel a little chilly on the inside and I rub my arms up and down out of habit.

"Do you want the heat?"

"No, I'm not really cold; we don't really…you know."

"I swear, Evelyn. We will beat this. All of us together, we'll find the cure—or at least something for the symptoms."

I smile into the mirror so he can see, but inside, I'm cringing. He's doing it again, making me feel needy and sick. I mean I love that he's so devoted to helping me, I love that he cares, but I hate feeling weak.

"Nicolas, if anyone is going to help rid the world of the Z-Virus, it's going to be you. It's going to be you because you care—and because you're brilliant."

He actually turns around so he can see me, not just my reflection through the mirror. "I do care."

"Thank you. For everything." I reach up and touch his shoulder and then lean back in my seat and listen to the road. "Nicolas. What did you say your Indian name is? The one your family calls you?"

"Sudhir."

"What does it mean?"

"Great Scholar."

"Ha!"

"Well, my parents were…"

"No, you are. You should go by your Indian name, Sudhir. It suits you. It's who you are." I glance at Greyson before I say, "Embrace what you are; make it work." Leaning up, I whisper in Nicolas's ear. "Don't let other people tell you who you are."

Greyson stirs behind me and I know he's not as asleep as I thought because there's this sexy, smug half-smile on his face.

FIN

ACKNOWLEDGEMENTS

Many thanks to my daughter Natalie, who supplied the raw material and encouragement to write this story. Thanks also to Elizabeth, Connor, Rebecca, and Esther who read for me, to Elena, Chris, and Jared, my accomplices in writing, and to Janie who shares my obsession. Deepest thanks to Curt who loves me despite the whole writing thing.

Amazon Reviews for the Walking Grey Series

—couldn't stop reading…hope there's a second one coming.

—turns the zombie genre upside down.

—a twist on the typical love story.

—perfect mixture of intense action and softly suspenseful moments.

—dying for the next one. And please for the love let there be a next one.

"Narrated with spunk and humor by a zombie who still has sex appeal, Grey Matters is a fresh take on the undead meme where the enemy comes from within, literally. One of the most original and shocking takes on zombie literature I've ever seen. Grey Matters is humorous, acutely terrifying, and thoroughly gripping from the first page to the last."
—Katherine Boyle, Veritas Literary

Rachel DeFriez

The WALKING GREY Series

Edgy romance embraced in raw suspense. The Walking Grey series chronicles the desperate story of Evelyn Cross and Greyson Childs in a dystopian world infected with the Zoser Virus. Infected, the virus has made them look like ZVs and crave human flesh like ZVs, but instead of slowly consuming their organs and brain, it has transformed them into super predators, fighting both sides of a looming conflict to protect Evelyn's uninfected little sister Amber.

GREY MATTERS

Book 1

They bash our heads and chain us up because we're different. Well, maybe knowing we would happily throw on a bib, rip out their guts, and devour them like hotdogs on a stick, without the stick--or the bib for that matter--probably has something to do with it. No one really wants to hang out with a girl whose idea of a Slurpee is grey matter and blood splashed in the snow, hold the straw.

Evelyn Cross has everything: shampoo commercial hair, a letterman jacket, a tiara, a 3.98 GPA, and now the Z-Virus that is infecting teenage couples in the small town of Eli. The virus has made her look like a ZV and crave human flesh like a ZV, but instead of slowly consuming her organs and brain, it has transformed her into a super predator, fighting both sides of a looming conflict. And she's not the only one of her kind—here's also Greyson Childs, the vicious pack-hunting player that dumped her best friend when they all got infected.

GREY KNIGHTS

Book 2

Angels or Demons? The grey is fading. The Z-Virus has mutated and the infection looms large on the Texas horizon. As the rushing tide of the apocalypse smears the lines between Heaven and hell, Evelyn and Greyson escape the fire of one quarantine zone, only to find themselves fugitives in the inferno of another.

GREY DAZE

Book 3

The chilling finale of Rachel DeFriez's award-winning series Walking Grey. Book 3: Grey Daze.

The Zoser Virus has gone global. It's not the first time mindless monsters have invaded France, set up defense positions, and devoured the inhabitants.

Evelyn Cross washes up alone on the Marseille coast. What she finds there is not exactly a dream vacation on the French Riviera. To make her way back to her little sister, she'll have to join the dystopian New Order that the greys of Marseille have raised up from the ashes of the apocalypse. And if she plays her part well, maybe, just maybe, somewhere in the rubble, she'll find love again.

OTHER BOOKS BY THIS AUTHOR

I AM KRONOS

It's not every day you get a friend request from a dead girl.

I Am Kronos is a thrilling blend of gaming, sci-fi, and supernatural romance.

Keven Meyers, gamer and classic underachiever on the fringe of cool, gets a friend request from Sierra Sands, recently deceased and haunting his video games. Sierra is stuck in the Nexus, the center where all the universes and realities collide. She desperately needs Keven's help to stop Silas, another lost soul using his diabolical understanding of the world between the worlds to prey on gamers.

When Silas attacks Keven in his video game, Sierra drags Keven's soul through the game and into the safety of the Nexus where he becomes painfully aware that he is inextricably connected, across universes and realities, to this dead girl. But with the infinite possibilities of multiple realities come options—options like his best friend Lexy Granger.

Only the strength of the ties that bind Keven, Sierra, and Lexy, on multiple levels, in and out of existences, are strong enough to overthrow Silas.

Rachel DeFriez brings us a spine-tingling supernatural thriller that delves into the metaphysical world of the multiverse.

ABOUT THE AUTHOR

Rachel DeFriez is the author of the chilling zombie romance series WALKING GREY: GREY MATTERS, GREY KNIGHTS, and GREY DAZE. She is also the author of the supernatural sci-fi thriller I AM KRONOS.

Coming Soon:
RAVENS AND LAVENDER in Romance
7 SECONDS in YA

Her books have won multiple prizes in the 2018 and 2019 League of Utah Writing Contests.

Due to her husband's nomadic nature, Rachel has taught French and Creative Writing in a variety of states including: Texas, Massachusetts, and Utah. She is particularly surprised to find herself writing YA horror since she's afraid of the dark. Visit her at www.racheldefriez.com